SAVAGE
DISCLOSURE
The Nickie Savage Series
Book Three

R.T. Wolfe

Photography by SL Jones Photography

Cover and Book design by eBook Prep
www.ebookprep.com

First Edition, November 2015
ISBN: 978-1-61417-799-9

ePublishing Works!
www.epublishingworks.com

THE NICKIE SAVAGE SERIES

DEDICATION

I would like to thank Jess and Jamie Larsen, CEO and co-founders of Child Rescue, for their help in creating this series but mostly for the tireless and dangerous work they do to save trafficking victims in the US and abroad.

CHAPTER 1

———◆ ◆ ◆ ◆———

Duncan woke before sunrise to an empty bed. Again. The faint lavender smell of his Nickie lingered, tempting him to remain right where he was. He stretched his arm over the empty space. Cold sheets. In the dim light, he thumbed the titanium wedding band that reminded him she was his even in her absence.

As he sat up, he spotted her, fully dressed with her nose buried in the oversized chart paper that rested on the easel reserved for her research. Her back faced him, but he could see she'd already tucked her .45 in her holster.

He stood, glancing to the grandfather clock barely lit from the glow of the floor lamp she preferred. Four thirty.

"I set the coffeemaker," she said without turning from her work. She didn't drink coffee.

He pulled on some sweats and walked to her instead of the coffeemaker. "You can't continue to keep these hours." He set his lips on the top of her head, smelling the lavender, smart and sophisticated. Her arm wandered behind and found his hand. As she drew a line connecting symbols to locations, her warm fingers brought his hand to her lips.

"What are these?" he asked. He didn't recognize the symbols she'd drawn.

"You might not want to know."

It took a lot for his detective to say this. "I fear I do."

"The double-heart thing means a pedophile who wants girls. The triangles mean the dude prefers boys. Four hearts that create butterfly wings mean either."

Once again, she was right. He might not have wanted to know. Reflexively, he winced and turned his head from the paper as if that might disengage his photographic memory. He distracted himself by meandering to the counter next to the wet bar and pressing the single button that started his morning coffee.

"The pictures you've tracked down of Zheng are priceless."

Zheng. His fingers clenched into fists at the sound of his name. Jun Zheng. The man who abducted Nickie from her home when she was a young teen. The one who forced her into eighteen months of prostitution before she escaped to freedom. To heal. To grow. To become the detective she was today.

She gestured to the map of lines and information on her chart paper as if she were providing a routine lecture regarding police procedure. "I'm tracking down the records of the men with him in the photographs. He may be in county waiting trial, but his crime ring is too big to dismantle in his absence. Some of the men in the pictures are serving time after they were caught with boys. If there truly are ten to twelve groups of captive children in Fu Haizi—"

"—Fu Haizi?"

"Yeah, I gave this mess a name. It means captive children. I'm taking it down, Duncan. All of it. Each day that passes, more children are taken."

He watched as she tilted her head, then wrote the words at the top of the paper. 'Fu Haizi.'

"I think he might have them divided by customer preference," she added as if she hadn't stopped. "All of the girls in my group were middle-to-upper-class females of nearly the same age. No one under ten. And if they survived to their upper teens, they were disposed of."

Odd way to say murdered. This time an involuntary shiver traveled from his hands and arms straight into his heart. Pulling up a stool, he sat next to her and noticed the beads of sweat that lined her forehead and upper lip. So much for routine.

"I'm expanding my search to include reports of missing boys. He might have groups of homeless children or runaways, too. Some johns prefer upper-class adults and some drive the streets looking for homeless prostitutes. Why not the same for the pedophiles?"

Ever since she learned her group of captive girls was only one of many, it was as if a portion of her life had been put on hold. She continued to function at her job and had agreed to a honeymoon, although shortened to five days. However, a portion of her focus consistently remained with rescuing each and every child as well as convicting the perpetrators.

He took the hand that held her black marker.

Steel-gray eyes turned to their joined hands, then lifted to meet his.

"I'm getting closer, Duncan. I can feel it."

"You'll be able to think more clearly if you rest." He used his free hand to tuck a stray piece of hair away from her beautiful face.

A small smile crept over her lips. "I'm too wired to sleep." Placing the palm of his hand against her warm cheek, she inhaled. "I love you."

She did. It was both cherished and reciprocated.

Nickie headed to the station in the unmarked sedan the Northridge Police Department had issued her.

Medium-sized, efficient. Great resale. She'd rather have a tooth pulled. Hoping no one would recognize her, she slid into a far spot at her favorite convenience store. She had just enough time to grab a giant Diet Coke and razz Slippery Jimbo before she had to be to work.

Next to her car, one of the last piles of snow left from winter lingered, dark gray and filled with rocks refusing to move on to a better place. She glanced at the waist-length leather jacket crumpled in the seat next to her, shrugged and left it.

The bell on the door rang as she entered. Jimbo stood behind the cash register and turned at the sound. Lifting his chin, he addressed her. "Mornin', Detective Dude."

"Slippery Jimbo," she answered as she headed for the fountain drinks. "How goes it?"

"You can't call me that here," he said, although his voice was loud enough that it carried across the length of the store. "I'm the manager of an upstanding business now."

Nickie wouldn't mention that managing a smelly convenience store complete with circles of old gum stuck to the floor might not be classified as upstanding.

Things had changed between her and Jimbo. He may have started as a thief who dabbled in dealing drugs. And he may have trashed her conviction record with the number of times he slipped by on technicalities. The brutal beating he took because of her trumped it all.

She grabbed the largest cup they had and filled it exactly three-quarters full with ice. The rest with the morning caffeine that would keep her from using unnecessary police brutality on anyone on the way to the station. Or, more importantly, once she got there.

Before paying, she took a deep drink and let the burn of carbonation mix with the chemical sweetener. She pressed the lid in place and paused to take a look at the thin band of yellow gold that rested next to her single-karat engagement ring. Air sucked slowly into her lungs and her eyes closed without her telling them to. Damn it if it didn't make her smile. At the risk of someone noticing, she brushed her thumb across the side of her nose and cussed.

When she stepped up to check out, Jimbo was explaining to a new guy something about how to juggle all the employee breaks. All four of them she wondered sarcastically.

"How's the arm?" Nickie asked and nodded toward the dingy cast that traveled from his knuckles to over his elbow. The only signature on it was that of 'his woman.' *Krystal* was written in black magic marker with several curly cues trailing from the K and the L. Barf.

"Cast comes off next week, Detective Dude. I can't wait. It itches like a mother fuck."

"Now, is that any way for the manager of an upstanding business to speak to his customers?" She threw him a five-dollar bill. "Keep the change, Jimbo. Stay out of trouble."

Her cell buzzed as she pushed open the glass door. Caller ID said it was her captain's station number. "Savage," she said as she took in the upstate New York morning air.

"It's me, Nick. We've got a disturbance."

Although she would never cross the line, there were certain benefits now that the captain's stepdaughter was Nickie's sister-in-law. Small town. One of the benefits was to call her captain out when he was dumping on her. "Sounds like a beat cop's job. Why me?"

Silence.

"It's…sensitive," he said finally.

Which meant it involved either a missing person or a possible sexual abuse victim.

"Come right to my office when you get here. I'll get you the address and details."

It couldn't be too bad if he was going to tell her at the office instead of sending her directly to the so-called disturbance. She pulled out of the store parking lot, imagining the captain's desk lined with the yellow sticky notes he used as his method of organization. Old dog. New tricks.

Carrying her nearly empty Styrofoam cup, Nickie marched into her office. She hoped she had time to harass Zheng before she went out. Having him so close was both torture and bliss. She'd barely flipped on her light and set down her soda when a knock rapped on her doorjamb.

Captain Dave Nolan stood towering at six-foot-four. "Come right to my office," he reminded her. Sheesh. She followed without even turning on her computer. He started talking before he reached his office. "The Stoner home. They've been calling every ten minutes for an hour. A female Heritage College student is picketing in front of it."

"*Thee* Stoner home?" Nickie asked.

"Dr. Stoner is a surgeon at the hospital. His wife doesn't work, but is on the school board and a member of city council. The missus says she's filing an order of protection as soon as we get the girl off her sidewalk."

Dave wouldn't send out one of his detectives for this unless there was more to it. There had to be. "The sidewalk is public property. And what kind of a last name is 'Stoner?'"

"I don't suspect they chose their last name."

Nickie had chosen hers the day she turned eighteen. And even chose to keep it after marriage. With Duncan's blessing. "Is this a repeat offense?"

His phone rang. "Since that's probably Mrs. Stoner again, maybe you could have a seat and let me do the talking."

He was right. She was wired and needed to bring it down a notch. Dave answered, then jerked the phone from his ear.

"I'll have your mother fucking badge."

Dave glanced over at Nickie. She lifted her brows at the noise.

"Do you realize this is the sixth fucking time I've called, and we still have no fucking emergency vehicle here?"

"There's no emergency," he mouthed to Nickie, but then answered Mrs. Stoner. "I have an officer on the way as we speak, ma'am."

Nickie put up three fingers and whispered, "Three fucks?"

"Well, it's about fucking time," were the words that came from the phone.

Nickie smiled and flipped up a fourth finger.

"What if the neighbors see this whore?"

Whore? The hair on the back of Nickie's neck prickled. A whore who pickets? Nickie's instincts woke. And it wasn't an instinct to protect *thee* Mrs. Stoner. Details from Dave weren't necessary at this point. If he needed her, he could call her cell.

As he placated the woman, Nickie dug the heels of her boots in the carpet and marched around his desk. She ran her eyes over the line of sticky notes and grabbed the one that had the name 'Stoner' along the top of it. Waving it over her shoulder, she strutted out of his office. She read the words as she headed to grab her Diet Coke on the way out.

Ah.

On the yellow paper, Dave had scribbled the words 'no consent' and 'no means no' below the words 'Dr. Eric, Sr. & Gertrude Stoner.' With a name like Gertrude, Nickie might fling the f-bomb around, too.

She almost bumped into him. Tall, dark as coal and wide as a barn. And dressed in jeans? Here in her office? Alone. It was all highly unorthodox. "Special Agent Hurst." She addressed him formally and knew the look on her face must have been a mixture of terrified and paranoid since that was exactly how she felt. He was undoubtedly here to pick up Jun Zheng who was still in county. Nickie's Jun Zheng. Hers. Not the FBI's. She'd waited seventeen years to take him in. Seventeen years of nightmares about the night he'd abducted her and forced her into sex trafficking for a year and a half. Jun Zheng who still had information about Fu Haizi. Information that could be crucial in rescuing each and every group of captive children.

He sat in jail on the adjoining premises. Handy for the times she wanted to question him. Or just sit outside his cell and see how he liked to be the one in the cage. His local trial for kidnapping, trespassing and attempted murder would take some time yet. She, her partner and the ADA were still working on securing the evidence to tie him to the explosions at the hospital weeks prior.

She also knew it was only a matter of time before the feds swept in and took him for the string of kidnappings and murders he'd committed across state lines. She'd known she was on borrowed time with Zheng but still she wasn't ready to give up the access she'd come to rely on.

"You're alone." It came out more of a question than statement.

"How's it goin', Detective? I was in the neighborhood."

She walked carefully around her desk. Hurst stared at her messy guest chairs, then picked up files from one and placed them on top of the other. He sat and swung an ankle on his knee.

Slowly, she sank in her chair, all but forgetting about the sticky note she held and the disturbance she was requisitioned to take care of. Why was he alone? In jeans? "In the neighborhood?" she asked.

He was slouching. FBI Special Agent Hurst was in her office without notice and unannounced. And alone. And slouching. Yes, highly unorthodox.

"I'm on vacation. Camping with the wife."

He camps?

"You have Jun Zheng," he said while checking out the backs of his fingers.

Here we go. "You wouldn't know about him if not for me." It came out overly defensive, but she couldn't help it. She clasped her hands to keep them from shaking.

He held his up like he was ready to stop her from a long tirade. "Which is why we haven't been up to get him." Leaning forward, he dropped his foot and placed his forearms on his thighs before adding, "Yet."

She kept her eyes on his, but she turned her head. His were black and matched the color of his short hair. And unfortunately, they were unreadable. So, they haven't come to get Zheng yet because they understand she needs and deserves to have him longer? Unorthodox doesn't even cut it. "Speaking of 'we,' where is your partner, Hurst?"

Swinging his ankle back on his leg, he sniffed and slung an arm over the back of his chair. This was a very different Special Agent Hurst than she remembered. Agents were all eerily similar. Stiff, bland, secretive. Hurst included. But this? She treaded lightly.

"I don't take Goodrich camping. I'm here on a courtesy call. To tell you Zheng might need to stay here a few more weeks. Maybe months." He held up his hand again, this time in surrender. "Not that I would know much about that." Then of all things, he winked at her. This was between her and him?

A few weeks? Months? How was that possible? Hurst was stalling for her? The sticky note crunched in her fingers. Zheng. In her grasp for months? A cautious smile spread across her face.

"As I said before, Detective, this whole thing ain't right. The Special Agents before me sold out. They betrayed you to Zheng. They are two in a long list of law enforcement and politicians who have done the same. So, I pulled some strings." His eyes turned consolatory. "This ain't right, and I hope at least some of it turns around for you."

And came the pity. It was patronizing and becoming tiresome.

Hurst changed his register of speech at the flip of a coin. She'd seen it before. He seemed to move into street mode when he was deep enough into a case that he didn't pay attention to impressing anyone with impeccable words. Nickie could relate since she did the same. "I could use your help." She knew she was pushing her luck, but it sort of just came out.

He lifted his brows like he read her expression and agreed with the absurdity of asking after what he'd just done for her.

"There's a mole in the station."

His look turned instantly into stereotypical special agent face. It was disconcerting to see him sit up ramrod straight in his civvies.

"What kind of mole?"

Either he had an excellent poker face or he honestly didn't know about the mole. She wished she wasn't so suspicious, but life experiences had taken their toll.

"The kind that is watching me and reporting my actions to someone else. We—I found an email." No sense bringing in the fact that it was Duncan who found the email. Less was more.

His shoulders dropped into a slouch as his chin moved from side to side. "This shit ain't right. One adult abducts you as a child. Another kidnaps you from foster care."

She didn't think it was worth it to mention Jun Zheng was the man who did both. No need to muddy the waters with conflict of interest.

"The assistant to the governor of New York secretly transfers you here so the crooked police chief can keep tabs on you. Now this? It ain't right," he repeated. "You sure?"

She couldn't tell him how she knew. Her husband

hacked into the NPD system and found the emails? And has hacked into the FBI database? Hurst's files even? Instead, she nodded.

"You had friggin' FBI special agents stab you in the back. How do you keep the faith, Nick? I know I'm losing mine. As far as the mole, I'll get somebody on—" His face turned pained. It was only for a second, but she saw it. "I'll get on this myself. Soon as I get to Langley." His eyes turned to hers. They were deep in…something. She wasn't exactly sure what. He hadn't even noticed his flippant use of her station nickname. He seemed like he was thinking of what to say. She was, too. Awkward. Instead, he shook his head and lifted from his chair.

He held out his hand, and she placed hers in it. He hung on. "This visit isn't a secret or anything, but you probably don't need to advertise it. Ya know what I'm getting at? Here." In his other hand, he held a business card with the back facing her. On it was a phone number written in pencil. "This is my personal cell. Use it if you need to."

She returned the eye contact and nodded once more. He left without another word. Her backside fell into her chair. Which one of her academy classes explained all the secrets/crooked cops/bullshit part of this job? Oh right, she thought sarcastically. None of them.

He was right. She'd been betrayed. Her parents turned away from her when she needed them the most. Her former captain and the fire chief. The frigging assistant to the governor of New York. The two FBI special agents assigned to work with her before Hurst and Goodrich.

The biggest question at this moment was if Hurst was friend or foe.

She looked down at her hands. They were clenched into fists so hard her knuckles were white. The sticky note. Oh shit. Bolting from her chair, she grabbed her keys on her way out.

CHAPTER 2

Her unmarked glided to a complete stop along the curb next to the Stoner home. Nickie decided against lights, and neither the college girl nor the screaming woman, who was apparently Mrs. Stoner, took notice. She took the incognito moment to assess.

The Stoner home was nestled between two Victorians in the most prestigious area of Northridge. It was a brightly painted white thing with columns and a long drive that wound to the sidewalk. Mrs. Stoner must have worked up a petite sweat walking all the way down here. Glancing out the passenger window, Nickie noticed the missus wore four-inch raspberry pumps. She corrected her assessment to include that the poor, poor woman must be sweaty and with sore ankles.

The girl craned her head away from Mrs. Stoner as she walked along the sidewalk. She wasn't marching necessarily. More like pacing. After about twenty-five feet, she rotated a hundred-eighty degrees, then turned her head away from Mrs. Stoner once more. The picket sign was big. It read 'NO CONSENT' on one side and 'NO MEANS NO' on the other. The girl was visibly shaken, but seemed determined to continue her march regardless of what Mrs. Stoner spewed at her.

She was a small thing and wore gray fleece sweatpants—the kind with elastic at the ankles—and the ugliest pair of Velcro shoes Nickie had ever seen. Sweatshirt with no hood. Low ponytail collecting dozens of braided extensions that seemed like they needed to be redone. No makeup from what Nickie could see. Bad signs. All very bad signs.

"Huh," Nickie said as she exited her unmarked. The girl had been raped and was picketing her rapist's home? She had to give her credit.

"…fucking arrested when—" Mrs. Stoner zipped her lips when her eyes met Nickie. Gun holsters had that effect. "Oh, Officer. Thank you for coming."

What? No ass-chewing? No f-bomb? And Nickie was so looking forward to it.

"This woman has been—"

"I'll take it from here, ma'am."

"My husband is at the police station filing an order of protection as we speak. This…this *girl*—"

"Can she do that?" Ah. The girl had a voice. "This is freedom of speech."

"Let's you and I talk about that." Nickie took her elbow and led her toward her police issued as Mrs. Stoner strutted on her pink spikes back up the drive.

"Are you arresting me?"

"Of course not. We're going to talk."

"At the police station?"

"How about coffee?"

The girl rode in Nickie's passenger seat without saying a word. She stared out the side window as Nickie turned into the parking lot of the Northridge downtown bakery. A nice, quiet booth should help. If the girl truly was a rape victim, she would want to avoid notice, wouldn't like talking about what happened and most definitely wouldn't picket the home of her attacker. This girl didn't fit all the stereotypes but enough of them that

Nickie felt at least part of her story was founded.

Pulling into a far parking spot, she turned off the engine.

"Are you hungry?" Nickie asked.

The girl shook her head.

"Coffee, then?"

"I don't drink coffee."

"Me either. Soda it is. How about you tell me your name."

For the first time, the girl looked Nickie in the eye. "You don't know who I am?"

It wasn't one of those I'm-so-important-you-should-know-who-I-am statements. It bothered Nickie. She decided on honesty. "No. Why do you think I should know who you are?"

"I just thought…" The girl shook her head and opened her door. "Never mind," she said as she got out. "My name is Nevaeh Thornton. I'm in my first year at Heritage Junior College."

Nevaeh. Nuh-vae-uh Nickie said in her head again and again. Nickie placed her hand on the girl's arm. Dark brown eyes nearly the color of Hurst's looked at her. The whites around the thick color had turned pink and glossy. "I'm Detective Nickie Savage, and I'm going to help you."

The girl stared at her for a moment, then nodded like she might believe her.

Silent mode kicked in as they walked through the door and Nickie chose a booth. It was mid-morning and the place was nearly empty. Good. The sweet smell of donuts, cinnamon rolls and caramel coffee filled the air. Even better.

"Diet or regular?" Nickie hoped they served soda here.

"Diet. Thank you."

"My kinda girl. Two diets on the way." Nickie ordered the sodas and two yeast donuts. She couldn't remember the last time she ate a donut, and she thought about the extra miles in the pool she would need that night because of it. As she handed the money to the barista, she glanced over her shoulder. Other than chewing her nails, Nevaeh sat completely still.

Sliding into the booth, Nickie placed each donut on a napkin and pushed one toward the girl. She didn't dare pull out her recorder, no matter how much she wanted to. But she did take out the mini-notepad she kept tucked in her holster.

It was almost like Nevaeh went into autopilot. She started before Nickie had a chance to click open her pen.

"I was at a party. A drama club party. I remember drinking but not that much. I was making out with Eric Stoner. He...grabbed my...you know. Hard."

"It's better if you tell me, Nevaeh. I've heard it all. And I've been through it myself."

That seemed to take her by surprise. She took a bite of her donut, then sipped on her Diet Coke. Nickie did the same.

"He grabbed my boobs. Hard. Right in front of everyone. He was laughing. I don't remember much of the rest of the night. Nothing actually. I woke up in Eric's apartment. My underwear was missing and I was bruised...down there." She clamped her eyes closed. "Both places. Some cuts, too."

"Down there?"

She shut her eyes. "Between my legs. My privates."

"Did you go to a hospital or the health center?"

Nevaeh shook her head. "I went to a counselor."

"One at the college?" Nickie scribbled feverously. So far, her story said she was given some kind of roofie, but the perp could be anyone.

Nevaeh nodded her head this time.

Nickie took another bite, another sip, giving Nevaeh time to regain her composure. The girl chewed on her nails between bites of the donut.

"Do you remember the counselor's name?"

"Janet Gillion. She took notes as I spoke. I found out later she left out some things I'd told her. She used the words 'insufficient evidence' and told me it was impossible to address the matter. That's how she said it. So, I'm picketing. Maybe the publicity will save a girl. A friend."

Nickie closed her eyes and took a breath. There weren't any news venues that were there to report the picket. No friends of hers would know.

"I'm not the only girl."

Nickie's eyes opened. Nevaeh looked as guilty as if she'd just betrayed a best friend's secret. She probably did. And if there were other victims, Stoner had earned himself a spot as top suspect.

"There are two that I know of. They're acting like nothing happened. Won't even go talk to a counselor, which I guess is a waste of time anyway. One of them still goes to the parties. Why would she do that?"

"If you think about it, Nevaeh, I suspect they aren't acting like *nothing* happened. Are they wearing less makeup? More conservative clothes?"

"Detective Savage?"

"Do you notice their eyes tracing the edge of the concrete as they walk to class? Do they hold their arms closer to their bodies? Hug their books as they amble along?"

A hand touched Nickie's forearm. "Detective Savage?"

Like a camera changing from a distant shot to close up, the hand on Nickie's arm sharpened into focus. Nickie glanced up. She'd been in a flashback. How long had she been like that? Nevaeh seemed to be deciding whether Nickie was competent.

Get in the game, Nick. Leaning away, she slipped her arm from the girl and slung a boot over her knee. "The girl who is going to the parties wants her life back. Wants to move on. She doesn't understand it's not going to happen until she deals with the now."

"I did research. In 2012, the laws were changed to say consent rather than only forced. How can I give consent if I don't remember?"

The girl was much like Nickie at that age. Not typical. Here she was fighting, even when she'd bared her story to an adult only to be turned away. Sometimes Nickie thought that kind of attitude was a good thing. Sometimes not so much.

"Is Mrs. Stoner really going to get an order of protection against me?"

Oh, jeez. She really thought that. "Did you do any physical harm or threaten her?"

The girl shook her head.

"Have you been picketing their house often?"

"Just the once."

"Then, she can file all she wants. It won't go through."

Nevaeh's lungs expanded and released. Nickie reached over and squeezed her dark fingers. "Is there someone you can talk to?"

The girl pulled her hand away. "No. I told you. I found other girls. Two of them. They won't even look at me now that they know I know."

"Just to tell you, that is the statistically typical response. Yours is not. Give me the names of the girls. You lie low for a while. Let me see what I can do."

"They won't talk to you. You're a cop."

"I'm a detective and I'm a woman. A woman who's been through what you've been through. Give me a chance."

Nevaeh seemed to consider before she answered. "They're in drama club, too."

"When is this drama club?"

"Monday afternoons at three."

Nevaeh's trust seemed sketchy. Who could blame her?

"Do you have someone you can talk to?" she repeated. "It's important that you reach out."

No nod or shake this time. The expression on Nevaeh's face told Nickie the girl might have just realized she had no one. Nice job, Nick. "I'm going to talk to a trusted friend who might have a resource for you. Look at me, Nevaeh." She did, with reluctance. Nickie took both of her hands this time. They were ice cubes. "I'm not going to let you down."

Nickie parked in no parking at the front of the main offices at Heritage College. Nevaeh was safe and sound at her apartment building across the street. Or maybe on her way to class by that time. Nickie would work a few angles before trying to find the other two girls.

It was warm for late April, so she rolled down the windows, pushed her seat back as far as it would go and propped her boots on the dash. She hoped they were muddy. Damned police-issued car. She pulled out her phone and dialed Dave's personal line. Nickie had the resources to hook Nevaeh up with nurses, shelters and protection. But the girl hadn't been rescued from a kidnapping or trafficking abduction. She needed rape counseling. The captain's wife ran a handful of homeless shelters. Maybe she could throw her a few names of counselors with a rape background.

She dialed his number.

"Hey, Nick. How'd it go?"

"Mrs. Stoner stopped her tirade of expletives as soon as she spotted me. Says her husband is filing a bat-shit-crazy-lady request for an order of protection. The girl appears legit. I'm at the college now. Gonna talk to the dean."

"You know he can't tell you anything."

"I'm persuasive."

"Be careful."

"Do you know who you're talking to?"

"Point taken."

"So, I get the impression this kid doesn't have anyone to…ya know…talk to. I was thinking maybe your wife could hook me up with a name or two."

"I'll text you her cell."

"I thought maybe you could—"

"Man up and get over your aversion to relationships with females."

"I do not have an aversion to relationships with females." Lie.

"Then, there's no problem. This is high profile, Nick. I want the report on Stoner by the end of the day."

Heat gathered on her shirt where her holster lay. She got out of her car and welcomed the sun and the sound of her boots as they echoed off the sidewalk instead of sloshing through puddles of slush. Life was good. Zheng was in custody. She was married to the best thing that had ever been given to her, and she had a new case. The fact that she wasn't so bad with the Rottweiler puppy Duncan had brought home for her was icing on her cake. Oh crap. The puppy. It was her turn to let Xena out over lunch.

She checked the time on her phone as she opened the paneled wooden door to the administration building. Her boots brushed across the plush carpet to reception. Pulling out her badge, she leaned over the counter. "I'm here to see the dean."

The gal lifted her chin and looked down her nose. "Do you have an appointment?"

"No, I have a badge. I know where his office is." Nickie walked around the desk and figured the woman would tell her if he was gone or with someone. Instead, she sat with her pink painted lips hanging in an O.

Nickie knocked as she walked in. Manners. He lifted his gaze and sighed. Good. He recognized her.

"Good morning, Detective. What can I do for you?"

"Yeah, good morning." Oh, how she did not want to

meet with this guy. She handed him a page from her mini-notebook. "I need the class schedules and addresses of these two girls."

He sighed, but the names of the two girls must not have rung any bells for him. She rocked on the balls of her feet as he began pecking at the keys on his keyboard. She looked around and felt like maybe she should have wiped her boots before entering. It wasn't her first time in his office, but she'd forgotten how plush it was. Plush carpet, linen blinds, dark polished desk with a matching wall of cabinets. Blah, blah, blah. She preferred her tiny office and splintered wooden desk.

"Anything else?" he asked as the printer on his desk woke.

"Nevaeh Thornton." She noted the recognition on his face this time.

"I can tell you her registration status and give you her class schedule."

"You know what I want."

"You know I cannot speak of it."

"I understand." Honestly, she did. "But you won't be breaking any confidentiality laws by listening."

The muscles in his jaw flexed, but he leaned forward and clasped his fingers, apparently ready to hear what she had to say.

"She shows all the signs. I met with her—"

"You met with her?"

"Yes, I met with her. See, that's what I can't stand about college rape. Girls all across the country get raped—not that I'm saying Nevaeh did. They go out on a limb to a college counselor, who turns around and makes the call as to whether the case has sufficient evidence. Who gives a college counselor the right to advise upon and decide whether there are grounds for an investigation? Then, we—the real police officers—don't hear about or know when a crime has been allegedly committed, because it isn't properly reported. So, yes. I met with her, and I—a Northridge Police Department detective—say there is sufficient evidence to proceed with an investigation."

He leaned toward her. She'd clearly hit a button. Good.

"What I can't stand," he said barely loud enough for her to hear, as if that might make it off the record. "Is that there are two sides to every story and one is often ignored. What if the hypothetical accused is a stellar honor student who organizes and participates in hours of community service each week?"

The puzzle pieces began to fit together. "She says she didn't give consent."

"There is no proof of that."

"She wasn't even conscious."

"There's no proof of that either."

"We'll see about that."

CHAPTER 3

——————•◆•◆•——————

The apartment building was typical for a college campus. Nickie stepped over the puke on the threadbare stairs that led to the second floor. Beer cans lined the window ledge. The faint odor of urine and the not-so-faint one of the puke wasn't so foreign to her, but she made sure to breathe through her mouth anyway. The first girl's apartment was on the left. Nickie figured someone was home since keys hung from the keyhole.

She knocked. Footsteps stopped at the door. Nickie held up her badge in front of the peephole.

The girl who opened the door matched the photo from the dean's printout. Caroline Studebaker. She wore chucks and jeans and a gray sweatshirt that read: *Drama kids fake it better.* Nice.

"Oh, thank you, Officer! I'm so embarrassed. I've been doing that all the time lately." She took the keys from the door and began to shut it once more.

Nickie placed the toe of her boot in the doorway, stopping it from closing. "That's not why I'm here, Caroline."

Understanding flooded the girl's face. Her gaze dropped to the floor. "Oh. Okay."

"May I come in?"

The girl glanced behind Nickie before answering. "Okay," she repeated.

Nickie sat on the edge of a gold couch that sank in the middle. The girl sat on the opposite end. Her knees stuck together. She picked up her backpack, hugging it close to her chest before slipping it over a single shoulder.

"My name is Nickie. Are you Caroline?" she asked even though she knew the answer.

Caroline nodded as she stared at the floor.

Nickie placed her forearms on her knees and folded her hands. She spoke lightly and started easy. "I'm here about drama club. Is that the team shirt?"

Crossing her arms over the words, Caroline continued to stare at a spot on the carpet and shook her head in quick succession. "Drama club is great." Her voice cracked.

"I didn't say it wasn't great. I'm here to help. You're safe."

Her lids closed and tears ran freely. "Did Nevaeh send you? I'm not safe, and I'm…I'm not talking. Do I have to talk?"

Nickie wanted to keep Nevaeh out of this. She tried her warmest smile. "It will help if you talk. It will help you, and it will help the other girls who are victims."

"The other girls don't want help."

"Everyone wants help, Caroline. I know. I've been where you are now."

Caroline's eyes turned to Nickie's. Nickie smiled and nodded. "I can help you," she repeated.

The girl stood, making her backpack fall to the floor. She picked it up and slung it over both shoulders this time. "I'm late for class."

She wasn't. Nickie had her schedule in the pocket of her slacks. "I want you to take my card. Please call me when you're ready."

The girl nodded, took the card and left without checking to see if Nickie shut the door behind them.

* * *

Damn, she was late. Nickie needed to make up for the days she shirked her turn in taking the puppy out at lunch. A stop at Mikey's to pick up a giant tenderloin for her lunch date with Duncan oughta do it.

The cleaning boys must have come that morning. Not a dish in the sink. Everything was shiny and clean. She'd stopped trying to convince Duncan not to have them come. Nickie was a slob. He wasn't. Compromise.

Xena's tail smacked the metal bars on the cage. The compromise meant she didn't have to vacuum puppy hair.

"Hey, baby girl. I'm coming. I'm coming."

Since the little girl couldn't keep her excitement in her bladder yet, Nickie and Duncan kept her cage in the kitchen next to the doors that led out back. Nickie noticed something out of the corner of her eye. Her feet stopped before they made it to the pup. Centered on the enormous kitchen table was a paper.

Ignoring the thumping tail, Nickie crept closer to the paper. She glanced over at the alarm to make sure nothing weird was blinking. A quick scan of her surroundings. Knee-jerk reaction. Nothing out of place. The paper was facedown. Picking it up, she recognized it as a print copy of the email sent from an undisclosed IP address at the station to the now missing crooked FBI agents. It wasn't new. She'd read it a thousand times. So, why was it sitting on her kitchen table? She read it again. Damned mole.

The subject still has the photograph on her computer. She continues to question the imprisoned and search for evidence.

Xena's whining brought her back to the reason she was home. "Here I am, girl. Let's get you outside." Nickie clicked a leash on the squirming mass of Rottweiler puppy. "Xena, calm," Nickie commanded as the trainer taught her to do. She was talking to a brick wall. Xena pawed at Nickie's slacks and head butted her as the pup's excitement leaked over the ceramic tiles as they made their way down the stairs of the deck. "Xena, heel." Yeah, right.

The dog may still be unruly when Nickie or anyone came into the house, but the time it took to calm became shorter each day. Progress. She did her business in the spot she and Duncan had taught her to, then came directly to Nickie and sat in the cool grass. Her ears twitched and her tail swept the ground, but her eyes were glued to Nickie's. "Such a good girl." Xena heeled at Nickie's left side and they made their way up the stairs. Nickie wouldn't say it was easy, but this dog-training thing was kick ass.

As Xena ate lunch, Nickie cleaned the floor then grabbed a half-full carton of Greek vanilla yogurt from the fridge, sprinkled a few blueberries over the top and her lunch was set.

A slimy, wet tongue licked the back of her dangling hand. "Eww, girl. Why do you do that?" Xena rolled over and stuck her feet in the air.

Duncan's stomach growled, reminding him it was well past noon. His part-time office assistant was long gone, so he'd turned on his security camera monitors. It was like watching a movie from his office chair. Nickie juggled a large take-out bag, a container of yogurt and a bottle of Diet Coke as she attempted the elevator button. He recognized the bag as one from Mikey's Bar and Grill, which made his stomach growl once more.

It wasn't like her to walk into anyone's office unannounced, especially when the door was closed. He crossed his floor and opened his door before she had the chance to drop his lunch.

He lifted a corner of his mouth as he took the Mikey's bag and the yogurt. His hand and arm were far too valuable for him to risk taking her Diet Coke for her.

With his free hand, he took hers and faintly twirled the wedding band that rested next to her engagement ring. Leaning in, he kissed her softly. "There you are," he said faintly.

She blinked three times before heading toward his desk.

"Am I so late that you waited by the door for your lunch?" she asked as she sank into one of his guest chairs. She lifted a boot as if she were going to plop it on his desk, then seemed to change her mind and let it fall in front of her.

Walking around to his chair, he gestured to the monitor at the side of his desk. "I saw you on the security cameras."

"Ah. Sorry for being late. And for my absence over the past few days. It doesn't look like the next few will be any better."

"Hmm," he said as he spread out his lunch on the paper bag. "That is a shame, actually, since I haven't seen you naked in—" He checked the watch on his wrist. "—seventy-two hours."

Opening her yogurt container, she scowled. "What about last night? On the stairs? Yum, by the way."

"You weren't naked."

She smiled for a solid ten seconds before her beautiful lips turned into a frown. "What's up with the copy of the email you left on the kitchen table?"

"You remembered to let out Xena."

"I did. We practiced sit, lay and stay. Smartest damned dog I've ever raised."

"The only dog you've raised," he corrected. After all the grief she gave him over the purchase of a puppy, Nickie turned out to be—with the help of training school—a natural.

"Email?" she repeated.

"I placed it there as a reminder that we need to discuss it."

"Again?"

"I haven't been able to detect the originator." It was the damnedest, most frustrating hack job he'd ever attempted.

"And that must really get you."

"It does, yes. It's as if he—"

"Or she."

"—or she knows I'm looking for him…or her. I need to tell you that Andy and I are going to take a road trip and dig deeper. It is well past time for disclosure on this front."

"I know you're working hard not to keep things from me anymore. And don't get me wrong, I appreciate it and all that, but you don't always need to tell your detective wife when you're going to commit a federal crime and hack into secure databases."

Ah, she knew what he meant by 'dig deeper,' then. It made him grin through his next bite.

Her head turned but her steel-gray eyes remained on his. "How can you talk the way you do, and look the way you do, yet eat that shit? It's all mixed up."

"Says the woman eating yogurt and blueberries, who just said, 'Eat that shit.'"

"Special Agent Hurst came by today."

He stopped mid-bite. "Singular?"

"See? You get that. Yes, just him. Dressed everyday like. It was creepy as hell. He asked me how I keep going after so many betrayals against me from colleagues within the legal system."

He nodded as he set down his lunch, every sight, smell and touch buzzing to attention. "He came all the way from Langley to tell you what you already know?"

"No. He stopped by to tell me we get to keep Zheng a while longer…weeks or maybe months. He said he was in the area. Vacation. Camping. I am *not* making this up."

His brows dropped. He wanted to check on her?

Recognized her long list of betrayals within the judicial system? "How do you feel about this?"

"See? You get that, too. Suspicious. Can't help it. Of course, I'm glad to have Zheng available for interrogation or the occasional needed bullying, but that's weird, right? Show up without his partner, in jeans and gives me more time? That's not what feds do."

"Possibly he appreciates what you've been through and believes you deserve this."

"Possibly he's like the rest of them." She shrugged and drowned some blueberries in her yogurt. "I have a new case," she said, flipping in typical character to her next subject change. "Alleged college rape. I'm at a road block already."

"You often include the word alleged."

Another shrug. "Innocent until proven guilty and all that. The girl seems legit, but no need to throw some dude under the bus until I'm sure. Which is where we come to my roadblock. I've got the girl. I've got the dude's ID." She dug in the pocket of her blouse and pulled out a photo. Waving it around with her free hand, she took another bite before continuing. "The student ID'd two other girls as possible victims. I visited one of them. She wouldn't talk to me."

"I'm surprised. You can be…convincing."

"That's what I thought, but she's scared stiff. Dean says the guy is all about community service and good student standing."

"You got the dean to give you that information? Why am I not surprised?"

"See? I can be—what word did you use?—convincing. The family is big in town. This could be harder than I expected. Statistically speaking, there should be more girls. I would really like to find more girls. I'm an NPD detective. I can't exactly stand in front of Drama Club practice and show this guy's picture to girls as they leave, judging their reactions to the sight of his face."

Duncan set the tenderloin on the paper bag and walked around his desk. He reached down and slid his hand beneath one of her muscled calves, lifting her leg to set her boot on top of his desk. Before repeating the process with the other, he snatched the photo from between her fingers. "I'm not a cop."

He barely had a chance to raise the photo over her head before she took hold of the inseam of his pants. The tug of her fingers sent him from zero to sixty in seconds. Pulling him toward her, she craned her head close to his, then grinned at him. "I didn't come here hoping to involve you. However, I'm truly grateful." She licked her lips and smiled. "Possibly enough for sexy outfits."

CHAPTER 4

—◆·◆·◆—

Nickie should have been dead on her feet, but for whatever reason, she was able to get up early, swim the extra two miles needed to make up for the donut she'd had with Nevaeh and do some extra training with the pup. She stopped her unmarked at the end of her long drive. Mother Nature kept up the warm spell, so she rolled down the windows of her wimpy station-issued car. The smell of spring morning dew was enough to put anyone in a good mood. In the neck of the black blouse she'd decided on that day, she tucked her hair to keep it from blowing over her face on the highway, then pulled away.

Her Bluetooth read her the emails she'd gotten throughout the night. If she was going to have to put up with such an embarrassing vehicle, it should at least come equipped with hands free. She pulled into Jimbo's convenience store and parked in her usual hiding spot. The absolute morning silence made the sound of her boots on the asphalt especially loud.

She ran over her list of things to do in her head as she walked. Try to catch other possible rape victim before the girl left for class. Do some digging on Eric Stoner and his family. Help her partner with his—Was Eddy

Lynx her partner? Fellow detective? Yes. Friend? Sure. Ex-lover? Unfortunately. But partner? It felt like it lately. But no one labeled them that way. Smart people.

The bell on the door wasn't enough to alert Jimbo of her entrance this time. He was too busy arguing on his cell.

"Good morning, ma'am." It was the new guy.

Nickie was in such a good mood, she didn't even threaten the kid with bodily harm if he ever called her, 'ma'am,' again. From the time she came in, to the time it took to fill her soda, all the way to check out, Jimbo had his back to the new guy, still barking into his phone. "What do you mean the door is unlocked, but she can't leave?" He hung up as she handed the new guy her money. "Hey, Nick."

'Hey, Nick'? Since when did he ever call her, Nick? "What's the matter with you, Jimbo? You're weird today."

His eyes met hers like he'd just seen her for the first time. "Can I ask you something?"

"You've got three minutes."

He looked at his new guy, then around the store. "Can I ask you something over there?" He motioned to a spot in front of the coolers. Was he serious? She pulled out her phone to check the time. Now, he had two minutes.

"S'up?" she said as they walked.

"I've got this friend, you see. His...uh...woman is in trouble."

Right. "What kind of trouble, Jimbo?"

"This girl, I mean, his woman, is with an injured kid...little girl. His woman says it's bad, and wants him to help."

He wouldn't bring this to her for some friend whose daughter fell down the stairs. There was generally only one reason why people ever brought shit like this to her. "Has he heard of a thing called 9-1-1? Is this little girl the woman's daughter? Relative?"

"No."

"How bad is the child hurt?"

"Sounds like real bad."

A few, quick flashes sped across the insides of her eyelids. A young black-haired girl who had been tied to the wall near a shower spigot that hung from the basement ceiling. She'd been beaten and hung there as an example to the other girls for displeasing one of her johns. Beads of sweat formed on Nickie's hairline. A flash of herself, as her yellow lingerie turned red and the smell of metal filled her nose from the blows she took to the side of her face.

Nickie lifted her forearm and pushed Jimbo against his beer fridge. "Enough cryptic shit, Jimbo. Tell me what's going on before I break your other arm."

"The girl." He shook his head. "The dude's woman," he corrected again. "She says she's with this kid. They can't leave. Says some door is unlocked, but they can't leave and she's worried about this kid. I don't know, Detective Dude. What do I tell him?"

The arm holding him against the cooler shook. She recognized the facts he was giving her. "You're coming with me." She grabbed him by his good arm and led the way out the door, leaving her soda by the new kid. "You're in charge," she yelled to the kid before the door closed behind them.

"Hey," Jimbo pleaded. "I don't know if he's ready for taking care of the whole place."

"He'll manage," she said and unlocked the passenger door of her car.

"But—"

"Shut up, and get in."

She marched around and slid into her seat, her only focus now was the possibility that a child had been taken.

Glancing at him, she started her car. He was checking out the instruments like a kid in a candy store. "I've never been in the front of one of these before."

There was no time for this shit. A girl could be dying. She peeled out of the lot. "The woman is a prostitute. Your friend is a john. The little girl is probably just that…a little girl."

"Wow," he said, drawing the word into three syllables. "You're like Sherman Holmes."

"Let me make this as clear as I can for you, Jimbo. A captive prostitute's description of the injured is in a completely different realm from the rest of the world. If she was desperate enough to call one of her johns for help, the kid might be near death. You're going to call the dude back and get the woman's location. Then, I want him to call 9-1-1."

"Why won't she just leave?" Jimbo asked.

The child might not have time for questions. "Make the call," she yelled.

"Yo, it's me," Jimbo said into his phone. "Yeah, I asked a…a friend what to do…who's been in the business, ya know?"

He wasn't wrong.

"I know, I know, but this friend. She knows. Listen. Where do you usually…ya know?" He glanced at Nickie.

She rolled her eyes. Her left leg started tapping the car floor mat.

"Meet up. Like, where is your friend." His shoulders drooped. "Manhattan?"

"Tell him he's got to call an ambulance. Give me the damned phone." She yanked it from him. "This is Detect—This is Nickie Savage. Do you have the location of the injured party?" Shit. She sounded like a cop. She was way off her game. Click. She handed the phone to Jimbo. "Call him back. I want to know if he knows where she's at, and have him write down the number she's calling from."

He called. She could hear yelling on the other end of

the phone. "I know. I know. Trust me, man. She's cool. Try to find out where she is."

The guy was loud enough on the other end of the phone now for Nickie to hear every word. "I said she won't tell me. Won't let me call an ambulance or the cops. She wants me to go over there. I ain't going over there. And she won't tell me where she's at unless I agree to go over there."

"Tell him to look at his Caller ID and write down the number."

She arrived at the station in record time. She squealed into her spot nose first.

Jimbo covered his phone with the palm of his hand and whispered, "Fuck, Detective Dude. The station? I hate this place. This is the icing on the dead horse. This day is shit."

Squeezing her eyes shut, she tried to keep her head. "There might not be much time before her pimp returns." She slammed her car into park and grabbed the phone from Jimbo's hand. "Hang up on me and I'll trace your number, hunt you down like a dog and rip out your throat."

"Listen, I don't know where she is." The guy didn't sound too young, maybe early/late thirties.

"She doesn't want me to call an ambulance or the police. She sounds scared, man. Why won't she just leave?"

Nickie's forehead sank to her steering wheel. She let the wave of grief encompass her arms and legs, then travel to her heart. "She's more scared to leave than she is to stay. How old is she?"

"What do you mean, how old is she? I don't…meet no kids. Get Jimbo on the phone."

Lifting her head, she shook it twice. "I'm what you've got, asshole. Tell me how old she is, or I'm hitting the highway to your place right now."

"I don't know how old she is. Maybe eighteen?"

"Freaking convenient." Manhattan. That familiar feeling of helplessness threatened to take over. She sensed as the veins in her forehead began to rise. "You got the name and number or what?"

"Yeah, I got it. I'll text it to Jimbo, then I'm out. I mean it. You call the police." Click.

If only it were that easy. Not her jurisdiction.

"The stairs, Detective Dude? I have a broken arm, ya know."

Losing her last thread of patience, Nickie gave Jimbo a push. She was due at the Heritage campus to check on the second college rape victim Nevaeh told her about.

This Manhattan thing wasn't Nickie's jurisdiction, but a girl was hurt. And both girls were in grave danger. The woman had crossed an uncrossable line by calling one of her johns for help. Nickie pictured how bad the child must be for the woman to make that call. And she doubted the legality of the age of the woman. Pimps didn't mix children with adult prostitutes.

As they reached the landing of the fourth floor, Jimbo stopped, nearly causing her to run into his back.

"No one's going to bite you, Jimbo. Walk." She gave him another push.

They may not have bitten him, but several recognized him. Nickie guided him—free of cuffs—and instead of heading to booking, went for the break room. She entered the room with her so-called partner taking up the spot behind them.

"This is where you eat, Detective Dude?" Jimbo rocked back on his heels. "It sucks."

She looked around. Cabinets, counter, sink, fridge, coffeemaker, microwave, table, chairs. What the hell more should there be? A loud thud shook the floor all the way to her feet.

Her head spun toward the noise and found Eddy holding Jimbo against the fridge. It was odd the way this was the second time that morning Jimbo had been held against a fridge. "There must be a good reason for Nick to have a slippery, drug-dealing thief in our break room. That doesn't mean we have to listen to you dis' the place," Eddy growled before finishing. "Do we understand each other?"

Jimbo kept his mouth shut and nodded quickly as he looked to the ground.

"This sucks? You work in a convenience store and hang out at titty bars," Nickie said, feeling suddenly satisfied. Thanks, Eddy.

Jimbo lifted the coffee carafe, smelled it and wrinkled his nose. "I just meant to say it's not like TV."

"He's stumbled across a situation," Nickie explained. "Possible captive child. Maybe ten-ish, I'm guessing. Allegedly beaten badly. And an older one who's scared enough to make a call."

"Why aren't you going in?" Eddy seemed to read her mind. "Oh. They aren't in the area, are they?"

Mind read again. "Nope. My hands are tied. I'm not thinking out of the damned freaking box. Not our jurisdiction. Cop territory and testosterone bullshit gets old sometimes, ya know?"

Jimbo's phone dinged. He patted his pockets, but she'd slipped the phone in hers. It was a text. "It's the phone number from the girl's cell. The john says she goes by 'Bianca.'" She dialed Duncan's number, but before she hit 'send' she turned to Eddy and Jimbo. "I'll be right back. No killing each other while I'm gone."

Duncan answered on the first ring. "Are you home?" she asked.

"No greeting. Is everything all right, Detective?"

"I've got a situation. Are you home?" she repeated.

"I'm working in my studio this morning, yes. What can I do for you?"

She could hear Xena whining in the background. "If I give you a phone number, can you find the location?"

"I can."

"Good. I'll text it to you."

Using her station cell this time, she called NYPD. A voice that needed to lay off the cigarettes answered. "New York Police Department."

"This is Detective Nickie Savage calling from the Northridge Police Department. I'd like to speak with one of the detectives on duty."

The raspy voice turned pleasant. "May I ask what this is in regards to?"

"Possible child kidnapping in your jurisdiction."

"I'll transfer you."

She waited six rings and almost gave up.

"Berkley," a male voice answered in the middle of the seventh.

"Detective Berkley, this is Detective Savage calling from the Northridge Police Department. Long story why I have this, but you have a probable child abduction and abuse case that came to me."

"NPD? Isn't that upstate?"

"It is. You have an alleged captive prostitute who called a john who called a friend. I have a number. If you could trace the call, it seems one or more of the girls is badly hurt and could use a look see."

"Listen, Detective. I don't know how they do things upstate, but here in the city, we don't have time to deal with women who call their johns for help instead of the police department. If the girl has access to a phone, she'll call the police when she wants or needs the help of the police."

"Ah!" Nickie yelled loud enough someone might come running. "Why is it so easy for your types to believe an adult woman is too scared to leave an abusive husband, but it's too hard to believe a child who's been forced into rape and has seen beatings and murders is too scared to betray her captor?"

Nickie thumped her forehead on her desk. The city

was four hours away. She could run her lights and make it in three. Duncan would find the address on the way. She could lose her badge for this. That scenario was becoming a habit. Lifting her head from her desk, she noticed several sets of eyes that stared at her from the commons area. Eddy was in the front. She stood, closed her plastic mini-blinds and shut the door.

Swiping her phone, she gingerly sank into her desk chair and dialed the victim's number. Goose bumps erupted over the cold sweat forming on her arms. The phone rang a dozen times with no answer. Her throat constricted. She pulled her head back to check and make sure she dialed the number correctly when the ringing stopped. She heard breathing.

CHAPTER 5

"Bianca?" Nickie assumed it wasn't her real name. "I'm here to help you."

Silence.

"I'm a friend of the john you called. Can you tell me if the young girl is still alive?"

"What's his name?"

"Whose name, honey?"

"The john."

Oh no. "I don't have it, but I can get—" Click. She pounded the side of her fist against the top of her desk, then cleared the contents in one swipe of her arm.

Hurst. Special Agent Hurst's card was in her desk. She slid open the rickety top right drawer. It stuck. She pulled harder. On top was the card, facedown, showing Hurst's chicken scratch handwriting of his personal cell. Frantic now, she dialed, not knowing if she was using her cell or the station's or Jimbo's.

"Nick?" He answered on the second ring.

Straightening, she wiped the sweat from her brow. "I have a situation I'm hoping you can help with."

"Are you hurt?"

"No, it's not me."

More frigging silence.

She clasped her fists and continued. "I have reason to believe at least two girls are being held captive and used in forced prostitution. One seems to be badly hurt."

"How does this involve me, Nick?"

This wasn't coming out as she'd planned. She stood to pace and gripped a chunk of her hair. "One of the girls called a john for help. She's too scared to call an ambulance or the police."

"Why aren't you with her?"

And there was the problem. "She's in the city."

"Did the girl cross state lines? Do you have an ID on the perp?"

No and no. "I called NYPD. We don't have an address." Yet. "NYPD can't understand why the girl won't call for help if she has a phone."

"Only ten percent of the police force has been trained in child trafficking, Nick. They don't get it."

Tears started dripping down her face.

"I have an idea, though. I know some people who might know some people. They're not cops or FBI. No jurisdiction. No bureaucracy. Let me make a call."

She grabbed all three phones and, ignoring the stares, took off out her office door.

"Stay," she barked to Jimbo as she passed the break room. One of the morning's donuts and a stale cup of coffee sat in front of him. That should keep him busy. She kept going to Dave's office.

She knocked on his open door and walked in before he could tell her not to. Even breathing was nearly impossible as she paced and gave him a summary of what had transpired. "I'm going out there."

"Nick, that's a four-hour drive."

"I know."

"Do you even know where you're going?"

She gave him a look that said she knew but couldn't tell him because she did. He must have read her face, because he held his hands up like he didn't want to know. "Okay, okay," he said. "I can move Lynx to the college rape case."

Not Eddy. He's a man. "No!" she said too earnestly and stopped her feet. Facing him, she tried to sound composed. "I will call the college girl and reassure her I'm taking care of the case. I've…got a plan for some recon on Monday." Or Duncan has a plan. "I can do research on the case just as easily on my tablet in the car as I can at the station."

Dave strode around his desk and hovered over her. Placing a hand on her shoulder, he spoke gently. "Do you have someone to go with you?"

She nodded quickly. "I'll be back bright and early Monday morning."

"Will you call before then and let me know you're okay?"

More tears threatened to escape. He was always more of a father to her than a captain. She nodded again, but this time less desperately.

She spun on her heels, grabbing Jimbo by the collar on the way toward the stairs.

A leg clothed in brown pants came out from the stairwell door, blocking her way. "You going rogue again?"

There was nothing she could tell Eddy, and instead, she lifted her eyes to him. He kissed her on the forehead and whispered, "Be careful."

Shoving open the stairwell door, she turned to Jimbo. The look on his face was judging. Eddy was forever a complication. She wasn't about to explain him to Jimbo. "I'm keeping your phone. I may need it."

"Man, Detective Dude," he said as his feet scraped the carpeted floor. "What if my woman calls?"

"I'll tell her you're working as an informant."

"Slippery Jimbo, official police informant. I like the sound of that."

* * *

Duncan's tablet lay open between them as he drove the 81 South. It blinked with the illegal trace he'd generated. His proximity was like blood pressure medicine. The calm he created in her didn't require physical touch. The scent of him. The slow and calculated way he moved. Watching her without watching her.

Her cell rang, sending her heart back to racing. Caller ID read: Special Agent Hurst.

"Savage," she answered after the first ring.

"It's me, Nick. I have a phone number for you. Child Rescue. It's a nonprofit that works specifically with trafficking. Some veteran delta force operatives who work with them live in the city. They might be able to help. I'm texting you the number of the CEO. He's expecting your call."

She recognized the organization. It couldn't hurt. "Thank you," she responded. "I'm sorry to bother you on your vacation."

She glanced to Duncan. He nodded the way he did that both reassured and gave her strength. Looking down at the phone in her hand, she opened the text. Jess Larsen, co-founder of Child Rescue. She clicked the link to the phone number.

"This is Jess." Nickie had expected a female. This was a man's voice.

"This is Detective Nickie Savage." She probably should have left off the title in this scenario. Habit.

"Detective, hello. Albert told me you might call. You have a lead on captive girls?"

"Yes. However, it's in Manhattan. I work upstate. There are two girls. Because they have access to a cell phone, NYPD doesn't understand why—if they're hurt—they don't call 9-1-1. They won't trace her—"

"She's scared," he interrupted.

Exactly.

"I'm afraid," he said before she could continue, "there

won't be much my friends can do without an address either."

"I've been able to access the address." Although she wouldn't be able to tell him how. "The girl—"

"What's the name she gave?"

He knew to say 'name she gave.' "Bianca. I can't tell NYPD how I acquired the address. I'm crossing into their turf." And because it was illegal. "The girl called her john. Some kid with her could be in bad shape. For all I know, the pimp is back."

"Text the address to this number, my friends said they are ready and willing, if needed."

She thought she should offer a disclaimer. "It will be highly dangerous."

"These guys are retired delta force. They've rescued girls in Peru and the city. Let's just hope they're in the area."

She hung up and let her head fall back on the passenger seat as Duncan drove her unmarked. Absentmindedly, he took her left hand and twirled the wedding and engagement rings between his thumb and forefinger.

"My car would have been faster," he complained.

But she didn't care. The feel of his fingers made her lids close and her lungs slowly expand. Two girls. They weren't included in the dozens held captive by Jun Zheng's Fu Haizi. She yearned to have the ability to be in several places at the same time. Solving the college rape case, saving the two girls in Manhattan as well as working the Fu Haizi case. She didn't have enough on Zheng yet to put him away for life for his involvement in the crime ring. And it wouldn't be enough to just put him away for life. He could be replaced. She needed the entire organization. It was time to interrogate Zheng again to see if she could get more out of him. She would. Soon after they got back to Northridge.

She forced herself to draw her focus back to the feel

of Duncan's fingers as they twirled her rings.

"I can get these soldered for you," he said seeming to notice when and where her focus moved.

Without opening her eyes, she smiled. "I'll pass."

The sigh that came from his lips was slight, but she knew everything about this man and decided she owed him an explanation. Her knee-jerk reaction was to keep it to herself. She wasn't worth this; he might think she was crazy and all that. It helped to keep her eyes closed as she spoke such out-of-character words. "I'm nowhere near ready to give them up yet. Not even the few days it would take to have them soldered."

His fingers let go of the rings. For that split second, she feared her knee jerk was spot on. Maybe her insecurities were too much for him. Then, he wrapped his long fingers all the way around hers and squeezed.

GPS told Duncan he had less than five miles to go. His Nickie rode this last leg of their journey with her head between her legs. He knew better than to rub her back. It would only serve to make her feel like a child. Instead, he rested his hand just above her gun belt. Her shirt was cool and tacky from the layer of sweat that covered her back.

"I'm okay," she said nearly loud enough for the neighboring cars to hear. "I'll be just fine. How much longer?"

"Four miles." He let his thumb circle a bump on her spine.

Her chest expanded one last time, then she raised her head and looked out the windshield. It might have been better they didn't take the Audi. The neighborhood was not one to accommodate a flat tire.

"No call from Mr. Delta Force." He noted the snark in her tone. You could take the cop out of her jurisdiction, but you couldn't take the resentment of the higher ups from said cop.

"There." She spotted them before Duncan's GPS had time to tell him he had reached his destination.

It was a two-story motel with access from the outside. Not bad for the neighborhood. New trim, newer paint job. Two muscle heads in dress pants and button-down shirts leaned close to one of the doors on the ground floor.

Nickie laced her fingers through her hair and shook it loose. Then, she unbuckled her gun belt and shoved it beneath her seat. "Looks like they haven't been here long." Her door opened before they came to a complete stop. She sank Slippery Jimbo's cell into her back pocket. Did she realize it wasn't hers? Pulling her shirttail from her slacks, she seemed to be attempting to hide her detective façade. Not bad.

He parked away from them and watched as she strutted to the two veteran delta force operatives. She was out of earshot, but he didn't need to hear her. Her presentation told him she didn't approve. He felt a small twinge of guilt for the veterans. It would be difficult to meet his detective's standards in such a scenario.

The two men glanced toward Nickie as she placed her hand on the doorknob. She turned, but her hand didn't twist. Ah. He imagined that would make her angry if the door had been unlocked all day until the veterans arrived.

As he approached, Duncan heard the one with a shaved head. "Got her to tell me the girl is ten. Says she's nineteen."

"Little too convenient," Nickie said.

"We agree."

"Let me try."

"You sure about this? Could cause you some steam this far away from home."

Ignoring the two, she dipped her head close to the door. "Bianca, it's me. We talked on the phone."

Silence.

CHAPTER 6

"I have the name you asked for," Nickie said through the door. "The name of your john." She looked pained as she glanced over her shoulder to the veterans. "He says his name is…John."

"My name's not Bianca. I'd like you to leave."

At least Nickie got her to say something.

"Is your friend still alive, honey? We can help her."

The veterans looked at Duncan as if they wanted to introduce themselves. Duncan felt the same. They all remained still.

The door clicked. Nickie moved forward, then pulled her hand back and held it up. The only sounds were the cars driving on the road behind them and some shouts from neighboring motels and apartment buildings. The light glide of a chain sliding was followed by a turn of the knob. The smell of urine and rotten food wafted as the door creaked open.

The girl had flat, brown hair. Dark rings circled beneath her big brown eyes. Her face was boney as was the little of her Duncan could see through the crack she'd made in the door.

"I think her arms are broken," the girl said. "She's asleep. I think. She feels hot."

"Will you open the door, honey? These men can help."

Her eyes darted from Nickie's to one of the veteran delta force, then the other.

The bald one stepped forward. "We can get the girl to a hospital. We have a safe place for both of you, Bianca. No one can hurt you. There are other girls like you there. Food. Safety."

The door shut. "My name is Mary. I don't know any Bianca. Please go away. My friend will be back anytime."

"You don't have to see your friend ever again," Nickie said. "Can I come in? Just me. I have no weapons. If he comes back, he can have me. I'll tell the men to hide. Please, Bianca. Mary. Let me help your friend. She could be dying."

When the door opened this time, Duncan noticed red in the girl's eyes. They'd turned glossy, but no tears escaped over her pink lids. This time her stare was fierce as it moved from him to the veterans.

Nickie nodded toward the end of the outside porch, then turned her head to the girl and smiled. Duncan and the veterans stepped toward the end. The door shut once more, but this time it opened without the chain.

No. Duncan did not want his Nickie in there. It took great restraint not to bust open the door and take the girls to safety over his shoulder. His trust in Nickie ran thin as the need to protect her fogged his mind. His feet no longer moved, but the door shrank as heat twirled around him. Heat, then sand. Sand, then mortar. Mortar, then blood. Blood that covered the inside of the Chinook. Why wasn't he dead? He should be dead. He stared uselessly at the lifeless bodies of his platoon. His commander spoke in his ear.

"PTSD."

Why would he say that?

A hand rested on his shoulder. He shook it off and

twirled to find the taller delta force veteran looking at him with the pity Duncan despised. "I've been there, man."

Nickie.

"Nickie?" he asked.

"She's been in for about ten minutes now. The area is still secure."

Duncan closed his eyes and felt the coolness caused by wind blowing on the perspiration covering his face. His Nickie. The sense of powerlessness was too familiar.

Nickie checked the scene. Two double beds. Stained. Two more mattresses tossed on the floor. Goose bumps erupted over her arms. The smell. Urine, the metallic odor of ancient blood. Her breaths quickened, but she forced herself to remain sharp. Television on with the sound muted. Ancient VHS player. Nothing dangerous. It was just the two of them. "Where are the others, honey?"

The girl kept her eyes on Nickie. They were a dark blue and completely dead. Suspicion the only sign of coherency.

The others must be out working. But why not Bianca? Or Mary? Or whatever her name was? "I'm going to check on the little girl now. Okay? Nice and easy."

Bianca clutched the cell in her hand like it was the only piece of safety she held in this world. It made Nickie realize she, too, clutched her belt where her gun usually rested.

The girl was alive but felt like she was on fire. Of Asian Indian decent, yet a flush colored her dark cheeks. Her clothes were lacey and loose and filthy. "You're right. She has a high fever. Will you let me call an ambulance?"

Bianca looked at her with lifeless eyes and shook her head.

It had to be now, had to be soon. "There's not much time, Bianca. You called for help. I know how much that took for you to do that. You are brave." Nickie tried to step closer to her, but Bianca stepped back and in front of the path to the door in response.

"I want to show you something, okay?" She lifted the tail of her shirt. "See? No weapons. No badge even. This is not my jurisdiction. I'm nothing here."

Bianca's eyes dropped toward Nickie's boots. Smart girl. "See?" Nickie lifted the cuffs of her pants. "No weapons here either."

Slowly, Nickie closed her eyes. Inadvertently, they squeezed shut as she rotated away from the girl. Reaching behind, she lifted the back of her blouse up to her shoulders. It was more than just exposing her back. It was exposing her life, her secrets. And it had to be worth it. Had to be. She made sure to display each of the six lines of scars. Each of the three cigarette burns raised over the flesh of her back. "I know why you're scared, Bianca. I got away. I got away, and I lived."

Turning back to her, Nickie noticed she had moved away from the path of the door.

"I'm calling an ambulance, honey. Can I let these men take you to a safe house before it gets here? The police will come. They are going to do everything they can to save this little girl." Nickie hoped she was right. "But I'm not sure if they will take you to a safe house or juvie." She pointed to the door. "Those men aren't cops." Anymore. "They can take you to a place with other girls who have escaped. There is food and shelter. They will let you call home."

Bianca's brows dipped low.

"When you're ready," Nickie amended, then straightened her shirt and stepped forward. Placing a hand on the girl's forearm, she whispered, "Let me have them hide you."

Nickie took the girl's lack of answer as affirmation.

Slowly, Nickie made her way to the door and nodded to the veterans. They knew enough to make their way slowly.

Her eyes met Duncan's. His were red, and his skin was covered in a sheen of sweat. 'Oh, Duncan,' she mouthed. He lifted his cell in question. She nodded and heard him dial the three numbers before hitting send.

He was coming. He was coming and Nicole was ready.

This one liked her. They'd brought him to her before. He called her Savage, just like the rest of them. She'd show him a savage. She scrambled to the edge of the bed and held her legs tightly to her body. It was only partially an act.

He huffed a half-laugh and emptied his pockets like her father did when he came home for the day. "I'd hoped you'd be that way, honey." He said it like she was some sort of little girl. They'd taken that away from her long ago. He took off his shirt. He was so fat, she couldn't tell if he wore a belt. The tie. He tossed the tie on the bed. She could reach it. She could. It was all she needed.

His arm. On his left forearm was a tattoo of a butterfly. It was more like four hearts made to look like butterfly wings. Where had she seen that before?

Gasping, Nickie sat up. Her eyes blinked through distorted visions as her lungs pounded. The tat. Forcing her eyes to focus on something…anything, she noticed Duncan sitting next to her. He didn't have his arm in front of his face ready to block a possible psychotic blow from his wife. She didn't know if that was a good sign or if he was stupid.

The sweat along her skin cooled, making her body let off small tremors. "The tat," she said aloud this time.

"You were having the dream."

The dream. Why did he put up with her? She looked

up to the skylights in their bedroom. They were still black. No stars out this night. No white clouds in the moonlight. Just black.

He didn't pull her into him. He knew to give her a chance to come around on her own. So, she took a cleansing breath and rested her cheek against his chest. He lay back and took her with him. His skin was warm and his heart quick. That sound. It kept her grounded in the back of her mind as decades-old memories raped her in her sleep.

"The john I killed." She nearly choked saying it aloud. Yes, she killed the john who raped her that night. Not that she wouldn't do it the same way all over again.

She let her lungs expand fully against Duncan's chest before she continued. "He had one of the symbols I showed you from my research. I hadn't remembered before now." Would he think she created this in her mind because of her research? A small smile tried to lift the corners of her mouth. He wouldn't. She turned her eyes to his. They were nearly onyx, the way they looked when his emotions were enraged. She lifted her hand and placed her chilled palm on the side of his face. "He had the tat that says he prefers either male or female. As long as they are children."

It was time.

She was going to research who this man was. Did Duncan read that decision in her face, because his turned pained as he covered her hand with his. She had to. Not to come to some kind of closure. She already had that. But what if this man led her to Fu Haizi. What if the key to bringing down this crime ring rested with the last man who would ever lay hands on her again?

She knew his face. She had that. An estimate on an age. Now, she knew to look for someone who died seventeen years ago and had a possible arrest record involving abuse of both boys and girls.

Duncan's arms wrapped around her. A steel curtain of

safety. He was allowing himself to show his reaction to her dream, to the way she spoke of her abuse like it was shop talk. It wasn't like him to do this. She placed her cheek on his shoulder above the tattoo of Black Creek on his pectoral. "I love everything about you," she whispered.

His long, lanky arms tightened around her. "We are quite a pair, you and I."

The comment could have a dozen different meanings. The vast differences between the two of them. Artist for the famous and the wealthy; small town detective. Polished etiquette; unrefined brass. Controlled and collected; reactive and explosive. None of it mattered at that moment. Yet she knew. It was his PTSD flashbacks and her dreams. He got it. Just like he got so much about her.

"Make love to me," she whispered and looked up to him.

In the dark, he lifted his brows and turned his eyes to hers. The color of them nearly matched the black of the skylight. "You're sure?"

Her dark lover. Her husband. Their differences meant nothing at this moment. "We might have to rain check the outfits I promised."

He rolled and tucked her beneath him. She felt him grow as he slipped his warm legs between hers.

Nickie had slipped out before Duncan woke. He'd roused her again after her surprising post-nightmare serenity. She was loose with that glorious unhinging in her joints. He needed rest. She'd watched him sleeping, half-naked and perfectly still, as she'd tiptoed around the open space of their bedroom.

Stifling a laugh, she packed some yogurt in a plastic grocery sack and grabbed the Jets apron Duncan's brother had gotten him last Christmas. The puppy lay on her back with her legs in the air as if to say, 'No one gets up before the sun.' Nickie placed the apron in the center of the kitchen table in the same spot Duncan had left the email from the department mole. Outfits. Let *that* be what they needed to discuss this evening.

As she pushed the garage door button, she thought of the other man she wanted to watch sleep. Only this one she would conveniently wake and not at all gently.

She had saved two girls from brutal captivity, didn't lose her job and had a few rounds of sex with the best thing that had ever been hers.

Life was good.

Today's list included Diet Coke, the station, harass the man who abducted her as he sat in his jail cell. Paperwork. Visit the second possible college rape victim Nevaeh had mentioned. All in that order.

She would bite her tongue for a whole day if it happened that way.

She decided against her favorite convenience store since Jimbo was the manager. She was still mad at him for holding back on her. The little Asian girl could have died if Nickie hadn't used police brutality to get information from him. Instead, she chose a fast food drive-thru and checked her email as she waited. Goal 1, complete. She forced herself to save some of the amazing caffeine before she hit goal 2, the station.

As she pulled out of the drive-thru, she reflected on each aspect of her crash-and-burn with the first potential college rape victim. Nickie would do her best not to let the situation repeat with the second. Instead, she went over her plan in her head and sipped on caffeine.

Today was the day Duncan would case the drama kids as they exited their club meeting. Most of the girls would swoon over him, like most every other female, but not the victims. He would see the signs, remember the faces and give her picture-perfect drawings of any he deemed as potential victims. As she pulled into the station drive, she shook her head at the thought of the girls who would be subjected to his charm.

First things first. Zheng. She bounced on her feet as she skipped the door to the station and went right to corrections. Down the stairs—never the elevator—and right to the Tompkins County Jail.

"Morning, Detective. The usual?"

"You bet." She took off her holster and set it on the check-in desk. She signed the register, trying not to smile, and made her way to Zheng's cell. On the way, she grabbed a folding chair. The one with the missing plastic feet. As she came to the cell, she watched him sleep. Yep. Nearly as fun as watching Duncan, but an entirely different kind of fun. She hoped she didn't wake the prisoners in the adjacent cells—not really—and scraped the bare, metal feet of the chair along the concrete floor.

He jumped and spun like a trapped animal. Oh right. He was a trapped animal. Yep, life was good. "How's the cage this fine morning, Zheng? It's different when you're the one on the inside, isn't it?"

He glanced over but didn't answer. Instead, he lay back and placed his pillow over his head. That was okay. He could still hear her.

"I saved two girls from captivity this weekend. Think of all the brutalized girls I've saved because of you. I should thank you. But then, no. I should just sit here and see how you like to be the one poked and prodded. Granted, I'm not going to inflict scars on your back, but…wait a minute. That's not a bad idea." She scooted her chair again, scraping the feet louder now that they held her frame. "I've learned that the latest customer you sicced on me liked both little girls and boys."

He moved the pillow from his ears.

"I'm closing in on you. You service all types, don't you?" She scraped the chair again.

"The double-triangle sick-os. The double-heart pedophiles. And of course the last one you gave to me—"

"The one you murdered."

That word. Her eyes squeezed shut. She wouldn't let him shake her. "Is that what you call it?" This time, she scraped her chair all the way to the bars. "Prove it."

He placed the pillow on his abs this time. "You have no idea what you're dealing with."

Her spine straightened against the hard back of the chair. Her incarcerated ex-captain had said the same thing to her when she'd visited him in federal prison.

"I'm getting closer," she growled. "And it doesn't look like you'll be going anywhere soon."

The lift in his head was slight, but she caught it.

She shouldn't have said that. She wasn't sure why, but she shouldn't have.

CHAPTER 7

And Nickie had been feeling so good. An epiphany—granted through a horrific nightmare—but still. Great middle-of-the-night sex with her husband. But harassing Zheng? It just didn't leave her with the happy feeling it usually did. Probably because she didn't get anything from him this time, not really. He verbally acknowledged that he knew of her abuse which resulted in the death of the last john. But she already had this information on him. And he reiterated that Fu Haizi, even though she was the only one who called it that, was big...possibly very big. But she'd suspected this, too. Ten to twelve groups of children as she'd learned from a previous visit to her federally imprisoned ex-captain.

As she reached for the light switch to her office, she noticed a figure sitting in one of her guest chairs. Pressed white blouse. Auburn hair slicked back into a low ponytail. Assistant District Attorney Miranda Vaughn. Nickie flicked the light as she checked the clock. She supposed it was about time for everyone to show up.

"Are you sure you need to turn that on? I'm hiding."

Nickie lifted her brows as she rounded her desk and

sat. "Is this because of my partner or Officer Parker?"

"Snort."

"Ya know," Nickie said as she slung one boot on her desk, then the other. "You really should either actually snort or use another word."

"I don't know how to snort."

"You could insert a good old-fashioned cuss word."

"I would never."

Together they laughed at that.

"What's really up, Vaughn?"

"You're right. It's Lynx."

"At least you're calling him by his last name now. It helps with the fitting in the department and all that."

Vaughn nodded. "He's becoming more aggressive. No. That's not the right word. More assertive."

And he'd just kissed Nickie on the forehead. "Do you want him to be more assertive? I told you from the start. You do work together, but if you're looking for a roll…"

"I'm not looking. Mixing work with pleasure isn't smart in my position."

Nickie guessed that would be true. They had to answer to her. Sort of.

"You're welcome to hide here, but I'm leaving the lights on."

"How much of an age difference is there between you and your husband?"

Ah. There it was. "Not enough to mention."

"Mmm."

Speak of the devil. Ten-years-younger-than-her Officer Parker passed Nickie's office. Probably on the way to get some coffee before he hit the streets. He didn't notice Vaughn sitting in the chair. Nickie slid her boots from her desk and let them smack the floor. Like a charm. He turned his head. Nickie lifted a corner of her mouth when he spotted Vaughn. His feet halted to a stop. He was one of the most coordinated people she knew. Tall, stoic, collected. And nearly tripping over his feet.

Drama. She rolled her eyes and booted up her computer. The other rape victim Nevaeh had hooked her onto didn't have class until nine a.m. Nickie would use the time to search for the man she killed as a young teen. Zheng called it murder. In some ways, it felt like it.

There was no statute of limitations for murder. She didn't remember the specific date she escaped. It would be easy enough to search, but why was it that she didn't remember? Was it one of those stuff-it-in-your-subconscious things? She shrugged.

She did a search for her birth name, Nicole Monticello. That in itself raised the hair on the back of her neck. Little came up. She knew this would be the case. Her parents had been so disgusted with what she had to do to survive during her time in captivity that they hid what files they could that might say she was anything more than a rich, spoiled runaway.

There it was. The air around her closed in and threatened to choke her. It was her. When they found her running for her life in yellow lingerie.

She pushed away from her desk and dropped her head between her knees. This was wrong. She was over this.

No one ever gets over something like that. Duncan's voice echoed softly. *They might move on but not over.*

Yeah, but she didn't have time for this. She had a college rape victim to help, a backstabbing department mole to find and possibly ten to twelve groups of captive children to save from Fu Haizi.

Taking a deep breath, she lifted her head, forcing herself back to the present. Miranda was gone. When did that happen? She shook her head, ran her thumb across her nose and turned to her desk computer.

She would cross-reference the date with death notices of anyone in the upstate New York area who had a record or suspicion in pedophilia.

It brushed through her mind to ask Duncan to do this.

Only for a moment, then it was gone. This, she needed to do on her own.

Determined to do this right, Nickie waited in the parking lot of the other potential college rape victim's apartment. Three girls, probably more. Similar MOs. All in the same junior college. All in drama club. All raped by the same man. Was it Eric Stoner?

She'd removed her holster and tucked her badge in the pocket of her slacks. One Starbucks coffee thing and she was ready to convince this girl to open up to her.

A young woman meeting the description Nevaeh had given came out right on time. Tall, blonde. However, unlike Nevaeh or the first gal Nickie had spoken to, this one had big hair and dressed like she was going to a rave.

Nickie stepped out of her car with the frappe. "Excuse me. Samantha? My name is Nickie. I'm with the Northridge Police Department."

The first reaction from Samantha was to dart her eyes around like she was considering a run for it. Then, there was a short moment of seemingly defeat. The girl's lungs emptied, making her backpack slide from her shoulder.

Nickie held out the coffee thing. The girl stared at it, then lifted her gaze.

"Can I walk with you to class? We could talk."

As if she'd just entered reality, the girl shoved her bag back up and straightened her shoulders. "Do I have a choice?" Sarcasm. Not good.

And no, she didn't have a choice. Nickie smiled her warmest smile and placed the coffee concoction in the girl's hand.

Nickie started with small talk. "It's chilly this morning." Maybe she shouldn't have chosen a cold drink. She sucked at coffee choices.

No answer from the girl. Glancing down, Nickie

noticed the heeled boots. Since Nickie wore heels as well, she probably shouldn't throw stones, but Nickie had ankles of steel and didn't have to walk around a campus all day.

They walked in silence for the first block, giving Nickie time to notice the tips of new grass that poked between the brown. "I've been working with some girls on campus." A stretch maybe, but necessary. Nickie made sure to keep it vague. "There seems to be a pattern of abuse that stems from drama club."

A heavy sigh came from Samantha, but she kept walking.

"Some counselors—" Or *a* counselor, "—seem to have misunderstood their role in determining the plausibility of investigative procedure."

Samantha stopped and turned. "I don't know what you're talking about."

The girl had a terrible poker face.

"This is Nevaeh, isn't it? That weirdo and her feminist bullshit."

The words were there, but the way Samantha's pupils dilated said otherwise. She became stiff and almost seemed like she was mentally leaving her body.

"It's drama club, Samantha." Nickie placed a hand on the girl's forearm, but she didn't seem to notice.

"She can't leave well enough alone."

"What's well enough to leave alone?"

Samantha's pupils enlarged, then focused on Nickie like she'd just remembered she was there. "You can tell Nevaeh if she wants to be part of the club, she'll mind her own fucking business."

Nickie started to stroll toward campus again, hoping Samantha would follow her lead. It was a crapshoot, but it worked.

"It's natural to want to be part of the club," Nickie said. "To want some semblance of your life back."

"I know what you're doing, okay. But it's not going to

work because there's nothing to talk about. If you don't mind, I want to walk alone."

Samantha hiked her backpack and strode away.

Nickie let her. Samantha's reaction was more dangerous than the victim who could hardly keep it together.

Waiting on the Heritage College quad felt a bit like stalking, but it needed to be done. Today was the first day the temperature hit the 60s. For upstate New York, that meant shorts and no-sleeve shirts. Add in the stares from the college girls, and it created one rather large box of awkwardness. For Duncan, the warmer air at least helped to calm his temper.

Drama club was over in ten. The back of the fine arts building didn't seem to lead anywhere useful. He hoped the students would use the front exit. In his right hand, he held the picture of Eric Stoner he'd gotten from his detective. Duncan didn't need it for himself. He would have every detail of the bastard's face etched in his mind until death. In fact, it would be fine with Duncan if Stoner used the back door. Keeping his fists from Stoner's face was going to take considerable constraint.

The door burst open and out came a group of students. Eccentric. Vast mix of styles. They had drama club written all over them. No sign of Stoner.

"Excuse me." He stepped into the path of a group of three of them. They looked at him and paused. They glanced at each other, then turned their eyes back to Duncan. "Can you tell me anything about this man?" He held up the picture of Stoner and smiled his best smile.

Two of the girls swooned over the photo. The third dropped her eyes. Duncan took mental note of the one whose eyes dropped.

"That's Eric," one cooed.

The other who still kept focus on Duncan spoke up. "What do you want with Eric?"

"I'm writing an article on students who excel." Others in the larger group stopped to stare, the guys as well.

Several turned and glanced at the exit. He must be coming out soon.

"Thank you," Duncan said and moved to the next cluster of girls. He was able to get through a few dozen of them before Stoner showed. Unfortunately, nine of the girls had raised red flags by that time.

"Eric." One of the students actually squealed. "This is a reporter." She slid her hand inside Duncan's arm. "He's here to interview you. How awesome is that?"

Stoner didn't flinch. It was like this sort of thing happened to him all the time. Stoner sauntered over to where the small hoard of girls circled Duncan. He looked at Duncan, and he must have decided he was of no contest as he stuck out his hand like a celebrity. Since Duncan worked for actual celebrities, he felt authorized to qualify that Stoner sucked at celebrity. He knew he shouldn't grab his hand as hard as he did, but a man could only exhibit so much restraint. "Good to meet you, Eric. My name is Duncan." He left out his last name. "I'm writing a piece on students who are locally involved in volunteering."

"I thought you said 'students who excel'?" It was the girl with her hand bound to Duncan's bicep.

Duncan smiled down at her. "And that as well," then winked.

Stoner stood taller. "Of course. What can I do for you?"

Duncan carefully slipped from the girl's vice grip, maneuvering Stoner into her spot. He asked the first question as he led Stoner away.

"I am taking the angle of students who live at the top yet mingle with the little guy. I'd love to get some pictures of you in your place."

"Yeah, sure. I live in the apartments across the street."

Such a regular guy, Duncan thought sardonically.

CHAPTER 8

The idiot still hadn't asked Duncan for identification or for a last name. Stoner was completely enamored with the idea of this fictional article. So much so that Duncan was able to pelt him with questions the entire distance to the apartment. He opened the front door and Duncan stood, casually allowing his eyes to roam every last inch. It wasn't because he was standing in the doorway of the apartment of a suspected rapist. Duncan used this procedure for any new room he entered. However, since the data gathered from these next few rooms might possibly include information that could convict a sick bastard, he took his time in memorizing each detail.

"This is perfect," Duncan said as he entered Stoner's bedroom. He hadn't considered bringing a camera. He wouldn't need one for himself, but a prop would have been useful. "Just what I need," he said as he noticed Sister Hazel and Def Leppard posters. That could be impressive if the boy wasn't a serial rapist. Duncan strolled toward his desk. "I have your past community services well documented. Any future plans?" He leaned over the desk, and started opening drawers.

"Whoa, dude. That's sort of my stuff, ya know?"

"My bad," Duncan said. "I tend to become overzealous when reporting on a topic of such interest." But it was all Duncan needed. In drawer number two was a small handful of women's jewelry. A bracelet, a few necklaces and earrings.

"I'm recruiting volunteers to help paint paws on the highways that lead into town. Go Heritage Dawgs." He lifted his hand to high-five. Duncan let the smack ring throughout the room. The wince on Stoner's face was followed by quick suspicion. Now, he wakes up?

"Hey, where's your camera, man?"

"In my phone." Duncan lied and pulled out his cell. "State of the art. Let's get you by your posters. Sister Hazel seems retro for you."

"No way, man. They fucking rock."

Duncan led Stoner next to his desk. "Here. Let me move you so I can get the posters as well." He took a few shots of Stoner next to the drawer that held the girl's artifacts. It would be one less picture for him to draw for Nickie.

Stoner actually took off his jacket, lifted his sleeve and flexed. Duncan would not have been able to hold back the sneer if not for the scratch on Stoner's bicep near his elbow. "You're bleeding." He wasn't, but Duncan needed to hear what he had to say about it.

"I am?" Stoner knew where to look. "Oh, that. Girls get excited, man. You know how it is."

Was that what they called serial rape these days? Duncan felt his expression fall. Heat radiated up his neck and over his face. He could imagine the current look in his eyes.

Stoner's expression fell as well. "What was your name again?"

"Duncan." He smiled wide, although it didn't reach his eyes. "I think I've got all I need for a kick-ass story. I'll send you a copy to look over when I'm done." Which would be never. He stuck out his hand and forced himself to shake like a man who didn't want to rip off Stoner's head.

Nickie sat in her car in the garage. She needed to make this phone call. Wanted to make it. And as soon as she walked in the door, Xena would be all over her and Duncan would understandably want her attention. She grinned and closed her eyes before dialing. When would the thought of Duncan's reaction to her daily homecoming wane? It would be okay when it did. Right? That was natural. Couples did that. What the hell did she know about being part of a couple?

Opening her eyes, she glanced at her cell and dialed the number.

"Thank you for calling Sunny Side Safe House. This is Tammy. How can I help you?"

Nickie's brows dropped. A safe house was something she had never been privy to. Thanks a lot, Mom and Dad. "This is Detective Nickie Savage calling to check on Bianca. How is she?"

"Oh, good evening, Detective. She's coming along. Started eating her meals in the dining room. Still not talking to anyone, though."

"Would you mind asking her if she would come to the phone? You can tell her it's me."

"I can tell her you're on the phone, but I won't make her talk."

"I understand," Nickie said. More than this Tammy person understood. She moved back the seat of her unmarked police car and propped her boots on the dash.

Next to her was Duncan's Audi R8 and next to that, his SUV. To the side was his Kawasaki. In the back rested the '72 Barracuda he was restoring that was responsible for the calluses covering his long fingers and hands. The sun had gone down, but it was still warm enough to keep the windows down. The air in the garage wasn't stale. Not this far away from Northridge.

She could see why Duncan chose this spot to build his house. Their home.

A distant voice came through the receiver. "Bianca, dear. This is Detective Savage."

Nickie dropped her boots to the floor. "Bianca? Are you there? It's me."

"I'm sorry, Detective," the receptionist said into the phone. "She is unresponsive."

"Give the phone back to her, please, Tammy. I don't mind doing the talking."

"Oh. Well, okay."

Nickie allowed enough time for Bianca to return the phone to her ear. "It's good to talk to you, Bianca. I've been thinking about you. Are you eating? Getting enough exercise?"

Silence, but Nickie expected it.

"I'm glad you have Sunny Side. A lot of success stories have come out of that place. Don't rush yourself, okay? You've got plenty of time. I know your parents are anxious to see you. They seem legit. Give them a chance when you're ready. Right now, you might be thinking that you made choices to do bad things, but the truth is you were groomed and manipulated. You are a child. Eventually, you will stop beating yourself up about things you did as a minor."

Nickie realized she was talking more about herself at this point than she was Bianca, but it was one in the same. She could hear Bianca's breathing. It sped up but seemed far from agitated. Because of that combined with the fact that the receptionist would take the phone if Nickie said anything that might hurt Bianca, she felt okay with continuing.

"I was younger than you when I was taken. They made me dress in yellow lingerie and put curls in my hair. Never any makeup. They sold me as the virgin child who fought back. You probably know there are men who like that."

"They dressed me like a grown-up."

The muscles in Nickie's body stilled. Her brain, her heart. A line of pain seared from head to toe. She shoved her seat back farther and dipped her head between her legs. "It's going to be okay, Bianca. We survived. I'm here for you. Do you still have my private cell number?"

No answer.

"I'll give it to Tammy again, just in case. I'm here. You're not alone. Remember that."

The expressions on the faces of the girls in the quad had been sadly classic. They burned permanent holes in Duncan's memory. Look down. Look to the side. No eye contact. Everything to hide.

He sighed as he glanced at the chalk in his hand. Changing his mind, he carefully placed it in the tray where it belonged and chose a darker piece. He created images of each of the girls he had flagged from his time at the college quad. If he finished this evening, tomorrow he would begin scanning the faces using public Internet sites to discover the identities of the potential victims. If needed, he would move to private databases. The illegal hacking would be worth it.

The faint lavender smell of Nickie's hair was a significant distraction. Her cello stood alone as she sat near the computer on the desk Duncan's uncle had made for him. His work would go exponentially faster if she played, but he wouldn't ask. Not tonight.

Tonight, she pounded away at the keyboard, searching arrest records for pedophiles caught with both male and female children. It was the MO of the john she killed.

The chalk in his hand broke in two pieces and fell to the floor. She turned her head and lifted her brows.

"I seem to have gotten carried away," he said and clasped his hands together in order to disguise the shaking. "I should be finished soon."

A small smile lifted the corners of her beautiful mouth. The bottom lip, which was slightly wider than the upper, curled enough to send a wave of much needed peace through his head. "You have your own work to do," she said and lifted from her chair. Her feet were bare and her jeans snug. She wore a raspberry flannel blouse with beige lace near her hips. He was hopelessly taken.

"I am thankful for you." In Nickie fashion, she slung a leg over his lap as if he was his Kawasaki. In seconds, he forgot his work and grew beneath her fine backside as she settled. "Shall I play?"

Her cello. She knew him well. "Only if you're finished."

"I'm at a good stopping point. I've got the addresses of eleven inmates and parolees I can interrogate—or I should say interview."

"You don't have to be politically correct with me."

This smile was brilliant, sarcastic and all Nickie. "So, should I say badger, bully or harass? I'm getting closer, Duncan. I can feel it." She shifted in his lap enough to make his eyes cross. "It's not all I can feel. You want me."

"I always want you."

"It's getting late. Can the cello and the drawings wait? I might be in need of a shower, and we should conserve water and share."

"Rose tells me we're hitting The Pub Friday night." Duncan's brother sat next to him at a corner table in the dumpiest coffee shop in Rochester.

"Yes. Nickie will be singing."

"It's been a while since we've gone to hear her sing."

"It's been a while since her foster brother has needed her to fill in as singer for his two man band." His forearms shook the rickety table as his fingers flew across the keyboards.

"I'm almost in," Andy added.

"I'm looking quite forward to it." Duncan sipped his black coffee as he waited for Andy to hack into the Northridge Police Department secured database. "Both The Pub and finding this damned mole."

He and his brother disagreed upon two things, yet agreed on them at the same time. Duncan agreed to the ridiculous false Internet trails Andy insisted on creating. Today it was through several states along with a few countries. Duncan thought of it as overkill.

Andy agreed to drive out of town to either Rochester or Binghamton and to use only their two laptops for the search. Adjusting his ball cap lower over his eyes, Duncan leaned back and propped his feet on a nearby chair. They would accomplish twice as much if Duncan allowed them to use their tablets as well, but that would draw additional attention. Duncan wasn't willing to put Andy in that kind of danger. Andy thought of it as overkill.

Agree. Disagree.

Today, they were here for the department mole who kept tabs on Duncan's detective. He released his mug before he squeezed hard enough for it to break.

Andy glanced over each shoulder without moving his head. Duncan could tell he was in. Dropping his feet to the floor, Duncan took a drink of his coffee and moved into the seat as Andy vacated it.

Duncan's turn.

Andy was the builder. He built the safety nets. Duncan was the one who could see IDs and passcodes in binary form for short moments in time and remember them. Now, they waited. Andy sat near him, serving as an extra set of eyes. Duncan may have an eidetic memory, but he still only had one set of eyes. Andy kept a watchful eye on the second laptop.

Andy spoke quietly with no expression. "There." Still, it caused a rise in Duncan's heart rate, his temperature.

Turning his eyes to the laptop in front of his brother, Duncan watched as some unsuspecting officer at the Northridge Police Department signed in. Duncan memorized the ID and passcode entered. Then, he used a new tab along with the ID and passcode to open a dummy login.

He repeated this process a dozen or so times. Drink coffee. Open new window. Wait for an NPD staff member to log in. Copy ID and passcode. Read through all old and incoming email messages. Leave window open in case said unsuspecting officer used his email at the very moment they spied on him.

With several windows and, therefore, email accounts open, Duncan and Andy spoke few words and instead concentrated on the open tabs while aiming to appear mildly interested as they drank their coffee.

Interrogated the prisoner again. Was visibly agitated upon return.

Duncan's vision blurred with a haze of red before refocusing on the words as they typed out on the screen in front of him.

Appears wrapped up in two larger cases right now. One is off the books.

Andy tugged at the fingers Duncan had clenched around the edge of the table. Duncan pulled his hands from the table but didn't take his eyes from the screen. The ID on this account was an I and a D. Without taking his eyes from the blinking icon, Duncan pounded the keyboard, tracing which IP address the email came from.

"It's changing," Andy said.

He was right. "What the hell?" IP addresses don't change.

"He knows we're watching."

Duncan pulled his hands back from the computer as if the person on the other end might somehow detect his movements. They'd hacked into the FBI, CIA and out-of-country government sites. Never once had anyone noticed their efforts.

Andy's hands, however, returned to his keyboard. "Let me try something."

Duncan needed to step back. His senses clouded with a cocktail of confusion, mad frustration and a primal need to protect his detective. Pushing from the table, he stood and gave Andy room. He paced, barely considering the attention he was drawing to the two of them and their illegal coffee shop hacking.

Andy was right again. He was right all these years to use his overkill safety nets and trails through dummy IP addresses.

"He's tracking us. Duncan, he's tracking backward through my maze."

Stuffing the rage, Duncan sank into the chair next to his brother and started closing everything down. Andy worked next to him just as fast.

Together, they sat, staring at the finally empty screens. He could hear Andy's breath working as fast as his. When they turned to each other, beads of sweat lined his brother's upper lip.

"Shit," Andy said.

"Yes."

"Did you get all the codes that flashed by?"

Did he just ask that? Duncan's brows fell. His expression gave away everything. He couldn't help it.

Holding out his hands in surrender, Andy backtracked. "Whoa, brother. No killer glare needed. I just don't know how that gift thing of yours works."

Gift? He knew? A tsunami of guilt sifted through Duncan. All of these years. He'd never told his brother, his friend. Gift? That was what Nickie called it.

CHAPTER 9

The music ran through her like a good bar fight. Nickie let her eyelids sink as she belted some old-school *Heartbreaker* to the crowd of mostly twenty-somethings. Behind her, her foster brother beat his drums as he sat crammed in the tiny triangle platform The Pub called a stage for the band. In front of her, the floor shook from the feet of buzzed dancers—Duncan's brother and his wife included. Rose was an especially spunky ball of fire tonight, even for her.

She'd like to tell Rose what she was doing on the dance floor with Andy was bordering on illegal. Except, as was customary, Nickie promised Gil she wouldn't be a cop—not even an off-duty one—the nights she filled in for Gil's wife. It probably wouldn't attract patrons if people knew the band's singer was NPD.

She played chords on the acoustic that was like an old friend to her. As she opened her eyes, she noticed Duncan sitting alone at the table in front of her. He wore his I'm-ready-to-hurt-someone face. She would definitely need to pick his brain about that at the next break. It was best to let her lids close again so she could concentrate on what she was doing instead of scanning the crowd. Once a cop. The next song would be a slow one. She wouldn't be able to drown out any mistakes with the quick steps of Gil's bass drum.

Just one quick peek. She squinted and let her gaze find Duncan once again. He was glaring at a group of older twenty-somethings at the table next to him. The muscles in his jaw clenched and released. Hey. She thought his jaw only did that when they were in bed and he was about to—

Good thing Rose was taking Andy's hand and leading him toward Duncan's table. Except, she planted it on her ass as she pulled him along, then tripped on the leg of a chair. Someone was going to have a headache in the morning.

It was difficult to focus, but Nickie spoke into the mic. "Now, for something a little lighter. Grab your girls, men."

Nickie propped a butt cheek on the wooden bar stool and started singing about how it's time to be a big girl.

"That's my woman you're talking about."

It was Duncan's voice. What did he just say? His what? His *woman*? Her eyes flew open, and she missed an entire line of the song.

A drumstick poked her lower back. Instead of nodding, she craned her head around and threw Gil her best buzz-off glare.

Forcing herself to both sing and find out why Duncan was talking about her like she was property, she saw that it was the two late twenty-somethings he'd been focused on. She was frigging NPD. Her shoulders fell as she thought of her promise to Gil. Her voice lifted from its usual alto tone as her breath quickened.

The men stood. One was blond with fake diamond earrings in each ear. The other had curly brown hair tied in a low tail.

Duncan stood and stepped toward them. Oh no. She knew that gait. No, no. Not now. Not here.

Rose stepped between them. Nickie cringed. The

blond dude looked down at her. From the look on his face, what he said to Rose was clearly inappropriate. Rose was small—115 pounds tops—but she was a third-degree black belt with a temper not at all as controlled as a black belt's should be. She took the guy's hand and bent back his fingers until his body bent with them. The ponytail dude put his hand on her shoulder. Did he not see Andy? Andy might be short, but he was thick as a building with bands of muscle covering every inch of him.

Screw it. Nickie dropped her mic and jumped off the stage.

Duncan stepped in front of her and growled, "He's mine."

The sudden silence from the music caused everyone to turn. Bartender, bouncer, waitresses. The manager-on-duty would be out any minute, but more importantly, Nickie's husband had just blocked her path after calling her his 'woman.'

The blond stood tall. Stupid testosterone was going to earn him a broken rib and a fist in his face. "Man up, Dustin." Blond told his friend. "We're not here to let a couple of old dudes and their hoes embarrass us."

Quick as lightning, Duncan twisted the dude's arm behind his back enough to make him buckle. She didn't miss the knee that slipped into his ribs and dropped him to the floor. The dude landed an elbow to the side of Duncan's face on his way down, but Duncan stood solid. He reared back his fist and got in two solid blows before the guy surrendered and fell.

Before Ponytail had a chance, Rose took both hands and pushed him in the chest, then followed with a push kick in the same spot. She knew how to use her 115 pounds to move a man. The guy looked down at her as he clutched the spot she struck. His eyes moved in disbelief to Andy and over to Duncan, whose chest was pounding and face was turning all sorts of colors.

Nickie knew that face and it was dangerous. She'd only seen Duncan lose control a few times and could live a long happy life if she never saw it again.

It was her turn to step in front of him. She held out her hands, palms forward. "It's okay. See? It's me. He's down. His friend is leaving." She said the last part as loud as she could and over her shoulder. Gently, she laid her hands on Duncan's arms. His eyes were crazed. Was he having a flashback? Was he in the desert in the Middle East watching his platoon bleed to death? "It's me," she repeated. His pupils dilated then contracted. The sight of his sinking shoulders relieved her as much as it brought back her irritation with him.

Rose and Andy stood strong yet still. They, too, knew to stand down and give Duncan room when he was like this.

"Nothing to see here, people. Time to dance!" As if on cue, Gil flipped on the DJ track they used during breaks. Nickie backed Duncan into his chair, allowing the idiot, gasping blond to make his escape.

Rose spoke up. "Andy, you take Duncan home. I'm riding with Nick."

Andy looked between Duncan and her and Rose, then shrugged. Duncan followed like a zombie.

Plopping down in Duncan's vacated seat, Rose whined, "He cheated me out of a good bar fight."

Nickie sat next to her. "How do you always make me smile at times like these?"

"I'm smart and witty." Rose took a swig from Duncan's untouched draft. "If we hurry, we might be able to catch up with the testosterone boys."

"Are you talking about the idiot boys, or our husbands?"

Rose threw back her head and laughed. "Ha! I meant the good fight I was screwed out of. I bet they're still hanging in the lot." Her eyes opened wide as she straightened in her chair. "You don't think Andy and

Duncan are—?" Her lids closed and sighed. "No. Andy would have seen that crazy-person look Duncan got and kept him clear. Duncan has done that since junior high. Did you know that?"

"Yes. You mentioned it once or twenty times."

"Just wanted to make sure you knew what you were getting yourself into."

"There is that."

"You're driving, friend," Rose said and downed more of the draft.

Nickie supposed she was.

"I'm completely sober yet being driven home by my little brother while my woman drives my car home." Duncan glanced out the passenger window of his brother's Jeep as he parked in front of Duncan's porch steps.

Andy shifted his Jeep into neutral and pulled the emergency brake. "You're not completely sober. You just drank two at my place. And, brother, I think 'my woman' is the phrase that got you into this mess."

"It was necessary." The blood threatened to churn in Duncan's mind once more. It swirled around like the hot desert sand. The look on Nickie's face pained him. It had been fear. Fear that he might have an episode right there in the bar. She wasn't far off.

He took a deep breath. Enough of the almost bar fight. Duncan needed to fix things with his brother. "Listen, Andy, I need to apologize about the gift thing."

Andy turned his head. "What gift? You got goods for me?"

The second deep breath helped as little as the first one. "My gift."

Still nothing.

"My memory."

"Oh, that," Andy said slowly, then shrugged. "I figure you've got your reasons for keeping it to yourself."

"It's not a gift."

"Like hell. You're like a freak. That is some crazy awesome shit you can do."

"Freak is the key word. It has been since we were kids."

They sat in silence in front of Duncan's porch steps for a long time before Andy spoke again. "I guess that makes sense. I never thought of it that way before. Does Nickie know?"

"Yes. She was able to determine the reason for my condition within the first two weeks of meeting her."

Andy laughed. "She's too smart for you."

"There is that." He looked at the lighted window in the third floor of their home. "I'm tired and going to bed, but I'm still sorry. I should have spoken with you about it long ago."

"We're brothers. Water under the bridge."

At that, Duncan opened the Jeep door to the clear night air. He stopped at the base of his flagstone steps as Andy completed a U-turn and made his way down the hill to his home.

He glanced toward the west at the edge of the woods that encompassed the house. There was no wind, which made it appear as if the world had stopped in order to give him ample time to regain the last piece of control he'd lost that evening.

Opening the front door, Duncan first glanced at the alarm, making sure it was set for the evening. He could hear Xena's nails on the metal of her cage in the back of the house. Not tonight, girl. It was long after bedtime for all of them.

As he climbed the stairs, he noticed there was no sound coming from above. No shower. No footsteps.

The door to the top floor was open and light poured out. He found her sitting in front of the easel that held the large chart paper tablet containing her notes on the Fu Haizi case, as she liked to call it. She didn't offer a greeting.

He tugged his shirt from his pants as he reached for a whiskey glass. Two fingers should be enough to settle his heart and his night.

The sound of magic marker scraped across Nickie's page. It ran through him like fingernails on a chalkboard.

He made his way toward his closet. She didn't turn her head or pause to acknowledge him. His head ached and he yearned for sleep, yet curiosity took him. "You're quiet."

More magic marker scraping. His right eyelid twitched as if he'd just eaten lime after a shot of tequila.

"Are you going to answer me?"

"You didn't ask me a question."

He spun on his heels and reached her in a half-dozen long strides.

Marker scrape.

He wasn't sure what came over him, but he took the marker from her hand, capped the lid and chucked it in the trash.

She sat with her hand in the air as if it still held the marker. His chest expanded and contracted as only her eyes turned toward him.

"Talk to me." It seemed more civilized than the silent treatment.

She stood and faced him, shoulders square. No words but at least the scraping marker was dead.

The steel gray in her eyes turned a shade darker as her lids dropped halfway.

"You called me your *woman.*"

Andy was right. That was what this was about.

"You're gonna need to make sure that doesn't happen again," she added in her condescending cop voice.

The swirling in his head returned. "That would be a problem since I will absolutely do it again if and when a similar situation arises."

"You called me your *woman* and stepped in front of

me in the middle of frigging police protocol."

He pulled his chin back. "Police protocol? You were singing at a bar with Gil." He took a step closer. "And when have you ever heard me refer to you as *my woman* before? It was contextual, and it was necessary. And you. Are. Mine. There are times when your badge has nothing to do with the fact that I'm going to protect *my woman*."

The blood spun in his brain, sucking the oxygen from his lungs that beat into his body. He needed sleep. He needed sleep and to be alone.

Her eyes tightened, then opened. "Well, hell. When you put it that way, it just makes me want you." Her gaze turned to his lips and the corners of her mouth turned up. She pulled her shirt over her head and dropped her slacks in seconds. Not the matching powder blue lace. He was useless against the powder blue lace.

The churning blood left his brain and filled other parts of his body.

He grabbed a shoulder and laced his other hand in her hair. He wrapped the locks of honey wheat twice around his hand, then pulled and turned to lead her back to the nearest wall. Her fingers dug into the muscles in his sides.

His Nickie. His wife. She was a swirling mass of confusing woman and all he wanted. He felt her heel lift and take purchase against his backside. Without letting go of her hair, he trailed his other hand to the warmth that radiated low between them. Her heel dug into his back as she pulsed, going over the edge in seconds. Her legs wavered as she shook. He pressed his weight against her, keeping her upright as she climbed, held then came down ever so slowly.

Her head moved back and forth against the wall as she groaned through the aftershocks, "Now, Duncan. I need it to be now."

He dug into her, sensing as his own legs threatened to

fail him. Both hands cupped her beautifully female backside, pulling her into the rhythm that was theirs.

Nickie felt that glorious edge threaten to take her again. She placed both hands on the wall behind her and pushed, toppling them both to the floor. He lay on his back with his hands outstretched, willing her to join him. She paused to inhale the sight of him. Lanky. Dark. He lay there. Ready for her. Dangerous. Wanting her.

She took his hands and took him in, watching as his eyes turned opaque then determined. Their fingers dug against each other as they moved until the physical threatened to consume. He released one of her hands and trailed his thumb over her stomach until he reached her. The euphoria was instant and violent. Her legs refused to sustain her as her body shook and her heart melted. He knew just when to pull away. She'd come down just enough, too weak to fight his escape.

She found herself with her back on the carpet as he cupped a hand over a shoulder while hiking her leg with the other. Fingertips grazed the inside of one thigh, his tongue down the other. He blew on the trail left behind, making her tremble with chills of every kind. Then, "Oh," she said. "There."

Her arms and legs were useless. His hands. His lips. His love for her. Her insides played a symphony of euphoria as she climbed like a concert toward the crescendo. She couldn't see, couldn't hear, couldn't create a complete sentence. Instead, she did what she only allowed with this man. She let go. Let go into a place of trust and raw ecstasy. Tears ran down the sides of her temples. Her hands found his hair and dug in. The cries that came from her throat seemed to make him give more. Then he was there.

His lips pressed against hers as she came down from one high and climbed another. More personal. More needy. Her nails dug holes in his shoulders. His fingers were surely leaving marks on her hips. They moved and moved until they were drenched in sweat, and she fell over that last peak. He made that perfect sound that told her he couldn't hold back any longer. Together, they pressed and held and pressed, then held the last piece of want.

The sudden weight of him grounded her. The kiss to the side of her head melted her into a sleepy pile of warmth. He traced feather light circles on her back until their breathing slowed to normal, and then he traced more.

"Am I too heavy?" In this position, he was, actually. His cheek rested on her shoulder.

"Don't move. I like you there."

"Keeping my woman down."

She felt his smile spread across her shoulder. Smiles were so rare with him, she wished she could see it, but not so much that she wanted him to move. "I'll kick your ass for that as soon as my arms and legs work again."

Duncan's eleven o'clock barely made it out the door before he loosened his tie and released the top button of his shirt. Real estate buyer. The thirty-five acres were rather difficult to navigate, yet it was beautiful land. Rolling hills, a creek, plenty of flat spots for camping. The buyer was a grandfather looking for a place to romp with his sons and grandsons.

Sons. Children. It was too soon to press the issue and yet…

CHAPTER 10

━━━━◆ • ◆ • ◆━━━━

Pushing back in his chair, he slid open the center desk drawer and pulled out his sketchpad. No more meetings for the day. Time alone had always been sacred to him. Now, it became tiresome.

He leaned back and started flipping pages. The first held an exact replica of the inside of Eric Stoner's apartment. The next seven were individual sketches of the trophies Duncan had discovered in it. At least he assumed they were Stoner's rape trophies. One silver heart necklace with the inscription, faith, hope, love, etched around the perimeter. He flipped the next page to the single large hoop silver earring. The next was a bracelet with alternating turquois and wooden beads. One-quarter-inch thick gold chain kinked in several spots. A thin silver chain with three loose pearls. A pair of florescent pink thong underwear. On the final page, he added some depth to a dangling copper earring with three small multicolored beads.

He turned his head and wiped the sweat from his hairline with the back of his hand. The next contained the faces of the girls he felt had an adverse reaction to his questioning when he met them in front of the fine arts building. Apparently, two of them were girls Nickie had already interviewed. And failed. It wasn't like her. There were nine he'd red-flagged that day on the quad. Nine. In one college club.

He lifted from his chair and paced a few slow laps around his office. How many girls had Stoner gotten his hands on? Were there more trophies hidden? Should he search Stoner's apartment further? His feet stopped in front of his sketchpad. He picked it up and made his way to his scanner. The trophies. The panties would be a wash but possibly the jewelry was unique or limited to a few retail sellers. He was privy to Internet sites that could search scanned images such as these.

Before digging in, he refilled his coffee with one hand and rubbed the other over his face and through his hair. Of all the times he pressured Nickie to get more rest, he really needed to follow his own advice. Between the station mole, Jun Zheng and now this…sleep was low on his list of priorities.

The pictures of the girls. Heritage College didn't include photos in their student database. Neither did the individual student accounts. He'd checked each of them. The drama club photo allowed him to label seven of the nine. A lengthy and tedious search on the most common late-teen social media venues IDed the other two.

His fingers hovered over his keyboard. He ached to check in on the NPD employee emails, but the mole was onto him. How to get around that? Maybe he would just use the fact. Yes. Let him or her trace the trace. Let the mole think Duncan had no idea he'd been discovered.

Ah. Not now. Not here. A new tablet. Cover the camera lens. New IP address. New access location. The tablet could be ditched at any time. Picking up his cell, he searched his brother's number and called.

"Andy, it's me. I have an idea."

Nickie didn't feel right taking any more station time to search for johns that might be associated with Zheng.

Even though they had him in county, it was technically for kidnapping, trespassing and attempted murder a few weeks back. And then there was the john Nickie killed.

She'd gotten up before dawn, swam a mile in the pool and left as Duncan got up. It was a bad sign when you had to schedule a coffee date with your husband to have time to see each other. Well, other than collapsing into bed for a round of sex in the dark before sleep. Or two rounds.

Leaning against the back of the chair in the downtown Northridge bakery, she propped her feet on the empty seat opposite her. The smell of the warm sugar and coffee wasn't so bad, even if she wouldn't eat or drink it. The sun was coming up, and she still had the current addresses of a dozen perps to add to her Fu Haizi spreadsheet. The thing was disgustingly long, and growing. Most of the creeps were still in prison, but the number who were out and living as free men was enough to make her squirm. She'd divided them up into categories. Those who preferred adult men or women. These were the easiest to service. Their prostitutes could be seen with them in public, sports venues mostly. Perps liked to get their rocks off watching hockey or boxing or the sport of the day then get their other rocks off with the illegal activity of their choice. Some dudes wanted teenagers. Girls. Boys. Either. Homeless types. Ritzy types. And then the younger children. Those who walked the sidewalks as free men after something like that. She needed to hit something or better yet, someone.

Closing her eyes, she dipped her head. Her fingers curled around the edges of the small table. She had work to get to. She had a job. A job that helped rectify what she'd done in her past.

No.

Not rectify. She couldn't go there. She'd been a kid. It was like what she said to Bianca. No more beating herself up for what she did as a child.

"Ma'am?"

Nickie opened her eyes to a young girl bending over the table.

"Ma'am, can I get you a refill?"

Turning her eyes to the half-empty glass in front of her, Nickie looked back up and blinked before nodding. She didn't have it in her to care about the ma'am comment.

The old school bell on the door rang. Instinctively, she turned to see who it was. Phil the barber. Go figure. The signature bags under his eyes were baggier than usual, and the hair on his balding head needed a cut. Irony.

Scanning the area like he was a cop, he spotted her but barely blinked. As he made his way to the counter, she considered how she could use him as an outlet to the frustration growing inside of her.

She waited for him to sit but he got his java to go.

"Phil!" she said in her most annoying voice as she made her way toward him.

The look on his face was part irritated, part jittery. Yet, he stopped and nodded.

"How's business? Any new guys?"

He moved his half-opened eyes around as he answered. "Business is good." His shoulder gave a slight shrug. "No new guys."

He looked worn, even for Phil. This wasn't nearly the fun it was supposed to be. "Keeping your nose clean?"

This time he looked her straight on. "Is this an interrogation, Detective?"

Ooh la la. He said her title through his teeth.

"Not at all, Phil the barber." She made a point to look over his unkempt hair. "Just two fellow citizens saying, 'Hello,' in the local bakery. Can I buy you a bagel?"

He shook his head, then took a sip of his coffee.

"Have a nice day."

His brows dropped. It was slight but she caught it. He

turned and sauntered out as slowly as he'd come in. Stopping his feet, he turned his head enough for her to view his profile. "Keep your eyes open, Detective." And he left.

Cryptic shit. Not like Phil at all. She pondered and banked it.

As she turned her head to the spreadsheet on her monitor, she realized it was time. Tragically, this list thing could go on forever. The names of men charged with illegal sexual acts were endless. She had a healthy list of men to begin her interrogations. The chart paper would have to wait. It was time to spend as many hours as she could in interviews. And she believed her theory that the ten to twelve groups of Fu Haizi prostitutes expanded beyond the group she'd already taken down.

The clock on the monitor said seven thirty. Damn, she was late. She flipped down the lid of her laptop and turned over her phone. Six missed text messages and a voice mail.

Her foster mother. *You have not come home for too long. I expect you to visit soon.*

Nickie smiled. She could hear Gloria's Hispanic accent in her text. It sent a wave of calm through her.

Duncan was next. *I can smell your lavender scent even though you're not here.*

Yum.

Eddy. *You showing up anytime today?*

Ugh. She didn't wait for the refill or to finish her messages.

Nickie had a day off coming to her. Several, actually. She shook her head and decided against the thought as she backed her unmarked into her parking spot at the station. Nights and weekends were going to have to do for interviewing the registered sex offenders in their homes or prisons. The inmates and parolees were scattered across the country, but there were plenty in state she could start with.

Tossing the gear into park, she stuffed her phone in her back pocket and locked up. The air was humid. Spring. Everything seemed to be a mint green. She took a late-for-work minute to look around. Little white things peeked out from the branches of the trees. Duncan's aunt would be thinking about this stuff 24/7 this time of year. How did Nickie end up in a normal family?

She made her way to the basement door. Skipping the elevator, she took the stairs, making sure to hit each one with her heel, letting the burn sink in her thighs. Never give up; never give in.

Eddy must have been watching for her. He came out of his office and met her at the door. "What the hell, Nick? You having breakfast dates with him now?"

Phil? What? The look on her face must have convinced Eddy she had no idea what he was talking about, because he stepped to the side and nodded his head toward the station break room.

Slippery Jimbo. Here. Uninvited. In her station. Forgetting all about Eddy, she made a beeline for the room.

Confused as hell, she leaned against the doorjamb. He was walking around, sniffing the coffee and opening cupboard doors.

"How...no...who in the hell let you in here?"

He jumped and turned. "Whoa! Detective Dude. You scared the fuck out of me."

"Thank you for the visual, Jimbo. What the hell are you doing in my break room, and I repeat, who let you in here?"

"I told the cranky lady I had an informant appointment with you."

She walked toward him. He backed up. She didn't stop.

"You. Came. To my station. And lied your way into my break room." She held his broken arm down by the cast and used her other arm to shove him against the fridge. Faintly, she heard something fall over inside.

A knock came from behind her. Keeping Jimbo in a chokehold, she turned her head. Eddy leaned against the doorjamb, where she'd been a minute ago. A large smile spread across his face. "Just checking to see if I could help."

"I don't need your help, Lynx."

"I wasn't offering. I was asking."

"Nope. He's all mine."

She felt jiggling beneath her arm and gave Jimbo a hard shake.

"Captain's got two house calls for us, Nick. Whenever you're done with your girlie talk there, let me know. I'm driving."

Shit. That was what she got for being late to work.

"Can we please," Jimbo choked, "talk about the camel in the room?"

Eddy pulled his chin back. "It's an elephant, dude. Elephant in the room."

Nickie grunted and pulled Jimbo away from the door.

"You." She pointed to Jimbo. "Sit."

She plopped a boot on the chair next to him. "You hate the police station. Talk."

"No, no, Detective Dude. This place is the bees' feet. I'm here for work."

"Knees, dude." Eddy was still in the doorway. "What's the matter with him?"

"I'm here for, ya know, work. Informant work. What've you got going on? What can I do for Detective Savage today?"

She ran both hands over her face. She really wanted to kick his ass, but he'd already had that done on her behalf. So instead, she sighed. "Phil."

"The barber?"

"The very one. Check in on him. Get a haircut. And don't come back unless I call you."

CHAPTER 11

———— ● ◆ ● ————

Duncan picked the local coffee shop that also had a soda machine with endless refills. He sat, using his phone to thumb through his portfolio as he waited for his detective. His coffee was hot. He had his recon with his brother planned and was about to meet with his wife. The meeting part shouldn't be as rare as it was, yet he was slowly becoming as busy as she was. Hopefully, it was all temporary.

The price of gold was significantly down, but silver was up. That didn't make sense, so he started searching through his favored sites to investigate as he waited for her. The steam from his coffee mug ceased before he realized how much time had passed. Still no Nickie.

It wasn't until he'd finished warming his coffee in the bakery microwave that she showed. Her boots dug into the carpet as she made her way to him.

"I'm late."

As if she was telling him something he didn't know.

She stopped her feet before she reached him. "You're angry."

"I didn't say that, and I'm not."

"I'm married to you. I know things."

It made the corner of his mouth lift, damn it. "I'm

frustrated."

"Potato, potahto."

That made him all out smile. She blinked three times.

"Why do you do that?" he asked as he gestured for her to sit.

"Be late? I don't know, and it seems to be getting worse." She opened the lid of the Styrofoam cup of Diet Coke he'd gotten her and looked in.

"Not the tardiness issue. And you might want to dump that. The ice is melted."

He couldn't help but admire her backside as she waltzed to the pop machine, dumped the contents of the cup and filled it with ice, then soda.

She slid back into the seat as if she hadn't left or been late. "Then what?"

"Hmm?"

"Why do I do what?"

"Oh, yes. Blink."

She lifted her brows as if he were dense.

"Blink *rapidly*." He said it as if she were dense. "Three times specifically."

"Oh, that."

Was she blushing? She was. Intriguing. She dropped her chin, so he leaned in to get a better look.

"It's embarrassing."

"After all we've been through—" He lifted her chin and assessed the steel gray, "—and done. Blinking is what embarrasses you?"

Her chest expanded slowly before releasing. "It's not the blinking. It's the why." She pressed her fingers against the side of her jaw, craning her neck until it cracked. Then did the same for the other side. "It's your…uh…smile."

"My smile." He said it as a statement, not a question.

"You hardly ever smile. It's beautiful. It takes my breath away. And if you ever repeat that, I'll break your nose in two places."

Only as his Nickie could illustrate. He relaxed into his best smoky gaze and smiled at her. Sure enough. Three blinks along with pulling her chin back and away.

"You're mocking me. Who does that to their wife? And now all I can think about is climbing over the table and straddling you in this booth."

He was sure the expression on his face fell immediately since all sense left his brain and traveled into his pants. Several images and...well...positions scattered through his mind before he realized it was she who smiled from ear to ear this time.

"You. You baited me." His smile came without intent this time. "Evil."

"Yes, and now that we're both not thinking straight, let's discuss Nevaeh Thornton's case."

Ah. The reason for a married couple to meet in coffee shop. Reluctantly, he removed his sketchpad from his briefcase. "This is what I saw." He handed the pad to her. She wouldn't need explanation.

He watched as she studied the drawings of the trophies and the girls for a solid ten minutes. Her facial expression remained consistent. She was in her autopilot mode. Stuff any feelings or memories the case ignites deep into the subconscious and get the job done. He used the tactic himself almost on a daily basis.

Her gaze turned to him. She must have assumed he had more. She was right.

"None of the jewelry or the panties is unique. Each either can, or could be purchased in a number of stores."

"How did you ID the girls? Or do I want to know?"

"All very legal. Well, except hacking into the Heritage College directory, but that was so easy it hardly suffices as—no, actually. I suppose you don't want to know."

"Nine potential victims. Plus Nevaeh. That's at least ten. Seven trophies. Okay." She leaned back and took a long swig. "Okay," she repeated. "I can track them down and talk to them during the day. Do the same for the johns in evenings and weeken—"

"What was that?"

Her blink was singular this time and not at all because she was taken with him. "I finished my spreadsheet of johns, or I should say I decided I have enough to get started. I'm going to see which ones recognize Zheng. Sort of do the same analyzing you did for me with the drama club girls. Thanks, by the way. I might get some intel on Zheng and Fu Haizi from these sickos."

She hadn't mentioned this plan. He felt his brows drop. "Nights and weekends." Again a statement. Now, he *was* angry. "To interview johns, where?"

She had the nerve to look offended, yet she answered anyway. "Around. Mostly in state. Some are in prison. Most in the registered sex offender program. What's your deal?"

"It could be that my wife has made extensive plans to interrogate felons without mentioning it to me."

"I'm *mentioning* it now."

"Moot point at this time."

"We've gotten off on the wrong foot more times than I can count on this coffee date."

"The necessity of a coffee date could be considered the first foot." He secured his briefcase, leaving the sketchpad for her to do with it what she would. "Followed by your lack of timeliness, absence in my life as of late and reluctance to share your plans regarding a topic of much interest to a husband." He was in no position to discuss this with her. Blood boiled from fear for her safety, the need to find who was betraying her and the man who abused her for eighteen months as a young girl who was locked away such a short distance from them. He took his things and walked out the door.

Determined not to fail this time, Nickie shoved her holster and badge beneath the seat of her unmarked. She pulled down her visor and flipped open the mirror.

Good hair day. Good makeup. Should be. It took her long enough.

She didn't look like a cop. Rarely was she called out for it. Jeans, black boots and belt, fuchsia buttoned-down blouse. What were the colors for Heritage College again? Too late for that. She was to meet with Nevaeh at fourteen hundred o'clock. That gave her exactly one hour to convince the next girl it was okay to come out, to come forward, and to ask for help. Come to some kind of healing and closure. What the hell did this Stoner have over these girls? There had to be more defectors than just Nevaeh. She'd been a rock. So damned impressive.

Caroline continued to tuck her arms around herself and run the other way each time she spotted Nickie. Samantha's method of coping continued to be showing herself as the classic bitch.

Nickie had parked in a no-parking spot that was as close to the science building entrance as possible. Yet, it was a hike and she didn't want to miss this next girl, so she got out and made her way up the walk. Nearly all the students who came out first wore shorts and t-shirts. It wasn't that warm yet.

Glancing down at Duncan's sketch one more time, Nickie looked up as she folded and stuffed it into the back pocket of her slacks. The girl came out alone. Head down. Arms crossed. Awful. Nickie understood why Duncan picked her out as a potential victim.

"Hello, my name is—"

She looked at Nickie and squinted. Before Nickie could finish, she said, "I know who you are." Then, the girl sighed. "Word gets around."

Nickie smirked. "Samantha."

"Yep. Good old Sam."

Taking a step next to her, Nickie gave her a moment to gather herself.

"You want me to talk," the girl said flatly.

"I want you to heal."

"How do you know I have anything to heal from?"

"Because I've been in your shoes."

The girl stopped, but it was a few moments before she turned to Nickie. "What can I do to help?"

Nickie closed her eyes and nodded, making sure to hold back the relieved smile aching to escape.

It was time to turn up the pressure on one Eric Stoner.

Steepling his fingers, the captain leaned back in his enormous vinyl chair. "His parents will create significant trouble. The city council. My boss. Possibly the media."

"I don't think the media," she disagreed. "Mom and Pop don't want this out. But yes to the rest."

"And you don't think you'll get a confession? Why are we doing this again?"

"Apparently, word is out that I'm nosing around. Major breakthrough with one of the newly interviewed victims yesterday." Time to play the big card. "Would you feel better if I ran this by the ADA?"

His elbow slipped from the armrest, the weight of his upper body followed. She kept a straight face and should get a medal for doing so.

"You're offering to speak with Vaughn?"

"Of course. I mean, she's growing on me. She's the real deal."

"That's a big accommodation, coming from you."

She didn't take it as an insult. "Yes. You'd be putting your neck out for me. I should make sure the backlash would be worth it."

Now she really needed to use her phone. "I'll just step out to call her right now, if that's okay with you."

Dave was a blessing. He knew something was up, but he trusted her.

Gently, she pulled his door shut, then yanked out her phone and pressed speed dial 2.

"Nick," Eddy answered. "I've got him in my sight."

"Abort, dude. The captain didn't bite just yet."

Silence. She hoped he wasn't too angry that she sent him out to get Stoner for nothing. Then, there was laughing. And more laughing.

"What's so funny?"

"I can't believe he said, 'No.' It's funny as shit."

"Glad I could be of amusement."

"Now you sound like that obsessive boyfriend of yours."

"He's my husband and not at all obsessive." Other than calling her his 'woman.' "And the captain didn't say, 'No,' exactly. I just have another hoop to jump through before we bring him in."

Harder laughing. What the hell?

"Vaughn. You have to speak with Vaughn before you can bring in Stoner. This is so making my day."

"You're an ass, Lynx. Be glad I can't reach you right now."

Again, the bed was empty when Duncan woke that morning. Faintly, he remembered Nickie squeezing his foot through the sheets. It must have been her way to say good-bye without saying good-bye.

He sat at his office desk in silence. It had been over a week since Nickie told him she was going out on her own to interrogate registered sex offenders and inmates.

His mind wandered to the time they'd vowed to kiss for six seconds each morning before they parted for work. She'd read it on the Internet somewhere. At the time, he'd understood the principle, yet thought leaving the house hard as steel wasn't always positive.

When had they gotten here?

She'd turned on the coffeemaker and placed his dark roast in the filter. He'd nearly forgotten to brew. On his way to the machine, he'd noticed the working document she'd left open on their desktop unit. He'd sat in his boxer briefs so long reading through it, he nearly missed his eight o'clock meeting with his portfolio manager.

Now, it was in front of him. Reading it as it was displayed on their desk unit felt honest. Copying it and sending it to his work email was another thing altogether. And yet, here he was. Staring at his emails.

He took a drink of his cold coffee, then opened the document. She'd made significant progress. At least her absent nights and weekends were paying off. But she hadn't shared this with him. Updates on the college rape case, yes. Times she'd spoken with the girl in trafficking rehab they'd saved from Manhattan, yes. But this? No. He had to wonder why.

From the looks of it, a number of those she interrogated recognized Zheng. It seemed as if she was under the impression there were possibly three rings of young female teens, the same for males, some younger children. How did she keep moving forward with all of this? He could barely read it, and he was not a victim of trafficking. Why wasn't she sharing it with him?

CHAPTER 12

———◆ ◆ ◆ ◆———

Miranda Vaughn sat at her desk, ramrod straight in her hard-back chair. Everything had its own little place. Pencil cup, standing file folder holder thing. Labels covered each of the drawers along the counter in back. Nickie could read them from where she sat. Blank warrants, pending caseload, cold cases of interest. Good grief. How could anyone work like this?

Nickie had felt like she needed to wipe her feet before entering. "Your office is too clean."

At least Vaughn's smile was sarcastic. Something Nickie could relate to in this mess of cleanness. "I'm told you initiated this meeting," Miranda said.

"Don't look at me like that. I can initiate meetings with an ADA, ya know." Nickie took a long sip from her Styrofoam cup of Diet Coke.

"Yes, of course."

Together, they laughed at that. It was odd having a normal conversation with a woman, although Nickie would never admit that to the captain. "I want to bring in the main suspect of the college rape case for interrogation."

"Why not question him on his turf?"

"Because it would be his turf."

"I see from your files that your evidence thus far is circumstantial, and that you have little hopes of obtaining a confession during this interview."

Another sarcastic smile. This one wasn't as appreciated.

"Your eyelid twitches when I use the word 'circumstantial.'"

"Does not," Nickie snapped.

"Yes. See? It's your left one."

"Then don't use that word, Vaughn." Nickie forced herself not to touch her left eye. "I know what circumstantial is and when it's all I have. Have you checked my track record?"

"A multitude of times. Have you checked my job description? This is what I do."

"Damn." Nickie said it using three syllables. "Your sassy gets better every day." She leaned back and slung a boot over her knee. "I've got nine victims—"

"Circumstan—"

"Don't go there, Vaughn. If you want to keep that ponytail and shirt all pretty and pressed, you won't go there. Two of the girls have inadvertently made it clear they are victims. Told me there's no use in pursuing Stoner. He's too big. Blah, blah, blah. Two have all out spilled and given detailed statements. He gets them tipsy in public enough that he has witnesses to it. Then, he drugs them. He keeps trophies—"

"About that. I see the drawings of the alleged trophies, but no explanation of how the drawings were obtained."

The word 'alleged' didn't sound nearly as bad when Nickie used it. "A friend—"

"You mean Duncan."

"Stop interrupting." Nickie's left eye twitched. Damn it. This was why she didn't like to meet with ADA types. Damned hoops. "Stoner let Duncan into his apartment. Duncan isn't a cop." As he so often reminds her.

"He's your husband. Conflict of interest."

"I just want to bring him in. Two girls are enough. I have four." Sort of. "I need him here." Why did she feel like she was asking her foster mom if she could go out on Saturday night? "Putting this spoiled wimpy boy in a Northridge Police Department interrogation room is going to change him. Whether I get a confession or not, he's guilty as shit. He's going to start trying to cover his tracks. He'll make mistakes, and that's when I'll go in for the kill."

Vaughn sat with her brows held high. "Wow. I get what they say about you."

What did they say about her? And who were they? At that moment, she didn't care. She wanted her green light.

"Twenty-four hours. I can make it stick for you."

Gee, thanks a frigging lot. "Thank you," Nickie said between her teeth before taking another swig.

"I went out with Parker."

Nickie nearly spit her soda all over Vaughn's perfect office. "Officer Parker? You cougar!"

"It was an accident."

"I get that." Not.

"It was just a beer after court. At The Pint. It turned into several that turned into an Irish bomb—"

"Irish car bomb, Vaughn. You're embarrassing me."

"Yeah, that. Then, there was walking downtown and a patio fire and a massage table—"

"Whoa. TMI. I get it. So, why are you telling me this?"

The look on her face was pained. What did Nickie say wrong? Shit. This was why she didn't make friends with women. "I mean, what are you...do you want to do about it?"

"Have it happen again." Her perfectly straight shoulders dropped. "Or crawl in a hole and die."

"Um. Well, you can't die because I need you to tell the

captain I can bring in Stoner. And Parker is sort of cute." Wow. Officer Parker. The real thing. Solid. She should have chosen one-night-stand Eddy. "Yeah, you're screwed."

Nickie sat in her office, making sure Stoner saw her as he was ushered to Interrogation 2. Eddy didn't have him cuffed, but the grip he had around his arm would be vice-like. She pretended to be working on some paperwork but made eye contact as he passed. His expression was cocky, you-can't-touch-me. She would have preferred scared shitless, but she could work with that. Only it meant he was going to sit waiting for a long time before Nickie moseyed her slow ass into his room.

First, she would take a few moments to plan her after-hours interrogation. Tonight's john served five of an eight-year sentence and was currently living in Rochester. Aggravated sexual assault of a male between the age of eight and thirteen. Plea bargain took down the battery to assault and the shorter term. What the hell were people thinking?

Her spreadsheet.

She had left it open on the desktop unit at home. Had she saved it? Duncan would have seen it that morning. A wave of guilt blew over her.

"Detective?"

She looked up to see the nosy desk clerk who sat just outside of Nickie's office. "Mr. Stoner is asking for a lawyer."

"Yep," Nickie said. Predictable.

"I gave him the station phone."

Blood pumped loud around Nickie's head. It swirled around until she could hardly see straight. "No, you did not." There went her time in stirring his temper and emotions. She could see the look on her face in the brawd's eyes. "Who the hell do you think you are, Lucinda. Not your decision to make. Get the hell out of my way."

Nickie grabbed a large, yellow notepad and marched toward Interrogation 2. Before entering, she dipped her head and forced her breathing to slow. Lifting her head, she cracked her neck then marched in, swung her leg over the metal chair on the opposite side of Eric Stoner and plopped her butt down. "So, Stoner. Why do we have you here today?"

He shrugged.

"Wrong answer, dude." She wrote some random shit onto the notepad.

"I called for my lawyer."

"Yeah, I know. We talk to each other around here." Even if some desk clerk oversteps her boundaries. "You've been read your rights, and you don't have to say a thing." Leaning back, she propped a boot on the metal table, then crossed it with the other and smiled.

He looked around like she was nuts.

Keep it vague, Nick. "We have a number of witnesses who have quite a bit to say about you." 'A' number could mean one.

Stoner remained silent.

"I'm supposed to give you a chance to save yourself and all that." She waved her hand around like she was conducting Beethoven's Fifth.

Oh, he was good. She was dropping the cryptic shit. He kept it together.

"You've got all that volunteer crap and good grade shit that can—"

"Good grade shit?" He speaks. "I'm practically summa cum laude."

"Yes, because that comes far above volunteering."

That shut him up. "You see, we're wrapping this up. Kidnapping, sexual assault and battery. Rape is a hefty sentence. The time, the paperwork. You're not such a bad guy. You're almost summa cum laude. We'd like to give you a chance to reduce your char—"

"Stop, Eric. Don't say another word."

Unfortunately, he hadn't really said anything as of yet. Nickie set her boots on the concrete floor and sat up. "And enters the lawyer." Mick Wanton. Of course. Damn. "Actually, your client and I were just about finished. Is there anything I can get for you? A plank? A noose?"

"Whatever he said is inadmissible."

'Don't say another word' *and* 'inadmissible?' Stoner must have a mouth on him. Nice. "As I said, Mick. It's all moot at this point. Have a nice day, Mr. Stoner." Nickie turned to him and held out a hand. She appreciated the confused gaze that stuck on his face at her sudden change of social register of speech. "We'll be in touch with your Mr. Wanton, here, when there is anything further to discuss."

"What further, Detective?" Wanton asked.

Nickie stood and smiled wide. "It's *inadmissible* anyway, Mr. Wanton. No worries."

Hills, winding roads and two-lane state highways. There was no good way to get to Liberty, New York. Nickie put her mind into her happy place and dug in for the drive to the prison. The dudes she'd tagged thus far all had pretty much the same MO. Yes, they were caught doing their sicko shit. Yes, they recognized Zheng. Yes, they shivered and clammed up at the sight of him. But she was able to start piecing together an estimate of how many of each type of groups of captive children or adults Zheng had organized. Tracking their base and method of coordinating was going to take more digging. Baby steps. She needed to keep reminding herself that Fu Haizi was big and no matter what part Zheng took in organizing it all, he could be replaced. She needed files. Computer hard drives, drop box accounts, iCloud data. Something that could connect it all together.

At least it was pretty out. The trees were exploding

with tiny bright green things. If Duncan were with her, he would stare out the window and memorize it all so he could go home and paint it.

Duncan.

How long had it been since he'd painted as she played her cello? How long had it been since she'd played her cello? She needed to focus. College rape case, list of johns, find john who she killed seventeen years ago and the mole in her department. And Bianca.

She activated her hands-free and directed it to call the Sunnyside Safe House.

"Good evening, this is Tammy."

"Hello, Tammy. It's Detective Savage. Can you get her on the phone, please?"

"Let me check if she's done with dinner. It's the third meal today she's attended in the dining hall. Such great progress."

The corners of Nickie's lips turned up. Progress.

Progress with the john she killed was not so good. There was no record of the death of a man near the john's age in Baltimore the night she killed him. Or the few days before or after. Let alone one with a record. Her search would need to expand around Baltimore. She would know him if she found his pic in an obit.

"I found her, Detective."

"Hmm? Oh yes. I'm still here. Put her on the phone." As expected, she received no greeting. When the rustling sound on the other end stopped, Nickie said, "How's it going, Bianca? I've been thinking about you." Nickie didn't wait too long for the answer she wasn't going to get. "I'm getting closer to saving more groups of children. I live for this shi—stuff."

"Have you found the man who raped you last?"

Nickie's back straightened. She felt her lids blink several times. She'd told Bianca about that? "Oh. Well. Um, no actually. No luck there." She knew she didn't tell Bianca that she'd killed him. "It's the damnedest thing. But I'm not giving up. I've got all the time in the world. Just like you. No one is in any hurry for you to get better. A wise man once told me you never get over something like what happened to us, but we can move on from it."

Duncan. She missed him like she'd been away from him for weeks. Maybe because she had. She ran her free hand over her face, then through her hair. She used her knuckles to press against her jaw, cracking her neck one way, then the other.

"They didn't take me by force. Not at first."

Whoa. Here we go.

"I went willingly. They seemed real nice."

Wait time. Wait time. Silence. Uh oh. "That's not so uncommon."

"But I wanted to go with them. Wanted to. The girls were nice and so pretty."

Scum. Nickie had to force her eyes from clamping shut.

"I think I would have known if they'd offered me a modeling job or something, but they didn't. I wasn't model material. I knew that. But they said I did my hair real nice and could use me for that."

"Tricky bastards, aren't they?"

No laugh from Bianca, not that Nickie was expecting one.

CHAPTER 13

———— •◆•◆• ————

"And they didn't even act super interested in me," Bianca went on. "They offered me a job. Told me to tell my parents and make sure it was okay, then I didn't hear from them for weeks."

At that, Nickie pulled to the highway shoulder and took the mini-notebook from the pocket of her blouse. She wrote down every detail. It was time to try and push. For the sake of the next victim.

"Where was this, honey?"

Silence. Expected silence. Nickie continued. "That's a pitch that I bet works with lots of girls. It's why I've devoted my life to helping girls like us, and anyone else taken against their will. And you *were* taken against your will. You were a child. *Are* a child. Just because I was taken at gun point doesn't make it any more justifiable." Nickie's head was between her knees by this point.

"The mall."

"Which mall, Bianca?"

"Uptowne River Shoppes."

"On the water. Nice place."

"The girls were clean. They had make up and nails. Their clothes were good, too."

She was justifying.

"They gave me a paper with phone numbers and addresses and everything. Made me give it to my parents. Told me it was an internship."

Nickie couldn't push her too hard, or Nickie would lose her. She would ask the parents about the paper later. Furiously, Nickie wrote every word.

"It was warm the day I met them to leave with them. It was at a room in the mall. When I realized I was in the mall with people I didn't know. I started to get nervous. I told them I forgot my other suitcase in my car, but I had taken a cab. They let me go to get it. No one went with me. I started to feel like I had overreacted until I got to the parking garage. I set my real suitcase down and was pacing next to a row of cars when the van drove next to me."

The van. Nickie shut her eyes and placed her forehead on the top of her steering wheel. She didn't need the rest of the story.

"The door opened and a man pulled me in. He left my suitcase on the concrete and stuck tape over my mouth. They threw me in the back, then acted like I wasn't there."

Nickie let the next space of silence go on more for herself than for Bianca. "I am here for you, Bianca. You're not alone. And you'll never have anyone make you do something you don't want, ever again."

"I know. I'm just not sure who I am anymore."

"You will be, honey. I promise."

Duncan kissed his aunt on the side of her head, then handed her a box of orange scones. "Your garden flowers are lovely."

"The early spring tulips are already losing their petals." She took his fingers and squeezed. "It's so very good to see you."

The look on her face didn't agree. "I smell coffee." He

paused, allowing her to lead the way toward the kitchen. He glanced at the painting of Niagara Falls he'd painted when he was a child. He cringed, yet refrained from offering to paint a better rendering. He'd tried that a number of times already.

"Yes. I just made a new pot. I'd tell you to sit and let me get it, but—"

"But I won't have any part of that." He opened the cabinet where his aunt and uncle kept their coffee mugs. He stood for a moment. They'd kept them in this cupboard since shortly after Nathan had taken him and his brother in as young children.

"We moved them. To the right cabinet."

He still couldn't quite move.

"It's closer to the dishwasher. More practical."

She'd moved the coffee mugs? How long had it been since he'd visited his aunt?

"Duncan?"

She'd raised him and taken him and Andy in as her own.

"Duncan, everything's okay. My tests show I am still in complete remission. How did you know?"

She had tests? He turned to face her now. Why did she have more tests? "Why did you have more tests?"

Her head turned away slightly, but her eyes didn't. "I thought that was why you came by. That you had heard."

He couldn't come by without a reason? He hadn't come by without a reason. That was the problem. She was family. His uncle was family.

"I wasn't keeping anything from you. I would never do that, Duncan. I just don't tell you unless there is something to tell. You get so worried."

She wasn't wrong.

"Except, it's a weekday and you're here. In the middle of the day. Is there something you wanted to talk about?"

Needed to talk about. He stepped to the side and opened the cupboard where she now kept her coffee mugs. He took down two and carried them to the refrigerator to get the cream Brie used.

He sank down on one of the kitchen chairs Nathan had made with his own hands and admitted to himself the accuracy of Brie's suspicion. She always knew everything. "I haven't been coming by."

She closed her eyes and nodded. It was more like a long blink.

"I've had a number of paintings due, plus the real estate market is pulling away."

Her new expression wasn't nearly as understanding.

"And I've been working nights on Nickie's child trafficking crime ring case."

She poured their coffee before sitting with him. He noted she didn't use the cream.

Time to buck up, as his Nickie would say. "I apologize. There is no excuse."

She placed her hand on top of his. He noted the age spot and slight wrinkles that began to give away the years. "You are forgiven."

"And it's Nickie."

"She's well, I hope?"

"Yes, yes. No physical issues. She's quite obsessed with her work as of late. She comes home late, leaves early. She's been gone the last few weekends." He expected Brie to be suspicious. Why was that? She knew Nickie was as loyal as the day was long. "She's been interviewing sex offender inmates and registered offenders. Traveling all over on weekends in doing so. Why doesn't she talk with me about it? Turn to me? She knows I could cut corners for her." He attempted his best apologetic expression at his reference to the illegal hacking Brie had known about for years.

She glanced into her black coffee before she took a sip. The dark liquid reminded him of the black creek that flowed behind the house. It would be roaring at this time from the snowmelt.

"What would be the difference for her if she asked for your help versus doing it on her own?"

"It would be a hell of a lot faster, for one thing." He felt his brows drop. "And she wouldn't have to do it on her own. She's asked for help with a college rape case she's been on, but not the rest."

"She is not a college rape victim," Brie said.

He looked into the beautiful moss green of his aunt's eyes and sighed. The betrayal and rejection left him, replaced with a palette of relief. It wasn't about him, it was about Nickie. She wanted to do this one on her own. This wasn't just a case. It was personal.

Nickie held the class schedules of the last two possible rape victims. She shouldn't be here. The captain gave her the afternoon to interview the girls, but she also had a truckload of paperwork, and after that, a drive to Ithaca to interrogate a registered sex offender Duncan had pegged long ago from a photo with Zheng. She would never have caught it. She wasn't the one with the eidetic memory.

And if she didn't either pull away from this driveway and get to it or get out and walk her ass into her foster mother's home, Gloria would soon be at the door, scolding her like a child for making her come outside to get her.

This was a place of peace for Nickie. Refuge. She gave in to the moment, closed her eyes and took a deep breath. She'd skipped her workout that morning, and she'd almost ordered a pecan roll at the bakery. The horror.

"Child!" Gloria yelled from the front door.

Nickie's eyes flew open. Shit. Throwing open her car door, she waved and planted her best smile on her face. Resting a hand on the butt of her gun, she clicked her boots along the tidy walk that led to Gloria's front door. Nickie would find her in the kitchen by the time she made it inside. Standing at the sink, specifically. Why did knowing this soothe her?

"Three Sundays. No daughter. No call on phone. Today you come?"

Normally, Nickie enjoyed when emotions caused her foster mother's Hispanic accent to become pronounced and her grammar to take a dive. Today was different. She entered the kitchen to find Gloria sitting at her small, kitchen table. No sink.

"Is life in danger?" Gloria asked.

Nickie didn't need proper English to recognize sarcasm. A mug of steamy tea sat in front of Gloria, a bottle of Diet Coke on the other side of the table. Nickie must not be in too much trouble if she wasn't going to be forced to drink tea.

"I apologize." It was sincere. "I've been busy with some important cases."

"Is someone's life in danger?" No sarcasm this time.

"Well, no—"

"Then, you come. You come or you call. No. No, you come."

Nickie felt a finger below her chin. When had she dipped her chin? Reflexively, she lifted to look into the smooth caramel skin of the only mother she truly knew. She felt her eyes fill but couldn't bring herself to allow a tear to spill.

"If you did not come this Sunday, I was coming to get you. Family first. You...you always go to your..." Gloria made an oval in the air with her hands.

"Cocoon," Nickie answered for her.

"Yes, your cocoon. You must reach out." Gloria's eyes were a deep chocolate brown, nearly the same as Duncan's. They squinted at her now. Gloria leaned back and slung an arm over the back of her chair. "You are doing this to your husband, yes? The cocoon? No phone calls? No show?"

"I live with him. I can't *not* show." But Gloria was right. They hadn't even made love in over a week. The space between them in their bed might have well been miles.

"He loves you. He protects you."

Did she know about the 'my woman' fight?

"Marriage takes work. Marriage should take work."

Nickie smiled. It didn't go over well. Gloria grunted and pushed away from the table. She stood at the kitchen sink and dug the stopper into the drain.

"I'm sorry."

"You said that."

"It's just that you generally sit without saying much of anything and somehow get me to work through what I don't even know I need working through."

"You did not come to my home in the middle of the day to hear nothing." She turned on the water and squirted dish soap in the sink.

"There are some things I need to do on my own."

"Pssh. You take that too far."

Probably. Nickie rested her elbows on the comfortably worn wooden table and let her face fall into her hands. "I don't know how to balance it."

"Pssh."

Nickie was home. It was still light outside and she was home. Duncan tried to continue his work on the landscape the Nevada legislator had hired him to do, but Xena heard her as well and was doing circles in front of the door leading down the stairs. He placed his brush in the can of solution near the sink and made his way to the dog. "Calm," he commanded to deaf ears. Only tell her once, as the trainer had taught them. As he took the sides of the dog's face, he stared in her eyes and gave her a shake as Nickie's email signaled. Out of habit, he glanced over to the large desk situated in the room.

Even squatting near the door, Duncan read the name, 'Hurst.' He could go down and tell Nickie, but how many times in the last few weeks had that even been possible? Or he could let her discover it when she was good and ready. Or he could walk over and read it. He thought of the conversation he'd just had with his aunt, and made his way to the computer anyhow.

The subject read: Mole. Any thought of what might be an appropriate reaction to this situation left him. He clicked open the email as he sank in the chair, all but ignoring Xena and the fact that Nickie could walk in at any moment.

'I'm sending this to your home email purposely. Don't ask how I got it. I've had a guy on this for weeks. He's safe; I'm sure of it. What he's found out is that the mole is working under a number of alias IDs. I can't get a hit on the IP address the emails are coming from. He/she runs them through a false maze that includes several IP addresses and networks, but my guy has two IP addresses the emails go to. Below, I've listed the aliases, IDs and IP addresses. See if the aliases or IDs ring a bell. I'll be working on tracing the IP addresses to see where this bastard is sending the intel.'

Duncan couldn't get his eyes to look at the list of aliases, or the dummy IDs. His focus zoomed on one of the two IP addresses. He knew it like the back of his hand—more like the curve of his detective's face—and he knew who it belonged to. His heart sank deeper than any pain the absence from Nickie could have caused.

CHAPTER 14

━━━━●◆●━━━━

Nickie ditched the Ithaca house call. It scratched the edge of her mind, but she ditched it anyway. She sat in her car in the garage of her home. Their home. The sun hadn't set yet. She missed her husband. She missed her dog. She missed her house.

She needed to expand her search on the john she killed. She had college girls to check on, and a rapist to stalk and badger. She needed to call Hurst and see how he was coming along with digging up the two-faced mole at her station. And Bianca. She absolutely had to call this Child Rescue thing and find out if they could do anything about a trafficking abduction group that hangs out at the Uptowne River Shoppes.

She was a terrible wife. Why did he ask her to marry him? Why did she agree? Balance. She could do this.

She opened her car door as Duncan opened the door leading from the house to the garage. His face was pained. Of course it was. It was the first time he'd seen her in the light in how long? She could hear Xena's tail beating against the metal bars of her crate. Why would he put her in there when she was coming home? It would drive the poor girl nuts.

His eyes. "Hi," she said cautiously. He stood and

stared. Something was off. Something that wasn't the strain she'd caused between them lately. "I'm sorry." It was an all-encompassing statement, and the softening of his expression told her he knew that. "I'm going to be better. Promise. Forgive me?"

"Nickie, I have something I have to tell you."

Oh, boy. Her cell rang in its holster. Now? She rolled her eyes. "It's Dave's ringtone." She said it with the most apologetic look she could come up with.

"I know that, but I have something I have to tell you."

Swiping it open, she hoped she didn't sound as irritated as she was. "Savage."

"I thought you'd want to know there is a vigil going on at the college. I think it's your girls."

"Shit, really? I can't decide whether to be happy or scared. I'm on my way. Thanks for calling." Duncan. She couldn't face him, so she closed her eyes as if that would make her disappear. "I have to—"

"I heard."

"Wanna come?" There was no way he was going to say, 'Yes.'

"Of course. Let me get my coat."

Oh, sure. Make her feel like shit.

He was back before she had time to get in the driver's side of her car. No argument about taking her unmarked or her driving. This was bad. This was very, very bad.

Silence filled the car as she pulled out of their drive. Whatever he had to say must not be too serious if he wasn't talking. He stared out the passenger window. That was normal. He did that. He liked to study the colors of the landscape and all that. He bounced his leg on the ball of his foot, shaking his knee. Not normal. When did he start doing that?

"I came home early," she said to break the awkward silence that didn't used to ever happen between them.

"You came home on time."

She deserved that. "Okay." And he didn't even

mention that she wasn't really home, but headed out to work again. "What painting do you have going on?"

"Hmm? Oh. A landscape."

"For who?"

"One of the legislators of Nevada."

Not something a person hears every day. "So, I'm not sure exactly what we're coming up against. Mrs. Stoner isn't going to like this. She might show up with some kind of muscle."

"Can she do that?"

"She can try. These things can be highly productive or a disaster. Let's hope for option number one."

"Nickie, I have something to tell you."

"I sort of got that. It's creeping me out a little." Not her cell again. This cannot be happening. It was Eddy's ringtone this time. "Savage," she said, not at all trying to sound pleasant.

"I heard," Eddy said. "You want me with you?"

"No, thanks. I have Duncan."

"Wouldn't let you out after dark alone?"

"Save it, Lynx."

"Are you and Pretty Boy having a fight? I could come out and make it all better."

She hung up on him and stuffed her phone back in her holster. As she turned onto campus, she glanced at Duncan. No clenched jaw. No tight fists. And he didn't make a comment about putting Eddy in his place.

The vigil was up ahead. Wow. She counted at least a dozen girls. "Looks peaceful enough." She parked in the closest no-parking spot she could find and shoved the gear into park. Fourteen girls. Half of them carried signs that read, 'no means no,' on one side and 'no consent,' on the other. The rest of the girls carried lit candles. Nice. The sun was setting. The lights of the quad were beginning to kick on. It looked as if they were slowly attracting a crowd.

No sign of Mrs. Stoner, but not everyone seemed

supportive. Could be hecklers. There were only three of these. If Nickie admitted it to herself, even three college-aged hecklers could do more harm to the girls than three Mrs. Stoners.

She opened her car door.

"Nickie."

She looked over to him and realized where his mind was. "Right. You're the magazine reporter. You can't come with me. I've got this."

The temperature dropped as quickly as the setting sun. Long shadows draped across the concrete, covering most of the girls. A trickling of students ignored the commotion and made their way along sidewalk perimeters with their backpacks on and earbuds dangling from their ears. A trio of men hung back, leaning against a lamppost. She would bet her paycheck it was Stoner. He was smart to stay clear.

The three girls she had pegged as potential hecklers stood in their stiletto boots and painted-on jeans. Samantha was one of them. Crossed arms. Hips cocked. She was the victim who did everything she could to not be the victim. It nearly broke Nickie's heart.

She didn't recognize the other two girls and had no idea whether they were any of Stoner's victims. As she got within range of the vigil, she heard it. "Why so bitter, girls? The best way to get over one guy is to get under another."

The circle of girls kept walking, but several of the faces fell. The heckling was as legal as the vigil. It didn't mean Nickie couldn't try to make it stop. She stepped next to the trio. When Samantha spotted her, Nickie swore she saw a quick wave of guilt cross her face. Had she been put up to this? Then, back to bitch face.

Samantha turned, giving Nickie a shove with her shoulder as she did. Nickie grabbed her upper arm but refrained from making it a point. Samantha was as much of a victim as Nevaeh. "Samantha. Be smart. I'm here to help you, but I am also an officer of the law."

Like a child, Samantha jerked her arm away and strutted down the sidewalk, her sidekicks following like baby ducks. Nickie kept an eye on the circle of girls as well as Samantha, who walked right to the trio of men. Stoner. He draped an arm over Samantha's shoulder and pulled her along. Oh, how Nickie hated him right now.

"Girls," Nickie said as if it were an announcement. "I'm Detective Nickie Savage." She heard a few distinct gasps. Most likely girls who thought they were in trouble for creating what they thought was a disturbance. "I'm impressed, I gotta say. Stay as long as you like. I'm going to give Nevaeh some of my business cards. Call me." She took out the few business cards she had from the back pocket of her slacks and handed them to Nevaeh.

Caroline passed. Nickie didn't have much of her focus on Caroline's expression or her stance or shoulders or how much her feet shuffled along the concrete as she walked. Nickie's main focus was the bracelet that hung around Caroline's wrist. It was a silver heart with etchings on it. She would also bet her paycheck the etchings read: faith, hope, love. An exact match to the necklace that sat in Stoner's desk. Oh, how she wanted to get a picture of it. The girls would flip if she took out her phone to do so.

"I'm going to let you do your thing, ladies. Call me if anyone gives you trouble. I mean that."

The temptation not to tell her tore at Duncan. He still didn't know who the mole was, but he knew the recipient of the emails. There was no question.

He could go see the woman, search her office, question her, and make her tell him who the mole was.

Then, he could tell Nickie. It would be smarter to do it in that order. Safer.

But their marriage, as all relationships, already had its share of struggles. Transparency was one of their larger issues. And that was his fault.

He poured himself a few fingers of whiskey as he listened to her work with Xena in the back of the kitchen. Nickie was a natural with her. The dog was pushing ninety pounds and was a gentle giant.

It went against all of his instincts, but he would tell Nickie. He would tell her that night. Now.

The telltale sounds of Xena's crate latch indicated Nickie was putting her to bed for the evening. Throwing back the liquor, he dug in his heels and headed for the kitchen.

And dropped to his knees.

Standing at the kitchen sink with her back to him was his detective, her feet bare. As well as her arms, legs, backside. Everything except the parts covered by his miniscule Jets apron. Had she been working with the dog in—? How did she change so—? Coherent thought left him. She turned her head enough for him to view the wicked profile of a smile that spread across her beautiful lips.

His hands couldn't get to her fast enough, couldn't cover her quickly enough. He spun her to face him, then picked her up, plopped her on the kitchen counter and dug in.

They weren't usually a couple that slept touching. Duncan was like a heater. In the back of Nickie's mind, she always feared waking up swinging from the dream. But she woke in the middle of the night on her side with Duncan curled in behind her. She had hold of his arm with both hands and tucked it under her cheek. His body was warm, too warm, but nothing could move her from her spot. She turned her head into his forearm and took a deep breath. It was just enough to wake him. He didn't move, but she sensed his change in breathing. Then, his lips pressed against the side of her head and kissed her hair. She squeezed her eyes shut and took in the moment.

It was still dark out. The clock read oh four hundred-fifteen. She would skip her workout, skip food and be late for work, so that she could stay right where she was.

He slipped his hand from her power grip and slid it down the middle of her chest, over her stomach. Yes. He was awake.

Her cell rang. She would drown it. Then, jump on it. Then, drown her captain since it was his ringtone. Duncan picked it up and handed it to her. Traitor.

"Savage," she whined.

"Nick. I'm afraid I have bad news."

She sat up and tucked her knees to her chest, propping her elbows on top of them. He had never said that to her before.

"I don't know how to tell you this. It's one of the college girls, honey."

Honey? Her hand flew to her mouth and covered it.

"They found her in her apartment, Nick. She took her life."

Tears pooled in her eyes. No. No, no, no. "Who was it?"

"Caroline Studebaker."

She nodded. Okay. Okay. Deep breath. "Is the scene secured?"

"Yes, but there are no signs of foul—"

"Don't let anyone touch anything. I'm on my way."

CHAPTER 15

———•◆•◆•———

It was still dark when Nickie arrived on campus. Duncan came with her again, and she was grateful. He drove, which provided her extra attention to assess the scene.

The streets and sidewalks were bare other than a group of students in their pajamas who stood around the quiet swirling lights of the squad cars, ambulance and fire truck. She recognized the coroner's car double-parked near the entrance to Caroline's apartment building. The air was thick with fog and dew and a deep, deep sadness.

He parked away from the crowd. They didn't speak as they exited his Audi and joined at the front of the car to walk through the mess. He placed a hand on her lower back as they maneuvered through college students and vehicles.

He gestured for her to duck under the yellow crime tape first. This was her turf. Everyone knew her. No one questioned her presence or the fact that she had a civilian with her.

She climbed the threadbare brown stairs and turned to the first door on the left. She was prepared for the worst. She'd worked dozens of murder scenes as well as some suicides. The apartment living room and kitchen area were as Nickie remembered them. Nasty gold couch that slouched in the middle. No signs of foul play or anything amiss. Other than the two uniforms that stood consoling the roommate. It would be a good idea to give the girl time to gather herself before Nickie had to interview her.

The uniforms nodded to Nickie. She returned the gesture before inhaling deeply. Her feet fought the way to the back bedroom. Duncan's hand burned strength and warmth into her back, and kept them moving at an even gait.

She turned into the doorway. Oh, Caroline. They left her hanging as Nickie had requested. Why did she request that again?

You sweet girl. You had your whole life in front of you. Why didn't you call me? Why didn't I see this in your eyes last night? Was I too busy dwelling on Stoner in the shadows? Too busy dwelling on the bracelet you wore that matched the necklace in Stoner's desk drawer at that moment? Circumstantial bullshit.

Duncan's hand wrapped around her upper arm. Her spine stiffened. It made the material of her blouse peel away from her sweaty back. "I'm fine."

Walking to the coroner, she listened as he gave his two cents. "Roommate says she found her like this when she got home from partying. Called 9-1-1 at 4 a.m. No foul play suspected. Suicide note's on the desk. She used the stool." He gestured to the small stool toppled on its side beneath her.

Nickie took out the camera from the front pocket of her slacks and started taking pictures.

"Nickie," Duncan whispered in her ear, close enough that his body brushed up against the entire side of her.

She turned to find his gaze gesturing to the bracelet Caroline still wore.

"I know. I meant to tell you last night." Last night.

She spent her evening having sex with her husband as
Caroline suffered enough to end her life.

She finished taking pictures, then stuffed the camera
back into her front pocket. Before she dug out her old
school recorder, she cracked her neck, one way, then the
other. Device in hand, she walked around the room and
pressed *record*.

"Caroline Studebaker. Age nineteen. Full-time student
at Heritage Junior College. Found hanging in the
bedroom of apartment 11, 624 Highcrest Avenue,
Northridge, New York. Wearing black Chuck Taylors,
faded blue jeans and a black hoodie with the words,
'Heritage College Drama Club' printed across the front.
Note that this is what the deceased wore the previous
evening at rape awareness vigil she participated in." The
suicide note sat on the white, chipped Formica desk.
Nickie wasn't ready to read it yet. "Nine eleven called
by roommate at oh four hundred. Taken down at—" She
gestured to the coroner, giving him the green light to do
so as she checked the time on her phone. "—oh six
hundred twelve. Deceased used a belt and stool, affixing
belt to the ceiling fan." Bile threatened deep in her
throat as her head threatened to spin. "Scene is
otherwise intact."

She wasn't sure why she was here. She just had to
make sure. The Stoners could be capable of anything in
Nickie's opinion. Samantha, too, for that matter. No foul
play. No need for her to check it out. Just a typical,
statistically cut-and-dry death of an emotionally tortured
victim. She reached out her hand, knowing he would be
there. Blind faith. Grabbing his forearm, she squeezed,
making the leather of his coat squeak.

"Thank you," Nickie said to the coroner. "Have the
parents been located?"

He nodded. "On their way."

"Good."

The note. She'd read them before. Why was this so

different? So hard. She walked to it in slow motion. It lay face-up on the white Formica. There was a crease across the center. Did they find it that way? Of course they did. She lifted it in her fingers and turned it over. On the bottom half, it read, 'Mom and Dad.' Nickie turned it back to the letter and forced her eyes across the lines of print.

Dear Mom and Dad and Sissie,
Please don't be sad. I am in a better place. I have nothing to offer this world. The hurt is too much. I love you.

The tears couldn't be contained. They were unprofessional, unhelpful and did nothing to help Caroline, her family or the other victims. And Nickie didn't care. She let them drip down her face and over her jaw. She had failed this young woman. Failed. Much like she had failed the nine girls she left when she escaped Zheng as a young teen. Why? What had she missed? What should she have done differently? She began retracing her decisions and the steps from the case when long, lanky fingers encompassed her shoulder.

She jerked away from them much like Samantha had done near last night's vigil. Then, her shoulders dropped and more tears streamed from her closed lids. He put his hand back on her shoulder and she sighed as she felt soft lips press against the side of her head. Okay. Okay. It was time. She opened her eyes, wiped the tears from her face and neck and set the note back on the desk.

She made her way to the roommate. Glancing over her shoulder, she noticed Duncan waited in the doorway. He was taking mental pictures, she knew. It would take him a few minutes. She left him to it.

The roommate was a brunette with large smudges of black makeup smeared around her cheeks. Nickie took the way of the walk-through kitchen to get a paper towel. She ran a corner of the towel under the kitchen sink, then slowly made her way to the girl. Like a catcher behind the plate, Nickie squatted in front of her. Puffy, red eyes looked up at her and blinked like coming outside after being in a dark movie theater. Nickie thought she herself may look much the same.

"Susie?"

The girl nodded.

"I'm Detective Savage. I'm here to ask you about Caroline."

First things first, though. It had to be done. She handed her the wet paper towel, then asked, "Were you in drama club with her?"

Susie's eyes squeezed shut as her chin dipped so far to her neck that Nickie could hardly recognize the nod. This time, when Nickie squeezed her eyes shut, she refused to let the tears take her.

"I never told her," Susie wailed. "I kept it to myself. If I only would have told her."

The girl threw her arms around Nickie, digging her face into Nickie's shoulder. Nickie didn't know what to do. Her arms stretched outward as the girl clung to her. She looked around at the two uniforms for some clue as to how to handle a sobbing girl. Then, she used her fingertips to pat her on the middle of her back.

"You can't go there, Susie. That's not helping Caroline." Was Nickie the pot or the kettle? "Right now, Caroline needs you to tell me what happened. Then, I need you to tell me the rest of what you know." They both knew what Nickie referred to. Susie was an Eric Stoner rape victim just like the rest of them.

It was past oh seven hundred before Nickie was able to leave the apartment building. The body was en route to the ME's lab. The gawkers were gone. All but the coroner's vehicle and Duncan's Audi had left the scene. A new BMW sat next to the coroner's vehicle.

Nickie spotted the dean almost immediately. Points for him, she supposed. "Detective." He held out his hand. "What can I do?"

Stop letting your counselors make police decisions?

He glanced around the area as he spoke to her. "I have my secretary lining up counselors for the students."

"How will the students access them?"

"The counselors? Oh, I'm not sure. What do you recommend?"

He was asking her what she recommended? Wow. "Set up a tent in the quad today and one in the student union tomorrow. Have hot chocolate and arrange private areas for students to talk to these people. And most of all, have them keep record of anyone who in any way seems like they may have been victim to the prick."

"Are you talking about Eric Stoner? Did Eric Stoner do this?"

"Caroline was one of his victims. She was part of the vigil last night."

"What vigil?"

Okay, points taken away. All of them. "On your campus. For over an hour. Over a dozen girls? Picket signs, candles. Enough heckling to send a young woman over the edge and hang herself?" She crossed a line. Why didn't she care? "I may have some of my own counselors I might want to include." She also didn't care if she crossed this line as well. "I'll have them in the quad today and union tomorrow, and you'll have accommodations for them if they show up." She would call Captain Dave's wife. She had connections with this sort of thing. Habitually, Nickie scanned her surroundings. A woman stood too far away to say for sure, but Nickie thought she looked like Samantha. Casually, she headed toward her. She passed the Audi on the way. Duncan sat working on his tablet. She thought he hadn't seen her, but without taking his eyes from his tablet, he rolled down his window as she neared.

"I'll be just a short while more. I see someone I'd like to talk to."

He didn't turn to gawk, but instead nodded and kept at his work.

It was indeed Samantha. She turned and took a step like she was ready to flee, but then she changed her mind. She actually stomped her ice pick heel on the concrete.

"Samantha," Nickie greeted her.

"What happened?"

"You haven't heard?"

"I did. I just can't believe it."

"I bet you can."

"It was that Caroline, wasn't it?" Tears dripped out of Samantha's painted eyes and poured over her cheeks. "Stupid, stupid girl."

"I'm here for you, Samantha." Nickie tucked her hand in her pocket, but realized she'd given all her cards out to the girls at the vigil the night before.

"I don't need you!" Samantha's ankle twisted and cracked as she spun on her heels. She hopped twice before catching herself and marching on.

CHAPTER 16

———— ◆ ◆ ◆ ————

"Brother, what the hell are you thinking?" Andy asked Duncan.

Duncan's brother sat at the kitchen table in the house he'd built. Andy junior, or A.J. as they called him now, clutched a bottle of formula in his chubby hands while staring at his dad, his blue eyes as big as saucers.

"You might not believe me, but I have made several attempts to tell her." There was the college rape vigil, the suicide. "She's...busier than usual." Jets apron sex in the kitchen.

"Stupid."

"I will tell her."

"You almost lost her the last time you did this." Andy didn't understand.

"I'm going to tell her," Duncan repeated, then added, "Today."

"Leslie Jacobsen is the one who is receiving the emails from the station mole? You've known this for two days and you haven't told her? The same Leslie Jacobsen who Nickie's father hired to conceal the records of Nickie's childhood abduction as well as escape?" Andy said her name with as much shock and distaste as Duncan had.

Duncan let his eyelids close as he nodded. "Yes. I'm finding difficulty focusing on the next step."

"You mean the next step after telling your wife."

Duncan hoped his glare answered Andy's question. The baby clung to his father's shirt as if it were his lifeline. "May I?" Duncan gestured to A.J.

"Yep."

Andy handed the baby over to him with a bit more speed and confidence than Duncan preferred.

"You want more coffee?" Andy asked, but Duncan wasn't truly listening. The baby smelled amazing. A combination of sweet and clean.

"Answer me, or I'm going to put French vanilla creamer in your mug."

A.J. looked up at Duncan with his mom's ice blue eyes as if he knew he was in the arms of family. As A.J. batted at the bottle with a fist, Duncan realized his nephew was still hungry. A.J. took the bottle and started chugging, then grabbed hold of Duncan's shirt with his tiny fist just as he'd done with his father.

Andy hovered a bottle of creamer over Duncan's mug. "Touch my coffee with that, and I'll break your hand."

"You want a warmer, or what?"

"I do, thank you. I'd like to approach Leslie away from her office."

"Hmm. Let me think on that one." Andy added enough cream and sugar to his mug, it could scarcely be called coffee any longer.

He heard footsteps. Both he and Andy became quiet as Rose entered the kitchen. Her tiny feet stopped. She looked from Andy to him to the baby and back again. Plopping her hands on her hips, she raised her voice. "Holy shit. You two are planning something illegal in front of my son."

Andy walked to her, slid his arms around her and placed them on her backside. "And you just said, 'Shit,' in front of my son."

They kissed quickly before she maneuvered around Andy and reached for the baby. "I'm headed to work. Give him here, Duncan. Off to the sitter."

A small hole in his heart threatened to open. It was short lived but most certainly was there.

"So, what? We go to this woman's house? And tell her what?"

"We have evidence of illegal surveillance. The trouble she and the mole have gone through to keep this covert, she must have a great reason to keep it that way."

As he sank into the chair opposite of him, Andy nodded in agreement. "And that is what we'll use to get her to tell us who she answers to."

"We already know who she answers to." Nickie's father. Her own flesh and blood.

Andy's face fell. "I'm sorry, man. This sucks on so many levels."

"Yes. However, we'll use it to convince her to tell us who the mole is."

Caroline's parents were in the basement, IDing the body of their youngest daughter. Nickie would give them time before she asked them the favor she needed. This was one of the worst parts of her job.

She sat at her desk, thinking of what legit NPD project she should work on. Screw it. Taking out her cell, she propped her boots—one, then the other—on the corner of her desk that was free of paperwork. "Jess Larsen," she spoke to Siri. "Child Rescue. Call."

She'd half expected to leave a message, but he answered on the second ring. "This is Jess."

"Jess. Hello. This is Detective Savage. I have a question for you."

"Nickie, it's good to hear from you. I heard the rescue was a success. One of the girls is reunited with her parents and the other is in a safe house."

"Yes, thank you for the help. I'm calling about the one

in the safe house, actually. She provided a decently detailed account and location of her abductor's MO. They use a mall...Uptowne River Shoppes." This was sounding more and more like a long shot. "I didn't get the phone number of the men you had help. Thanks, by the way. Do you think they might be up for a stakeout?"

"I'm sorry, Detective. They are unavailable."

Long shot or no, disappointment took over.

"They are en route to Peru as part of a trafficking rescue jump team."

"Peru? Jump team? Nice. How many children?"

"It seems I don't need to explain a trafficking rescue jump team to you. Also, nice. We believe at least two dozen, mostly girls."

Her disappointment was misplaced. Over two dozen children would be saved. "Wow. Very, very nice. How did former delta force agents end up as part of a jump team in Peru?"

"These are men who became tired of the red tape and bureaucracy it takes when in the system."

"I suppose those of us still in the system can relate to that. Thank you for your time. Good luck with the mission."

"You're welcome, Detective. I'm sorry I couldn't help."

Oh nine hundred twenty-five. She would head down to the basement and grab the Studebakers on their way out. Leaving her Diet Coke behind, she grabbed the copy of the suicide note, then stuffed her phone in her back pocket. The walk down the stairs would be helpful.

Jump team. No bureaucracy. It sounded too good to be true. The sound of her boots thumped along the Berber carpet.

High profile be damned, she had the thumbs up from her captain and the ADA to bring Stoner back in. It was iffy. She didn't like iffy. She was more of a going-to-break-the-suspect-in-minutes kind of girl. Better yet, she liked not having the need to break the suspect, because the evidence she'd collected was so outstanding it sealed the arrest and conviction.

The basement door led out of the last set of stairs. Mr. and Mrs. Studebaker, and what looked like maybe an older sister, were still in the medical examiner's lab. She would give the basement wall a lean as she waited.

She had the accounts of two victims that came down to he said/she said. She didn't get the impression Stoner was going to go all guilty conscience because of Caroline's death. She had trophies that she couldn't access. Even if she got the warrant, they would need to have blood on them not to be circumstantial, and these girls didn't walk away with those kinds of wounds.

It was time. As the Studebakers shoved open the glass door that led out of the ME's lab, Nickie pushed off the wall. Their faces displayed the shock they experienced. White, almost gray.

She held out a hand. "Good morning, Mr. and Mrs. Studebaker." She nodded to the potential sister. "My name is Detective Savage. I am sorry for your loss."

The missus nodded, then started a new round of crying. She turned and dug her face into the shoulder of her husband. "What can we do for you?" he asked.

"Would you mind stepping into our consultation room?" Nickie placed her hand on his elbow and pointed with the other. "It's right here. It will take only a few minutes of your time." Hopefully.

He nodded and allowed her to lead his family into the room.

Neither the mister nor the missus could be expected to think of introductions, so Nickie held out her hand once more to the younger woman. "I'm Detective Savage."

The girl didn't shake Nickie's hand, but answered, at least. "I'm Caroline's sister, Marlene."

Still present tense. Nickie got that. "Thank you for your time. Do you have any questions for me? Is there anything I can do for you?"

"Are you the one who found her?" asked Mr. Studebaker.

Nickie assumed he was asking if she was first on scene. "No." She would be as honest as she could. "I did assess the sce—her room, however. She passed quickly and with little suffering." So much for honest. There was no way for her to know that.

Mrs. Studebaker threw her arms around Nickie. The woman was clammy and chilled and hung on like Nickie was a long lost friend. Her cries raked through Nickie like hot coals. Nickie's arms laid lifeless to her side as the woman shook with sobs.

"Oh, Detective. Why? Why would she do this?" Her shoulders trembled against Nickie's. Glancing over at the dad and sister, Nickie noticed them embrace and sobbing as well. "She's gone," Mrs. Studebaker muffled.

Nickie was the worst human on the face of the planet for what she had to ask next. Waiting for Caroline's mother to pull away, she tried to smile warmly. She didn't want to give out more information about the rape than Caroline would have wanted her parents to know. "I would like to ask your permission to use her bracelet for a few days. I promise to have it back before the funeral."

"Her bracelet?" Mrs. Studebaker said and wiped her nose with the tissue Nickie handed her. "Why?"

Damn. "It will help me piece some things together. For her."

The father was more intuitive. "Piece what together?"

Time to go out on a limb. "I think I may have found the necklace that matches it."

Caroline's mother turned to her husband. "The necklace is missing? I didn't even notice."

"Me, either." He moved his gaze to Nickie. "I still don't understand."

Nickie was out of ideas. All she had left was

transparency. "Your daughter was previously raped. I believe she wanted to tell you but wasn't sure how to go about it. I'm so very sorry."

For Nickie, the roomed seemed to go silent, although she could clearly see as the mother and daughter clung to the father and cried. It wasn't that loud, uncontrolled sobbing you hear on television. It was subdued and that of deep grief.

Mr. Studebaker looked over them into Nickie's eyes as he held them in his arms. His eyes were filled with rage and despair as he nodded his approval of taking the bracelet.

The family was still where she left them even after retrieving the bracelet from evidence. Nickie paused to watch them through the glass. Was this what family was like? Was this what people did for each other when the ends of the rope were frayed beyond repair? By this time, Nickie's wonderment had her facing them full on, watching this foreign scene of love and grief as it unfolded before her. Part of her wanted this so badly she could taste it. Not the grief. It moved beyond unnatural, beyond wrong. But the love and commitment between family in that room was something Nickie had never known. Would she? Could she?

"Detective, there you are." The look on Nickie's face must have read murder, because that was what she felt. Of all the people to interrupt her displaced moment with this grieving family, bitchy, nosy desk clerk Lucinda was not who she wanted to see.

"You have a crazy woman in high heels demanding to see you."

"Crazy woman in high heels doesn't cut it, Lucinda." Do not strangle NPD employees. Do not strangle NPD employees. "Did you get a name?"

"Samantha Collins."

Samantha? Was here? Nickie looked through the glass door at the Studebakers. They stood in a tight football huddle with their arms draped over the backs of each other.

Nickie bolted through the door and took the stairs two at a time. As she came through the door to the top floor of the station, Nickie might not have recognized Samantha if not for the ice pick heels and painted-on jeans. They had her sitting in the chair next to Lucinda's desk. As soon as Samantha spotted her, she sprung from her chair, startling the poor guy assigned to babysit her.

Black makeup smudged her cheeks and her hair looked like something nested in it. "Detective Savage, please. I killed her."

Nickie took her by the arm as she looked around to see who'd heard that. Only everyone. "Calm down, Samantha. We'll talk about it." She took her to her office instead of interrogation. Nickie shut the door as Samantha grabbed her arms like she was drowning. Her body shook from head to toe.

"Did you hear what I said? Caroline died because of me."

"Here, honey. Sit here." Nickie peeled Samantha's arms from around her neck but carefully hung onto her wrists. "There you go. Right here. Sit down."

Samantha's shoulders shook with grief as Nickie released one of her wrists and reached for a box of tissue. "Look at me, Samantha. Honey, look at me."

She grabbed her upper arms as Samantha clung to the tissue without using it.

Samantha stopped. A few quick intakes of air and she looked up to Nickie. "I have something," she whispered like they were in a room full of people. She dug her shaky hands in the pocket of her coat and pulled out a Ziploc bag. Nickie could tell what was crumpled inside. She didn't. Did she? Female underwear.

Samantha's eyes were crazed and opened wide. "I don't know why I saved them."

Nickie knew. Victims' actions varied and could be

bizarre. Deep in Samantha's heart, she knew what she exactly was doing. Glancing down, Nickie noted the blood and what looked like semen stains.

"It happened again."

"Oh, honey. When?"

"A few weeks ago. I took this." She pulled another Ziploc bag from her other pocket, but Nickie couldn't see anything in it. "I scratched him."

The scratch on Stoner's bicep. "Where, Samantha?"

"On the inside of his upper arm. I knew what he was going to do, and I went with him anyway. And I went back again after that." She shook her head as the tears flowed freely now. "Why would I do that?"

"Because he tricked you. He drugged you, and he raped you, then he used your pain to manipulate you again. What's in the bag, Samantha?"

"His skin."

His what?

"I just thought." She sobbed between syllables now. "I might need it. I dug his skin from beneath my nail and put it in here."

Nickie was speechless. She dropped to one knee and awkwardly wrapped her arms around Samantha, letting her cry until Nickie's shoulder was wet with tears. "It's going to be okay. There, there. We're going to take care of you. You're not alone anymore."

CHAPTER 17

The morning would soon turn into afternoon and Nickie still hadn't answered Duncan's calls. Each time he checked his phone, it still held the original message. *Can't talk right now. I'll call you later.*

Duncan parked his Audi across the street from the station.

"You want me to wait here?" Andy said from the passenger seat.

"Whichever you prefer."

Andy shrugged and got out. The rain was starting and made the gravel dust stick to the bottom of their shoes. "This is smart, brother. We have plenty of time to make the drive."

Andy was right, but Duncan didn't give him the satisfaction of agreement since he would have told Nickie about Leslie Jacobsen before they left anyway.

Nickie would insist on coming with them. It was too dangerous. He didn't like it.

As they entered the ground floor of the police station, he shook the droplets from his coat, then headed for screening. Keys, coins, phone in the bin. Metal detector, then reverse the process. Andy followed in silence as they made their way to the elevator. Arriving at Leslie's place of residence was going to be risky, but since he and Andy had already infiltrated her office, that option was too dangerous.

The elevator doors barely opened before Duncan sensed something was happening. From his vantage point, he could see Nickie's, Lynx's and the captain's offices. Each was dark. No one questioned his presence. Had he and Nickie been together so long that no one questioned his presence? So, he kept walking with Andy next to him as if they knew where they were going, which Duncan had a hunch he did.

Officer Parker stood outside one of the interrogation rooms. He turned his head as soon as Duncan and Andy rounded the corner. Damn, Parker was tall. He stood ramrod straight, but rotated his head enough to nod at the question on Duncan's face.

Duncan held out his hand. "Hello, Officer. This is my brother, Andy. Andy...Officer Parker."

"Good to meet you, sir."

"No sir necessary. Just Andy. Thanks."

They shook and Duncan forced himself not to wince at the grip. "Is she in there?"

"Yes, sir."

He wouldn't correct him for the 'sir,' but it was disconcerting, especially since they'd shared drinks at The Pint together in the past.

"I'm afraid she can't be bothered."

"Of course. I was hoping we might step into the observation room."

Parker looked pained but stepped in front of the small glass panel looking into the interrogation room. "Detective Lynx, Captain Nolan and Assistant District Attorney Vaughn are all in there. I suppose they'll tell you if you're not allowed."

"I suppose they will. Thank you for your time."

They didn't knock. Duncan honestly wasn't sure if he would be allowed. It didn't hurt that Andy's wife was the captain's stepdaughter.

The captain spotted him first. "Duncan," he said in a low voice. "Come on in. She just started."

All Duncan heard through the one-way speaker was rustling papers. Duncan had no idea who she just started with, but didn't question.

"Is that Andy?" Dave asked. "Come in. We'll find room."

The disgusted look on Lynx's face was satisfying to say the least. Duncan still owed him for his comment about coming out to 'make Nickie all better.'

Nickie moved enough for Duncan to spot the suspect. He faced the one-way mirror. Eric Stoner. Duncan's senses came alive. Every one of them. Stoner had you-can't-touch-me arrogance written all over his face. He obviously didn't know Nickie.

She had her back to the one-way mirror. Hair straight in a low ponytail. Chair squared and sitting ramrod straight in the center. Legs crossed and forearms resting on the table. Not her usual MO.

He'd seen her use her sexuality a plethora of times in order to achieve her desired outcome. Flip chair backward, sling leg over the top. Snug slacks and large, wavy hair draped around her shoulders and down her back. And it worked. Stoner types who thought little of women dropped their guard around females, especially those perceived as loose or dense. That was when his detective went in for the kill.

Today was apparently straightforward business.

The edge of a manila file folder rested in front of her. On the floor next to her foot was a brown cardboard box. Not knowing the contents might very well make Duncan insane.

"She has to talk fast," Lynx said. "He's already lawyered up. Wanton should be here any minute."

"Mr. Stoner, we have two victims who recount the same scenario for the rapes you wreaked upon them and others." Her voice was distorted through the speaker, but Duncan recognized the controlled monotone in her inflection.

Ice-cold confidence in his eyes, Stoner replied, "You don't have shit."

"Choose your victim using a public arena. Determine that victim is at least partially intoxicated. Show evidence thereof to potential witnesses, then drug the girl, take her to a back room and sodomize and rape her."

"Prove it," Stoner spat.

Keeping her neck stiff and head held high, she casually dipped into the cardboard box and removed a manila envelope. Duncan knew they would all see the contents soon enough, but that fact did little to ease his burning curiosity.

Pushing from her chair, she walked with purpose around to him, then propped a hip on the metal table. "You have some leverage to your advantage, Mr. Stoner."

"Not." It was Lynx, and for once, Duncan was thankful he spoke.

She folded her hands on her lap. "Ideally, this process will go as quickly as possible with no need for the victims to face the stand. That is our objective, Mr. Stoner. For the sake of these victims, I am going to offer as much transparency as possible and tell you each of them has expressed a willingness to testify."

"I want my lawyer."

"As you have stated previously and after hearing and agreeing to your Miranda rights. Mr. Wanton will be escorted into the room as soon as he steps onto department property. You are not obligated to speak, Mr. Stoner. My purpose at this time is to offer you leniency. I won't be able to do that once Mr. Wanton intercedes."

His face turned away from her like a teenager

planning to shut out an adult. Slowly, she pulled out a photograph. Duncan didn't remember any photograph and nearly forgot his entire reason for coming to the station in the first place.

She held it out and waited. It took some time, but curiosity got the better of Stoner and he glanced at it.

Duncan asked, "Does anyone know what's on the picture?"

Lynx answered. "She took a picture of the dead girl's bracelet."

Ah. His Nickie was a genius.

"Do you know who I am?" Stoner said between his teeth. "I'm not stupid, you know. That fake reporter you sent took that picture."

"I'm sorry, Mr. Stoner. I'm not sure what you're talking about. Are you referring to the jewelry items you have in your clothing drawer?"

Duncan's brows dropped. Nickie knew it wasn't his clothing drawer. She wouldn't make a mistake like that.

"Desk drawer, you dumb brawd. You can't even get your facts straight. The jewelry is in my desk drawer." He said those last few words through his teeth and loud and slow as if Nickie were dense. "I knew he was a fake the whole time. I wanted to see how long I could keep him going. It doesn't matter anyway. My dad says you didn't have a warrant, so you can't use anything from that."

She turned her chin to face the one-way mirror. "Please take note," she said, raising her voice, "that the suspect states under his Miranda rights that the artifacts are or have previously been located in the drawer of the desk in his apartment. Send a warrant to the judge on hold. Thank you."

Stoner jumped to his feet. Duncan, along with everyone else in the interrogation room, stood as well. Duncan's gaze turned to Parker at the door. He was facing the suspect now. Duncan didn't think Nickie would need assistance, but it killed him to see this prick come after his wife. It helped to know Parker was on top of his game.

The captain turned to the ADA, who was already rising from her chair. "Vaughn—"

"I'm on it."

He turned to Duncan and answered the question that must have been on his face. "We have a judge on call for the warrant."

Stoner's chest rose and fell. He was inches from Nickie, but she didn't move. However, he didn't notice her body morph into a defensive or aggressive stance either.

"I am an honor student with more clout and hours of community service than you can count."

Nickie lifted her chin a fraction as she did when she was holding her tongue.

"I've talked to my lawyer and all you have is circumstantial bullshit. Your so-called testimonies are he-said/she-said. The photo of the necklace, nothing."

"I never said the photo was of a necklace." She cocked her head. "Eric." She cracked the last C. Without taking her eyes from his, she blindly reached inside the envelope and pulled out the bracelet. Dangling it over her forefinger, she took a step forward and nearly closed the small distance between them. "This is the bracelet that goes with the necklace. Too bad you didn't take the matching set."

The hook came out of nowhere and landed squarely on Nickie's temple. Her head spun and dipped from the force.

Duncan started for the door, only to have the captain growl, "Sit."

He didn't see exactly what happened, but none of it happened above the shoulders. Apparently, she clamped a vice grip on Stoner's jewels, because he buckled at the waist and face-planted the metal table. She held up her free hand to the rushing Parker. "I've got this," she yelled over Stoner's cries.

Her face. Duncan needed to see the side of her face and couldn't from this angle. He glanced around, trying to make a plan to get to her. Everyone was on alert and staring with wide eyes at the two of them.

"I'm going to ease up now, Eric."

She didn't take her hands from his crotch, but she must have lightened up, because she was able to lead him back to an upright position. "Your ass lifts from that chair again, and I'm cuffing you to it."

No need for threats. The look in Stoner's eyes said it all. He knew he'd lost his temper and that he was going to pay for it now.

She made her way around the table. Her face. It was already bright red and swelling. "She needs to see a doctor," Duncan said to the captain.

"Agreed, Duncan. But we're giving her more time. She knows what she's doing."

Duncan's leg started shaking again.

She pulled out another envelope from the box, then calmly sank into her seat. One of Stoner's hands was between his legs and the other gripped the arm of the chair. Precisely, Nickie laid out the photograph and the bracelet.

"She went for the nuts," Lynx said. "No marks. That's my girl."

"Eddy," the captain barked. "Go find Vaughn. Take the warrant she gets and haul ass to the apartment before the lawyer thinks of a loophole."

Duncan would deal with Lynx later. And he was right. Her choice in target must have been premeditated. "Do we know if she has anything substantial?"

"We have enough for a trial," the captain said. "And thanks to his slip about the necklace and its location in his apartment bedroom, cause for a warrant."

"So, what's the deal?" It was Andy. Duncan nearly

forgot he was there. "Her face is swelling like hell. I can see it from here."

"What she has is still gray," Duncan said. "Nickie likes black and white."

"I have something you're not going to like, Eric. I want you to know before I show you. I am willing to offer the option of leniency if you cooperate. Again, to save the girls from testifying in court, not for you, your grades or your pathetic community service. I can't do this for you if you take another swing at a department detective."

Stoner remained quiet. Who said you couldn't teach a dumb dog new tricks?

She pulled out a pair of black panties, lace.

"So, I've had sex with girls—I mean women."

Stoner must have realized there would be semen on them. Duncan supposed his honor roll status might be justified.

"Eric, there's blood on them as well. You're not going to like who it belongs to."

"Me? That's not possible."

"Not you." She turned her head and raised her voice. "Parker," she called over her shoulder.

Duncan asked Captain Nolan, "Does she have a DNA match?"

"No. She's bluffing, but we may have enough to get a warrant for a sample."

The door opened, but Duncan felt confident the person who came through wasn't who Nickie had hoped. An Asian man sporting a suit and tie burst through the door. All eyes, including Nickie's and Stoner's, turned to see. The Asian man stopped short in the center of the room. He looked to Nickie, whose bruise turned a deeper red with swelling that had nearly closed her eye. The man turned his head to Stoner, who had both hands gripping the chair now, then back to Nickie.

"This is illegal. This is all illegal. All you have on my client is assaulting a police officer." He didn't keep his poker face for that statement. "I was called less than an hour ago. Whatever he said, I'll have it thrown out before any case begins."

"It's all been video and audio recorded, Mr. Wanton. Including a repeat of his Miranda rights. There are three witnesses behind the glass." She sat back in her chair and crossed her legs. "And I haven't asked him a single question."

The girl with the makeup and spiked heels Duncan remembered from campus stepped into the doorway. It was Samantha. Samantha? The one who continued to side with Stoner? The one who heckled the suicide girl? Ah. Yes. She must have been who Nickie wanted in the room. The lawyer's back was to her. Stoner had his face buried in his arms. Nickie held up a hand toward the door, making Parker quickly pull her away.

"Two victims who recount similar MOs. Choose an intoxicated female in a public venue who you've already groomed."

Duncan assumed she was summarizing for the attorney's sake.

"Drug them, take them in a back room and sodomize and rape them. Keep a trophy, which you've stated of your own free will a few moments ago would be located in a drawer in the desk in your apartment. If I know my captain, he's already attained a warrant and has a detective on the way to complete a legal search. We have fluid samples on panties worn by victim number two that show semen and blood evidence of both rape and sodomizing."

Andy spoke from behind Duncan. "Why didn't she mention the bracelet?"

Duncan answered before the captain had a chance. "The bracelet is common and therefore circumstantial. The victim who wore it is dead and never officially came out as a victim."

Stoner set both hands on the table, then plopped his head into them. It was muffled, but Duncan heard a distinct, "I want to hear what the detective has to offer."

"You're looking at predatory sexual assault. In the state of New York, we call that a Class A-2 felony. That's three years to life, depending on how the jury feels about drugging, raping and sodomizing college girls. I'm putting Class B on the table, Eric. That reduces your sentence to first-degree rape with a sentence of one to twenty-five. I'm only offering this on behalf of the girls, Stoner. Not you. You give a detailed, written confession that keeps them off the stand. My offer expires in ten minutes."

Wanton stepped to the table, placing both hands flat near Nickie. "You're crazy, Savage. You think this man, this...this *boy* with no record, outstanding lineage and community service is going to be convicted in the eyes of a jury?"

Behind her back, Nickie signaled to Officer Parker as she spoke to Wanton. "Did you really just say, 'lineage'?"

It was then that Samantha walked into the room. She was visibly shaking and a much different Samantha than the one Duncan witnessed in front of the Fine Arts Building and during Nevaeh's vigil. Her arms hugged her body, but she was fuming.

Stoner's face fell. Ah. He hadn't known who victim number two was. He would be able to put together the fact that the panties belonged to her.

Wanton's eyes darted between Samantha, Stoner and Nickie. "Someone tell me what the hell is going on here!"

CHAPTER 18

Nickie left her captain's office with a strange mixture of serene closure and intense drive.

Closure from landing a confession from Stoner, definitely. It was as if his weasel lawyer wasn't even in the room. He couldn't write his story on paper and get the plea deal fast enough. His parents and all their money would figure out a way to appeal, but the evidence was solid. And the girls wouldn't have to testify. Closure and closure.

The drive part would have to come after a stop at the soda machine. Diet Coke, then onto her work in tracking down the crime ring that abducted girls like Bianca. She would skip Stoner's confession celebratory drinks at The Pint, then get home to pack. A weekend staking out the Uptowne River Shoppes would give her time to surf for records of the death of the john she killed. Stake outs were like that. Duncan. She would positively make sure to tell him, no *ask* him, if he would come with.

Eddy would give her shit for not showing up at a happy hour in her honor. She couldn't think about drinking when girls were being abducted and she knew where and how.

She rounded the corner to her office and noticed two more men sitting in her guest chairs. Where had they put the crap that was on the chairs? She needed that crap.

Speak of the devil. "Duncan. Andy." Duncan *and* Andy? "What's up?" She linked fingers with Duncan and squeezed before walking around the desk to her chair.

"Andy." Duncan spoke to his brother but was looking at her. The expression on his face sent chills down her spine, not the good kind. "I appreciate the time you've sacrificed already, but could you give us a few moments, please?"

Oh, boy.

"Good to see ya, Nick. Rose says, 'Hey.'"

Nickie lifted her chin toward Andy in response but wasn't about to take her eyes off Duncan. As it became just the two of them, her brows rose. "So?"

"I have something I need to tell you."

"Me, too. I mean I have something to tell you. And although I appreciate your transparency, you don't have to tell me every—"

"Nickie."

Her chin pulled back in response to his abruptness. Now, she really was scared. "Okay."

"Come sit next to me."

"I'm fine right where I am. You're starting to freak me out."

He sighed and lifted from his chair. As he walked around the desk to her, she leaned back and slung a boot over her knee, then rested an arm on the back of her chair. He sat a hip on her desk close enough that she sensed the faint smell of his cologne.

"I found the recipient of the emails."

Really? "You found the mole?" She let her leg drop and sat up straight in her chair. "This is perfect. This is a perfect day. Who is the slippery, backstabbing jerk? I'm ready for a good ass-kicking."

"The recipient, Nickie."

"Oh, right. You said that. How did you...never mind. What now?"

"I read your email."

Her eyes rolled around in her head. He had such little willpower when it came to snooping. "That is really irritating, ya know." She stood now, and wiggled her way between his legs. "Tell me who the recipient is. Maybe I can still kick someone's ass. Are they close?"

He ringed his hands around both of her upper arms and stilled her high.

"Why are you so sad?" she asked.

"I read an email from Hurst to you that came through yesterday."

"You read an email from Special Agent Hurst? That's not irritating, Duncan. That's wrong." Especially since she'd been way too busy in the last twenty-four hours to be reading email.

"It was wrong, yes. He's been searching for the mole."

She knew that. And she didn't tell Duncan. Shit. Now, she was the one who was wrong.

"He does not have the identity of the mole in the station, but the email included the IP address of the recipient. I recognized it."

Of course he did. Eidetic memory. She looked down at her arms. "You're hurting me." He let go and held up his hands in surrender.

"I'm sorry. I didn't... The emails are going to Leslie Jacobsen."

She knew that name. Her brows dropped. "Wait. What? Jacobsen? But that means—How can—?"

She fell into her chair. Possibilities spun circles in her head. "Leslie Jacobsen works in my father's building." Her eyes turned to him. His were nearly black and screamed pain. "Someone in the station answers to someone who works for my father?" Her eyes moved along the carpet in her office, searching for an answer. "My father is the one who has a mole keeping tabs on me? Is he that scared I might rat him out for ditching me after my teenage escape from Zheng? For hiding the files on my time in captivity? Ruin his spoiled-runaway-daughter cover for the time I was in captivity?" Her eyes found an answer and found Duncan. "Where is she?"

"Nickie."

She stood now and paced. "I'm going to see her. I'm going to interrogate her, then make a visit to my father." His grip was gentle this time but enough to stop her pacing.

"Nickie. She was put in charge of the hidden files from your teenage escape and rehabilitation."

"Rehabilitation? Did you just say rehabilitation? I didn't have day one of any kind of rehabilitation. You mean estrangement from a family because of what I had to do to survive, then tossed into the foster care system."

"I apologize. You're right. Please let me rephrase. Put in charge of the hidden files regarding your escape, abandonment and neglect. I don't think you should be the one to question her."

Breathe, Nick. Closing her eyes, she inhaled. "It's me who's sorry. You know all of this. I'm barking at you for syntax. I know the semantics."

So much spun in her head. Memories of her escape. The disgust on her parents' faces after her escape. The way they couldn't look at her at the press conference celebrating her return. The way they cast her off into the system after a few short months, then erased all cyber evidence of her abduction and escape and placed paper copies in the hands of... Leslie Jacobsen. Her forehead fell into his chest, and his long arms wrapped around her.

Her arms hung loose at her sides. "You're saying she will recognize me. She'll see me coming and clam up or run."

"Yes."

She lifted her head. "You, too. She'll know you, too, then."

"Yes."

The lightbulb went off in her head. She looked from one of his eyes to the other. "Andy."

"Yes. He has agreed to come with me. We plan…we'd *like* to approach her at her home. Tomorrow morning. We want to leave right away. It's why I came by, but you were busy with Eric Stoner." He moved his hand to her face and rubbed a thumb across her cheek. "You were amazing. Will Eric Stoner go to jail for rape?"

Duncan had been watching? Her chest expanded and released. "Yes. For a long time. Not long enough, but no one has to testify." Her eyes squinted. "I'm still coming. To hell if she tries to run. There are three of us. I'm going with you. We're going to nail her to a wall, then I'm going to Manhattan to stake out the Uptowne River Shoppes mall for Bianca's abductors. And when I get some free time, I'm going to give my father a visit."

He pressed his forehead to hers. The corners of his lips lifted, almost making everything okay. "I'm so in love with you."

"Back at you."

"Are you sure that is the best course of action? Your father is a powerful man. He will have resources."

"Bring it."

Records indicated that Leslie Jacobsen lived alone in an upper-middle class, single-family home on the outskirts of Baltimore. Andy insisted he ride in the back and Nickie shotgun in the sedan rental Duncan made them get.

"Recap," she announced as Duncan pulled to the curb down the street from her place. "Duncan, you're taking the back of the house in case she tries to make a run for it. I'll stand to the side and out of the way as Andy takes point." She tossed her coat next to Andy. It was nearly sixty-five degrees already that morning. She checked her gun. Loaded. Safety on. Phone, camera. "Just basic shit, An—"

"I've got this, Nick," Andy interrupted. "She'll tell us what we want to know. Have a little faith."

Oh, to finally know who the mole is in the department. "Right. Okay." Her mind was clear, her emotions in check. Or else at least stuffed in that place she often used.

Duncan exited the car first. The faded blue jeans, work boots, gray hoodie and plain, black ball cap he wore were nothing like her Duncan. Perfect. She waited the agreed upon ten minutes, then made her way up the street. Duncan took the long route around the back of the house. He was military. She doubted he would be detected. She took a less winding route, but approached the house from the side and took out her phone like she was reading a meter. Andy approached shortly after.

Nickie wasn't about to stand so far away that she couldn't hear and stepped into range near a front window. Andy was good. He didn't glance her way or show any indication he knew she was right there near him. His shoulders filled out his brown leather jacket. Sunglasses rested backward on his head. Designer blue jeans hugged his muscled thighs. She never noticed how good-looking he was. That could work to his advantage. He was a man. Of course he knew this.

He knocked and waited perfectly still. When the door opened, Nickie wanted to fist bump the air, then she wanted to barge forward. But she maintained their plan and, therefore, her cool.

Andy turned on a brilliant smile. Very, very good looking. He held out his hand. "Leslie Jacobsen? I'm—"

"Oh, I'm not Leslie. She went into work this morning. You are?"

Oh no. Heat ran up Nickie's spine and over her scalp.

She needed to intercede. Andy wasn't trained for this.

He paused for only a moment. His smile dissipated but didn't go away completely. He didn't balk. No glancing to Nickie for what to do. Not even a blink.

He held out a hand. "My name is Sylvester."

Sylvester?

"I'm an old high school friend. I should have called first. I was hoping to surprise her. Who's out this early on a Saturday morning? Speaking of, I am bothering you early on a Saturday morning."

"I'll tell her you came by."

"I would appreciate that. I'm sorry. I didn't get your name."

"Liza."

"It's nice to meet you, Liza. If you wouldn't mind, tell her I'll be in town through the weekend. She knows how to get ahold of me."

The door shut. He turned and headed down the sidewalk just like a regular guy who just missed catching an old high school friend at home. She texted Duncan, waited her ten minutes, then took the long way back to the car.

She found Andy waiting in the driver's seat. She slid in and turned to him.

"That may have been a friend or her partner. Let's hit the office. I bet Duncan can bust us in if it's locked."

"Bust us in?" Andy asked. "I can see why he thinks he needs to protect you all the time."

"What's the big deal? We were coming to catch her alone at home. So she's alone at the office."

"It's a Saturday," she argued. "Locked building. Home is legal. Breaking in is illegal."

Duncan slid in the backseat. "Talk while you drive, brother."

Andy pulled away from the curb, speaking a mile a minute. He never was the stoic, quiet type like Duncan. "A Liza person answered the door. She's gay. Maybe

Leslie's partner."

That must have been the reason for the quickly deflated killer smile he tried at the door. "How do you know she's gay?" Nickie asked.

Andy looked over to her, then rolled his eyes. "Leslie is at work." He held his smartphone in his free hand and illegally punched some keys as he drove.

"I can give you a ticket for that."

He shrugged. "I know a detective who could get me out of it."

"Could you please continue?" Mister stoic, quiet type wasn't nearly as much fun.

"We're on our way to catch her at work." Just as Andy finished this ridiculous statement, he brought the butt of the phone to his lips. "Address. IEM. Import and Export Services."

The name of her father's business sent harsh chords of childhood memories over her. "Andy. You've already broken into her office."

"No, I didn't. Your cranky husband in the backseat did that all on his own."

"Aiding and abetting," she said, but had to admit it was actually beginning to sound like an intriguing idea.

"Not if I don't get caught."

"I can't take the chance," she said.

"You are not going to." It was the cranky husband in the backseat.

She knew she wasn't going to, but she really hated when he did this. "Excuse me?"

"You're not going to," he repeated, making her decide to, just to spite him.

"Whoa, guys. I did not sign up to be mediator on this trip. Duncan and I know where the cameras are located. We have hats and hoods if needed."

Oh, how she wasn't in the mood for a pissing match. "Did we not have this conversation the other night? Don't get in my way, Duncan."

"Andy," Duncan barked from the back. "Pull over."

She was trying to be patient and a better wife; she truly was. "Don't you dare, Andy. We're going to the office building. No more drama."

"Sorry, Nick. Bros before—Well, Duncan trumps you, man. Forgive me."

He pulled to the frigging curb before exiting the subdivision. She opened her door while the car was still rolling. Duncan was out before she was. She paced as she ran her hand over her face, then the top of her hair. Possessively, he took hold of one of her shoulders, then the other and turned her to face him.

He didn't look like he was ready for a fight. He looked...scared?

His fingers wrapped around her arms, and he set his forehead on hers. "I love you."

Her hands slid up his forearms and hung on as she melted into him. Her body was a traitor.

"I've spent over a year watching the people you love betray you." His hands slid up her shoulders and cupped her neck. "I've seen a gun pointed at your head, listened on the other end of the phone as you were caught in a car explosion. I thought you were dead when I found you upside down in your car after the reckless stunt you pulled with Zheng."

She couldn't open her eyes for fear the tears that were building would betray her.

"The idea of you jeopardizing your job by breaking and entering is not going to happen. Even if the building is unlocked, it's likely some items are going to go missing and offices may be broken into. Security cameras won't be able to detect the identity of Andy and me, but you and I together are too easy to identify, even with our faces covered."

She opened her eyes to the beautiful chocolate brown in his. She was helpless against them. "Okay."

His face pulled away enough to make her want to pull

him back to her.

"Did you just say, 'Okay'?"

A traitorous smile escaped her lips as a much more traitorous tear tipped over her eyelid. He pressed his lips to hers, making her forget why they were standing there.

"Oh shit, guys. Get a room." She glanced over to see Andy climbing into the backseat.

Duncan used his thumb to brush away her tear, then kissed her cheek where it had been. "You're driving."

"You're willingly giving up driving? Oh right. I'm the lookout getaway driver. The guys at the station would never let me live this down."

CHAPTER 19

————— ◆ ◆ ◆ —————

"The city has cameras on the streetlights." While sitting shotgun, Nickie pulled down the ridiculous straw hat Duncan had given her. "I can see them at the corners of the strip malls, too." On the way, Duncan and Andy had traded their hideous ball caps and hoodies for what she considered private eye hats and jackets. Duncan wore a jean jacket and Andy a medium brown trench coat.

"Pull over here," Duncan said. She did. Before opening his door, he took her fingers and squeezed. And then he was gone.

"He's going to check out the alarm system," Andy explained.

Traffic had picked up as the morning drew on. She watched as Duncan made his way toward her father's building, then turned down an alley. Rotating in her seat, she faced Andy so she didn't have to talk through the rearview mirror. "So, you're just going to waltz in past weekend security detail and knock on Leslie Jacobsen's door?" She was green with envy.

"Pretty much, yeah." A toothy smile spread across his face. "The plan is to have Duncan stand out of the way while I weasel into her office. She'll recognize him and might make that security call before we get a chance to corner her about the dirt we have." Unexpectedly, he frowned. "Except, I won't be able to use my charming smile and good looks."

Ha. The gay thing.

"Imagine her face when we tell her what we know," he added.

"What are you going to do when she turns you in?"

"After all the illegal shit she's done? Hiding public files about your abduction and release? And now taking part in spying on a cop? While the cop is at work in a police station? Oh yeah, she's not going to turn in anyone."

She wanted to go with them. From the corner of her eye, she noticed movement from the alley. Duncan came around and tugged on the front entrance door like he expected it to be unlocked on a Saturday morning. It was. No doorman. No valet. No security detail.

"So, what's this thing we're doing later?"

"The mall stake out? Oh, we're staking out a mall." She smiled at him.

He looked amused at her jest, but then moved his hand in large circles as his way of gesturing for her to elaborate.

"It looks like there's a potential group of scum grooming girls for trafficking at Uptowne River Shoppes Mall."

He made a face like he'd just eaten a slice of lemon. "Sheesh. How do you do this shit?"

She shrugged. "It's a job. The least I can do. You know I got away. Others didn't."

He lifted his brows, nodded and shrugged at the same time. It amazed her how different he and Duncan's mannerisms were. Yet, their personalities were much the same. Loyal, dedicated, fearless.

Duncan made his way to the car, rapping on the window as he passed.

"That's my cue, dude." Andy got out of the backseat and made his way to the trunk of the rental.

He held an...umbrella? She wasn't missing this and followed. He opened the umbrella, then the trunk. Oh umbrella. A camera must be pointing at the back of the car. She got it and made sure not to look up. Andy tilted the umbrella so it covered most of the view inside. Duncan's trench coat-wearing body did the rest. "This car may be in some fake name, but the plates and serial number will be easy to trace back to Binghamton where you got it," she said to him as he approached.

"I changed plates and covered the serial number on the dash before we left."

She lifted her brows. "Nice."

He opened his coat and pulled out—"Hey! That's my tranq gun." Her eyes moved to his. "What have you done?"

"Time to move, Andy." Duncan slid off the jean jacket and replaced it with a long, black coat he got from the trunk. "I clipped the outside alarm and monitor connection wires. It allowed me inside and to the security room. No telling if the now-sleeping security guard in the surveillance room had called for help before I got to him. The rest of the screens are frozen, but his body could be discovered at any time."

Her ears listened to what he said, but her eyes couldn't leave the contents of the trunk. "You brought all this? I've been driving in a rental with C4?"

"Just a small amount." He stuck tiny vials of the putty substance into his pockets, followed by his Beretta, a lighter and some other things she wasn't able to identify as he stuffed his pockets.

He opened a small box. "And grenades? You brought grenades."

"V-40s. They, too, are small."

Andy slung a case over his right shoulder.

"Do you plan to have time to surf the Net while you're

in there?"

Andy shrugged and smiled. "Never know."

Duncan paused to look at her. He mouthed, "Be safe," before taking off down the street. "Move the car two blocks northeast of the entrance, please. We'll look for you there," he called as he went.

She kept her head down but nodded as she peered under the lip of her stupid hat and headed for the driver's seat.

Duncan checked his surroundings as he pulled open the front door to IEM, Edward Monticello's import/export business building.

Game on.

This time, Leslie Jacobsen would pay. It was one thing for her to hide files on Nickie's abduction and escape. It was another altogether to be in charge of a mole who keeps track of Nickie.

A thin sheet of sweat covered his hands and neck, yet his head was as clear as day.

He maintained an awareness of his surroundings without appearing to do so. The elevators were adjacent to the marble floor and to the left past the unmanned, marble reception counter. No need to tell Andy where to dodge his image from any cameras. Duncan had frozen the motherboard that supplied power and direction to each.

He punched the elevator button, then folded his hands in front of him. "You get us in, then let me do the talking."

"You keeping your cool, brother?" Andy asked from his side as they waited.

Looking down, he realized he'd been clenching his fists. His jaw ached as well, letting on that he must have been grinding his teeth. "I won't lose it if that's what you fear."

"If that's what you fear." Andy said it as Duncan did.

"Don't be an ass. I'm not like that."

He was right. "I apologize. Are we good?"

"We're good."

"I am grateful for your time, Andy. I am putting you at risk. Again."

"No way, man. This is all on me. I live for this shit."

They entered the elevator and pressed the button up to Leslie's floor. As they had agreed, they kept their heads down. No need to take any risks that a camera might pick up a head shot. When the doors opened, he took a left and Andy a right. The long way for Duncan would give Andy time to get into Leslie Jacobsen's office and Duncan a way to remain unseen. The lights were off but plenty of light spilled through the walls of glass that surrounded the area. Sleeping monitors glowed lazily in their weekend rest.

Duncan's phone buzzed in his pocket. It was from Andy. 'Get your ass over here. Now.'

Curiosity picked up Duncan's pace until he passed the last desk before Jacobsen's office. The top half of the enclosed office was glass. The office back wall was ceiling-to-floor windows. What a bad place to be in high winds. File cabinets lined the right side of the spacious room. In this day and age of Dropbox and iCloud, how could anyone possibly need so many file cabinets? Was Jacobsen in charge of storing more covert files illegally than just Nickie's? In the center of the office sat a conservative dark oak desk with two guest chairs.

Andy stood just inside the room. His back was to Duncan, his head held low and his arms out to the sides of him like he didn't want to touch anything. He had on plastic gloves. No Jacobsen. What the hell?

Andy's stance. He wasn't moving. Something was wrong. Very, very wrong. Duncan's heart jumped, then sped. As he approached, he realized why. The door was open and inside the office, lying on the floor was a large pool of deep red with Jacobsen's head resting in the middle.

"Shit, Duncan. Shit," Andy said as Duncan stepped next to him. "What the hell do we do now?"

"You get the hell out of here. Go find Nickie."

Andy turned his head enough to meet Duncan's eyes. "Are you kidding me? I'm not going anywhere."

Duncan pulled out his flash drive. His body morphed into autopilot. He rushed to Jacobsen's computer and shoved in the flash drive. They couldn't question Jacobsen. She'd gotten herself involved with something horribly wrong. Duncan would at least gather as much information as he could in the time he and Andy had.

He was startled to sense Andy follow, pushing him away from the computer. "Out of my way, brother. This is my thing."

Pain threatened Duncan's gut. Andy had never experienced the death that came with war, never found his wife tied and beaten...twice. The sight of a dead body surely made it difficult to focus.

Wearily, Duncan went to the body. A close-range gunshot between the eyes. Hollow bullet. The back of her head was wide open. Later, he would dwell on the fact that it didn't affect him. He looked around, making sure to memorize the location of each chair and lamp, right down to any pencil or paper clip that had dropped to the floor. All evidence that might be of use.

His eyes turned to the wall of file cabinets. Would the key that opened them be in the same spot as the last time he'd broken in here? Surely not. Using the C4 would be risky. He did a quick and careful search while Andy manned the download. No key.

"I'm in," Andy said in a nearly inaudible voice.

"Copy everything you can find," Duncan said. "The flash drive has more gigabytes than my hard drive."

Duncan pulled out his C4 stick and broke off a small piece. He stuffed it into the lock of the first file cabinet, then repeated the process with the rest. Pulling out his lighter, he blew on the small puffs of smoke as he lit them, releasing the locks to the cabinets. He slid open the first drawer and skimmed through files. One drawer after another. He didn't have time for this. "We need to get out of here, Andy."

"I need five more minutes," Andy said.

"Agreed." Duncan peered down the row of cabinets, and started pulling open drawers. He decided on taking the entire group of 'M,' 'N' and 'S.' Nicole, Nickie, Monticello, Savage. The inside pockets of his coat were compatible with the size of the file folders, but the number of files he needed to secure was nearly unreasonable. The left side of his coat pulled awkwardly to the side from the weight. He had just enough time to do a check in the back of each file drawer. He ran a hand over the back of each, and that was where he found an envelope. Glancing over the lid of the drawer, he was able to rip it from the back. Masking tape clung to the sides of the envelope. Carefully, he tucked it alongside the already too heavy pocket full of file folders.

Movement from the corner of his eye made him drop to the floor and growl, "Andy, duck." Goosebumps erupted across Duncan's arms. Andy couldn't get caught, he just couldn't.

As Duncan lowered to the floor, Jacobsen was close enough for him to smell the blood. Her eyes were frozen in time, staring at the ceiling with an expression mixed between confusion and fear. He reached out a gloved hand and felt her cheek. She lay cold in her pantsuit complete with jacket and pumps. "Andy."

"I know, I know. It's almost done."

Duncan lifted his head enough to access the scene. The movement was a security guard. Definitely not alarmed. Making his rounds. For a lazy Saturday afternoon, the man was annoyingly diligent. He looked in each office and around each cubicle. And he was getting closer. "Andy," Duncan said with more force.

Andy pulled the flash drive and shoved it in his pocket, then began to army crawl toward Duncan. His shoulder bag dragged next to him. Duncan kept an eye on the guard at the same time as he motioned for Andy to hurry up. They could press themselves along the lower half wall that concealed them from the main area, but Jacobsen's body lay sprawled in clear view to anyone who walked within ten feet of her door.

Duncan slid the gun from the back of his pants. Andy's eyes grew large. This was all wrong. Andy should be home with his wife and baby. What had Duncan done? He was responsible. Responsible for the life of his infant nephew's father. Responsible for the lives of his platoon as the Chinook spun, hurdling toward the desert sand, the gaping hole in the side casing, the blood that covered everything. Responsible for the screaming that came from their bodies that were just as lifeless as Jacobsen's.

"Duncan!"

He shook his head, confused at how dead people could screech like a machine.

CHAPTER 20

———— • ♦ • ————

"Duncan, the alarm." Andy punched him in the shoulder.

He looked up as the security guard disappeared into the elevator. Shoving the gun back into his belt, Duncan yelled, "Move."

They bolted for the stairs on the other side of the elevator. The cameras could well be up and running by then. He heard another ding of the twin elevator as they dove through the door of the stairwell.

The stairway door slid closed as Duncan held out his arm, keeping Andy behind him. He leaned over the cold, metal rail to check below. The stairwell was empty. Duncan dropped his arm and they began their race down the stairs. Duncan held onto the files in the pocket of his jacket as if it was a book bag. He took two stairs at a time with Andy close on his heels. The ground-level door flew open and banged against the concrete wall.

Andy and Duncan halted their descent. They were halfway between floors and decided to tiptoe back up to the next level. As they listened to the sound of pounding feet, they pressed the fourth floor door open, slipped through, then eased it shut again.

"Elevator," Andy said as he took off.

The elevator would be risky, but without the stairs, their options were limited.

"There can't be more than a few at the most," Andy whispered. "Did you catch how many are in the stairwell?"

"Two sets of footsteps," Duncan answered.

Andy shook his head as he pressed the down button. Duncan kept his eye on the stairwell door. As they waited for the elevator, Duncan pulled him behind a desk.

Duncan leaned close to his brother. "We'll take it down to two and hope they are well past there by that time."

As the elevator bell rang, Andy began to rise. Duncan held out an arm to stop him much like he'd done in the stairwell. The doors opened. It was empty, so he started to rise.

This time Andy's arm stopped Duncan. The stairwell. The door opened and the two sets of footprints entered the area. The files in Duncan's inside pocket were cumbersome as he and Andy crawled around to the farthest side of the desk. Duncan pointed to the northeast corner of the area as a reminder to Andy of the security camera located there. Both sets of footsteps came closer. Just like he and Andy, the men didn't speak.

Andy gestured to the stairwell. Duncan nodded. Silently, they crawled through the maze of cubicles. The distinct sound of a walkie talkie buzzed twice. "BPD has back up on the way."

Duncan reached in his inside pocket and clutched one of the V-40 mini-grenades. He glanced at Andy, then to the stairwell door, then back to Andy. If they could make it to level two, they could use a north window and jump. The alley where Nickie hopefully waited was along the north side of the building. Before they went for it, Duncan texted her and told her the plan. An explanation would have to come later. Andy must have read his thoughts, because he darted from cover and sprinted for the stairwell.

"Freeze!" The voice. It was too close to Andy.

Duncan ripped the pin from the grenade.

Andy didn't freeze. Gunshots blew holes in the drywall, following the path of his brother's escape. Duncan hurled the grenade toward the voice and dove over a desk that stood between him and his little brother. The rush of air from a bullet buzzed past the side of Duncan's head. He landed and rolled low before making it through the door after Andy. The grenade explosion sounded as Andy and Duncan grabbed the handrail, then the wall, and jumped. Shots came from above. More men in the stairwell.

Explosions. Shots. Footsteps. His mind threatened to take him back to his stint in the Middle East. Not now. He wouldn't let it.

"Second floor, Andy," he said low alerting Andy to where they were.

Andy obeyed and abruptly stopped at the second floor door. Duncan nearly plowed into him. Andy creaked open the door and peered around at the narrow hallway that lined the office doors.

"Go north," Duncan whispered to him.

He did and Duncan followed closely. Duncan heard something faint and paused to assess. "Those are sirens. Move, Andy." The area was dark other than the light from the wall of windows at the end of the hallway in front of them.

"There." Duncan pointed to a women's restroom on the north side of the building as the elevator bell sounded. "They're following our trail. They must have the cameras working again."

The window in the bathroom was opaque with no way to open it. For sunlight purposes only.

"C4," Andy suggested.

"No time." Duncan pulled out his Beretta and blew holes in the window until it shattered. He tucked his hand inside his sleeve and used his elbow to remove the leftover shards from the perimeter of the window frame. Lights from police cars in front and back of the building moved across the alley. "Go," he commanded Andy before it was too late.

"You first," Andy argued.

"I've got the ammo. Go!"

Duncan pulled the pin of the next V-40 as Andy jumped. He tossed the grenade toward the door, then glanced out the window to the alley below. Andy landed and rolled. The rental car crawled down the alley toward him as Duncan jumped. The air was hot on his neck. Bits of fine sand threatened to invade his eyes, nose and ears. His mind dizzied as it tried to pull him back to memories of the desert floor. He wouldn't let it take him. The grenade explosion sent smoke and bits of debris out the window.

He landed on his feet, letting the bend in his knees absorb the impact. He welcomed the jarring pain it created. "They're coming." Duncan wasn't sure if he was referring to imaginary Middle Eastern insurgents or the police, but he ran for Nickie and the rental car regardless.

Andy was already entering the back seat. Duncan slid along the hood and yelled through the open window, "Move over. I'm driving."

"Not gonna happen," Nickie yelled back and pulled away before he had the door fully closed behind him.

"Why couldn't you rent a better car?" she whined as she quietly crawled down the alley. "Get down. I doubt they'll be stupid enough to let me pass without checking out the car."

He did as she suggested but not without reminding her: "Pull your hat down around your face."

"Like that won't bring more attention to me?"

"The first priority is your confidentiality. This is nonnegotiable."

"Bite me," she growled but complied. Crawling onto the main street, he heard it.

"Excuse me, ma'am," a voice yelled from behind. Duncan reached up and adjusted the rearview mirror so he could see behind them. With a hand on the butt of his gun, an officer approached. "Hey, you."

"Ma'am? Ma'am?" Nickie murmured out loud to herself. "Do I look like I'm old enough to be a ma'am?" Her foot buried the gas pedal into the floorboard. The officers ran to their cars. Nickie spun around the first corner.

Duncan analyzed the sounds. "I hear sirens coming from the south."

"I'll go north, then," she said with too much joy and turned again.

He sat up and noticed Andy had already done so. Murder. They found a murdered Jacobsen. He couldn't allow Andy to be caught up in this. "She's dead, Nickie."

"Jacobsen? Holy shit." She turned once more. "Perfect."

He hoped the perfect comment wasn't about the murder and then recognized the used car lot as she darted in and stopped between a Buick and an ancient Chrysler. "Duck," she said. This time all three did.

The sirens came from around the last corner and buzzed past. The three of them waited a solid five minutes before Nickie took off. "We have to move fast. Once they find the body, more muscle will show up, including helicopters. They have the make and model of the car. We'll take the highway. They'll keep an eye on the interstate but can't possibly man all the highways leading out of town."

About halfway to Manhattan, they stopped for gas. Nickie agreed to let Duncan drive. "Jacobsen is dead," she said more to herself. "What are the possibilities?" She didn't want to think of the possibilities. Her father had been a terrible role model. He never loved her, never cared for her. But a murderer? She couldn't remember a single time he showed signs of violence and certainly never the backbone needed for murder, even if it was for hire.

"I'm afraid I can only think of one." He clasped his warm fingers around hers. "Someone wanted her silenced."

"Did you take pictures of the body?"

He tapped his right temple with his forefinger.

"I took real pictures," Andy said from the back.

"You what?" Duncan asked. "When?"

"While you were busy blowing up file cabinet locks. What else did I have to do while I waited for her personal and secure files to download?"

This time, Nickie had no aversion to hearing about their illegal hacking.

"I thought an actual photograph might be better than a drawing. No offense, brother."

"None taken," Duncan answered.

Andy handed his phone up to her. On it was a picture of a dead Leslie Jacobsen. "She's dressed in a suit." Her brows fell low. "On a Saturday morning."

"I noted that," Duncan said.

"So, she had a pre-arranged meeting with someone."

Andy added, "Her friend at the house didn't say that. She said Jacobsen had some work to do. I remember it clearly."

"She had a secret pre-arranged meeting with someone."

He'd taken a few photos. Five, to be exact. Jacobsen had been shot in the head. Her body lay unnaturally, as many did after an instantaneous fall from a kill shot.

Her eyes stared unbelievingly at the ceiling.

Nickie's phone rang, making everyone jump. "Savage."

"Detective? It's me, Nevaeh. I'm so glad I caught you. I hope it's okay to call. You said I could call."

Nickie glanced from Duncan to Andy and gave them a shake of her head that said the call didn't pertain to their situation. "Did something happen? Are you okay?"

"Oh, it's nothing like that. I want to do something on campus. Ya know, for the victims. Maybe ways to help other girls be safe. I'm not sure where to start. I feel empty. I've got to do something."

"I understand, honey. Are you seeing your counselor?"

"I am, but still…"

"You've been going hard for months, and now it's over. You feel relieved yet it's unsettling. I'm sort of in the middle of something this weekend. Can you come in and see me Monday morning? I'll make some calls in the meantime."

"Yes, of course. I have class. Is after that okay?"

"Absolutely. Take care, Nevaeh. You're going to be okay. Everything is going to be okay."

She hung up and turned to Andy. "Can you send those pictures to me?"

He nodded and got busy. She pulled out her laptop as she considered her father. A heavy sigh filled her chest. It wasn't something she ever wanted to do again, but it was necessary. She would corner her father the first chance she got.

"I think we should split up." Andy stayed on one side of her, Duncan on the other. They entered the mall using the main entrance. It was sparse for a Saturday. Could be a good thing. Could be bad.

"Good idea," Duncan said.

"Agreed," she said. "But if we're going to do this, I

need to talk to both of you first." She motioned toward a few tables in front of a set of lockers. "Are you going to be okay? You just found a murder victim. You ran from the police." Knowing it wouldn't faze Duncan, she was talking to only Andy but tried not to look like she was.

"I've seen dead bodies before," Andy said. He seemed to figure it out. "And I don't think they're going to ID us in the B & E. We were careful."

She nodded but didn't agree. The chances they weren't IDed sometime on some camera was between slim and none. "I'm here if you freak. So, in a perfect world, we find the lair of the scum who abducted Bianca today. Since that's not likely, plan B is to plant a bug on one of the players while they are out of their lair and trying to groom girls."

They sat on the bench around a circle of tables. Digging in her pocket, she pulled out a handful of audio bugs. "These are stickers—"

Duncan's face lit. "You brought electronics?"

"Boys and their toys." The look on his face was telling.

She propped a boot on her seat and remained standing. "Sticking one on a perp beneath a lapel or hem of a shirt would be ideal, but you can plop one in a pocket if need be." She handed two to Duncan and three to Andy.

"Why does Andy have more than me?"

He'd been smiling when he said it, but she knew it was an honest question.

Andy grinned from ear to ear. He straightened, then laced his fingers behind his head.

"You two are children," she said as she rolled her eyes. "I have eight. They don't divide evenly between the three of us."

Duncan lifted his brows to her. "You have three as well?"

"Andy gets three because he's new at this."

"Hey!"

"I get three because I'm the cop." She took the small receiver box from the inside pocket of her leather jacket. Flipping the on switch, she said, "Each is set to the channel on this box. I tested them all, but go ahead and give them a try."

They spoke into each. She was able to decipher who was who and which was which.

"If we don't find where they bring the girls and we aren't able to plant any bugs, plan C is recon. Take notes of what you see."

"Some will need paper for that," Andy said. "Some won't."

She blew over the eidetic memory jab. "We'll each take a floor of the mall. You're looking for teens and young women who are made up and dressed well. They will be approaching young teen females who either are made up, too, or are the opposite and seem socially awkward. We meet back here at twenty-one hundred."

"Deal," Andy said as he stood. "I'm taking my three bugs, not two, and heading for the top floor."

Duncan kissed the side of her head as he passed. She lifted her chin once making sure not to show the warmth that filled her heart.

Since the boys headed for the elevator, she started her surveillance on the ground floor. It was hard to focus. She yearned to dig into the files Duncan had lifted from Leslie Jacobsen's office. Who killed her? Why? Nickie needed to question her father. Jacobsen was his employee. Unless he's being scammed, he hired her to keep an eye on Nickie.

She passed a cinnamon roll bakery. Evil sabotage. No young females sitting alone or in small groups. No young females period. Just elderly people walking the corridors and young mothers with babies. It was a frigging Saturday. Wasn't this what average teenage girls did? Hang out at malls? How would Nickie know?

She was never an average teenage girl, not even before she'd been abducted.

Who at the station was feeding Jacobsen the intel? She assumed Duncan would be able to trace him or her better now that he had the IP address of the computer the emails ended up at.

As she contemplated, she found herself standing instead of walking. Generally, she was excellent at multitasking during a stakeout. But this time she wasn't even facing the open hallways of the mall. She stood facing the display of a maternity shop. She physically shivered and moved her feet along so fast she nearly left the rest of her body behind.

CHAPTER 21

———— •••• ————

Duncan realized he didn't seem to be the type to order a smoothie and sit at a brightly colored Formica table by himself to drink it. Yet, that was where he'd noticed a younger girl who sat with a college-aged woman. Sisters? They didn't look alike.

The bookstore next to the smoothie shop would need to suffice. There were a few magazine displays outside the doors.

The younger girl didn't seem scared or awkward. She seemed flattered. It was a risk. The chances were near zero the young woman would be part of an abduction ring. If she were, he was being watched at that moment. And if he tried and failed, they would likely never come back to this spot and be lost forever. Or if they truly were sisters having a smoothie at the mall, he might be arrested for approaching a minor.

Overtly, he grabbed his crotch, attempting to appear as if he were adjusting a hard on. Better to appear to be a child-molesting bastard than a man helping a cop on a stake out.

Approaching the girls, he reached and scratched the back of his head. "Oh, hey. Excuse me."

The older of the two glared at him as if she might

scratch his eyes out.

"Hello," he said. "My phone is dead. Do you happen to have the time?"

Her eyes darted over his shoulder. It was slight, but he didn't miss it. She pulled out her phone and checked. Her nails were manicured ruby red with rhinestones embedded in the polish. "Straight up noon." Her eyes moved to the young girl sitting next to her.

Duncan's did as well. The girl appeared confused. Was it the reaction the woman had to his presence? A bright, artificial smile erupted over the woman's face.

"Is there anything else I can help you with, sir," she asked.

He sat down at the table next to theirs and turned the chair to face them. "Yes, actually." He didn't need the additional shift in her eyes over his shoulder; Duncan could hear the shuffle of soft shoes moving quickly toward him.

He continued as if he hadn't noticed. "I was hoping you might—"

"Excuse me, miss." It was a man who looked to be about thirty. "Is this man bothering you?"

Nodding as she looked away, the woman tucked a strand of hair behind her ear.

The man had black hair, buzzed and curly. He wore a short, brown trench coat. Wrapping his fingers around Duncan's biceps, he squeezed and lifted. Duncan succumbed, purposely leaving the muscles in his arms loose.

"Whoa, dude," Duncan said in his best Andy Reed voice. "I'm just talkin' to these—"

The man ignored Duncan, dragging him away while reassuring the girls. "No worries, ladies. I'll help this man out."

Duncan was sure 'out' had a special meaning. "Hey! Wait, wait, wait." Sticking his free hand in his pocket, he flicked off the backing from the audio bug and stuck it between his thumb and forefinger. The sticky backing pressed to his forefinger, helping him from dropping it as the man dragged him past the bookstore magazine stands.

Holding out his hand in surrender, Duncan turned on his heels. "I'm sorry, man. I didn't mean no harm." He patted the shoulder of the man's coat, firmly sticking the bug under the collar.

The man gave him a healthy shove. Duncan raised his shoulders and ducked his head, shirking away toward the elevators.

Duncan had been amazing. Nickie could almost squeal if she did stuff like that. His show was genius. There was little chance he was pegged as undercover.

She didn't want to text him until he was well away from the suspect. So, she texted Andy instead. 'Meet at the car in 5.'

With the earbud from the receiver her ear, she headed there herself. The thug was on the move. He didn't speak but that didn't mean he was alone. Duncan must have placed the bug between materials because the rustle of fabric caused a consistent, rattled noise.

Her phone buzzed. The display read: Andy Reed, and said, 'K.'

She was halfway through the parking garage before it buzzed again. This time the display told her it was Duncan. 'Bug planted.'

Nickie responded, 'Yes. Listening in now. Big points for you.'

'When do I get to redeem said points?'

A surge of electricity ran through her like she'd just nailed the cello solo in Bach's Suite No. 1. 'Soon. Meeting Andy at the car now.'

'Outfits?'

She smiled. 'Whipped cream.'

'Damn.'

She squinted her eyes. 'Good damn? Or bad damn?'

'Good damn. Definitely good.'

The breeze from the nearby Hudson River made the air cool quickly in the late afternoon. She started the rental, then paced next to it and listened to the trafficker in her earbud. She nearly missed the sound of boots as they approached.

"S'up, Nick?" She jumped at the sound of Andy's voice.

"Duncan scored a plant."

"What? Damn. I'll never hear the end of it."

She stopped pacing and lifted her brows to him. "Saving children. Remember?"

His head swung back and forth twice before he amended, "I know, I know. It's good. I mean it. I'm happy. You listening now? I just...ya know...I'm a dude. I wanted to plant a frigging bug."

Using her free hand, she patted him on the shoulder, then leaned in to kiss him on the cheek.

"Get your hands off my wife, little brother."

Andy held up his hands. "Not even touching her. I can't help it if she throws herself at me."

"Standing right here," she said, then lifted her hand and stuck up her forefinger. Through the earbud, she heard the distinct ding of an elevator. She closed her eyes as if it might help her hear better. Footsteps. The slide of a keycard. A room that takes a keycard in a mall? Clicks. Then, the opening of a door. Upstairs office? Maybe the basement?

Her eyes opened to the feel of Duncan tugging on the spare earbud so he and Andy could hear, too.

"Julia crashed and burned. Let a man into it and freaked the kid. She'll pay for that later." The man's voice was close. It must have been the one who carried the bug. His voice was baritone and raspy. A smoker?

A loud rustling made her pull the earbud from her ear. "Where did you plant the bug?" she whispered to

Duncan as if the thug might hear her.

Duncan leaned in to listen and gestured to the inside of the left collar of his coat.

"I think he just took it off and threw it on a chair. Where would there be meeting rooms with hotel-type key locks?" she said the last part mostly to herself.

The three of them stood in the cold, listening to the new sound of plucking on a keyboard.

"Email?" Andy asked.

She shrugged at the possibility. "Database," she countered. "Or both. That would be more plausible under the circumstances."

"Trinity landed two bites," the voice said. "Here are the names and numbers. Get them in the spreadsheet. She got the age on just the one. The other is an estimated fifteen."

Yes. Database.

The muscles in Andy's jaw flexed. He turned his head to the side like he'd just seen a crash. Duncan was used to it, although his eyes did that thing where the color seemed to darken from deep chocolate to nearly black.

"We give them one more hour. If Julia doesn't redeem herself, I want you to take care of her." More rustling, then the sound of a television.

Nickie didn't explain to Andy what it meant to 'take care of her' and feared Duncan already knew. He endured much for her.

"An hour," she said. "They might move out of range—"

"What is the range?" Andy asked. The last time she saw that look in his light brown eyes was the night she broke up a fight involving him and Duncan behind The Pub.

"About ten miles," Duncan answered, tilting the box to read the make and model. "Can you rig it?"

"Pssh," Andy said and pulled out his phone.

"Who are you calling?" Nickie asked. "What rigging?"

"I'm searching for the nearest electronics store."

She didn't like the cryptic shit. Not now. "What rigging," she asked louder this time.

Focusing on his phone, Andy ignored her. She might kick his ass for this.

"He's going to rig a satellite feed," Duncan answered for him.

"He can do that?"

"We'll have to keep it in range until the connection is complete."

"We need another car," Andy said. "Two of us go shopping. The other stays to keep an eye, or ear, on the perps. If they try to take off, that person follows by car and keeps us informed through our cells."

"That would be ideal, yes." The way Duncan's eyes traveled up and down the rows of cars was unsettling.

Oh no, Nickie thought. "You're not stealing a car."

"Borrowing." He walked down the inside of the aisle, touching an occasional hood. "We'll put it right back where we found it."

"Bingo." The GPS on Andy's phone voiced the first road to take.

Nickie shook her head clear. "What are you doing?"

"What?" they answered in unison.

"You." She pointed to Duncan as he walked farther between cars.

"I'm looking for an older model that is still warm."

"Older models are easier to jump," Andy explained.

She tried to give him a look like she wasn't stupid, but apparently he didn't follow, because he continued.

"A warm car means the occupant just got—"

"Yeah. I get it. Except there are cameras all over this parking lot that have already seen us without wearing your stupid Sherlock Holmes hats."

"Whoa. Sherlock Holmes?" Andy shook his head as he opened the driver's side of the rental. "Those hats are GQ."

"Says the dude that just said, 'GQ.'"

"Found one," Duncan said, heading back to her. "Give me the receiver. I'll stay while you two get the equipment. I'll use the rental to follow them if needed."

"Two don't need to go on a shopping trip," she said. "I'm staying."

Duncan squared his shoulders. She was so not in the mood for a fight. "You could go to jail and lose your job. That trumps just going to jail, which is what I face."

"I need to hear what's going on. You're the one who thought the perps were simply sending emails."

"Duncan," Andy whined. "The clock is ticking, man."

Nickie sat at the end of the long drive. A familiar dark cloud threatened to take her. Take her back to before she'd moved on, before she'd become Nickie Savage. Instead, she cracked her neck, one way then the other, and got out of her car.

This time the images of the eight-foot brick walls seemed like overkill. The wrought iron gate an embarrassment. She dug out her badge and approached the security camera and buzzer. She didn't have the chance to identify herself before the gate slid open almost without a sound.

The enormous manor she'd grown up in hadn't changed from the few short months since she'd been there. Well, except for the twin rows of twenty-foot-tall evergreens. They lined the sides of the long drive like they were knights leading the way to their king who sat on a throne. The one that had been missing had been replaced. Which one was it, again? With her Diet Coke in hand, she entered through the open gate and crawled along the smooth drive, trying to determine which enormous tree had been replaced. How did a person replace a tree that big? She nearly snorted her soda through her nose.

It was Sunday. Her parents would likely be there,

unless they were on a trip. She wasn't about to call first. The drive was fine. It gave her a chance to sort through all she was juggling. The intel she was gathering on the Uptown River Shoppe's traffickers. Taking down Zheng's Fu Haizi child trafficking crime ring. The mole at the department. And now she was at the house she'd grown up in and had sworn never to return to.

Security cameras stared at her from the trees. The pillars around the place looked like they belonged at the White House as they flanked the entrance. She parked with one tire purposely on the bottom step that led to the front door.

The man who answered the door was the same one as the last time she'd been there. He was just as gray and just as old. "Yo, dude. Here we are again."

He didn't acknowledge her but stepped to the side to let her in. Her eyes all but ignored the cathedral ceilings and balconies on the second and third floor landings. This time they went straight to the tiles that covered the entire space of the entrance. The falcon thing. Where had she seen that before?

"Mr. and Mrs. Monticello will see you now."

She followed, knowing the cameras would see her mocking the dude behind his back. "Mr. and Mrs. Monticello will see you now," she mouthed as she tilted her head.

The feel of the place. The smell. She was way too tired and cranky to let it take her down. It was cool and damp. Stone lined the floors and many of the walls like a castle. Who lived like this? Oh right, she did for the first fourteen years of her life.

The butler took her to the kitchen nook this time. Her parents sat drinking tea like sweet elderly grandparents just home from church.

"Detective Nickie Savage to see you, sir. Ma'am." The butler bowed and left.

"Edward." Nickie nodded. "Ivanna."

"Oh, Nicole dear." Her mother was nearly crooning. "Did you come to offer your condolences regarding the tragic death of our employee?"

Nickie could puke.

"About that." Since it wasn't going to be offered, she pulled out her own chair. The feet slid smoothly along the heated ceramic floor. She couldn't help herself and asked, "Hey, what magic is on the feet of this chair?" She tilted it to see for herself. Felt covered the bottoms of each of the four feet. She picked at the side of one. "Is this permanent? Nailed on? Stapled? Ingenious."

"Nicole," her father scolded.

Snort.

"Oh right, right. Jacobsen. Yes. So, you hired her to keep an eye on me." She kept pretending to fool with the felt bottoms on the chair. They were actually the same kind she and Duncan used on their kitchen chairs. And then, she saw it. Her mother's eyes flicked to her father. It was quick but Nickie was quicker.

"Nicole." Her father sighed overtly. "I'm not sure how to respond to this nonsense anymore."

As if she came to question them more than one other time before. "Twice doesn't really count as 'this nonsense anymore,' but okay, I'll bite." She turned the chair backward and slung a boot over the top, then plopped her butt down. "Let's say you're not paying her to keep an eye on me. Let's say she's salary, and it's an all-inclusive deal. Ya know, work on a little payroll, illegally delete and store files and details regarding the disappearance of your only daughter...maybe some interviews on hiring some new office scrubs, then keep an eye on me through Jacobsen and a mole at my station."

Both tried to protest, but Nickie held up a hand and stood. "But the mole at the station..." Her mother was much more careful this time. Both stopped trying to interrupt, stopped to look down their snooty noses.

"Now, that had to be a hire. Please tell me you don't have a salary employee working at my station. That seems like a waste of money." She kept eye contact with both of them as she started pacing the length of the ridiculously large nook table. "That would be illegal. A felony, actually."

Her mother started to speak, but her father silenced her by holding out the palm of his hand. "If a person has hired a mole within your department, Nicole, shouldn't you be investigating him?"

Him. Damn. Nickie had really hoped it was Lucinda, the nosy desk clerk. She so wanted to kick her ass.

"Why?"

He gave her a look like she was dense, then spoke slowly. "Because he's the one tracking you?"

"Tracking." She bobbed her head back and forth. "He." Then, nodded. "Okay, let's pretend. Say, a person had hired a mole to keep an eye on his daugh—on a cop. Why?"

"Let's say a daugh—cop," he said, mocking her, "broke into a business, stole files and killed a woman."

Blood rushed to her head. She could feel the heat move over her skin from her neck to her face. Placing her fingertips on the table, she leaned into her mother, then over to her father and growled, "Prove it."

CHAPTER 22

———— • ♦ • ————

Nickie took a swig of her plastic bottle of Diet Coke. "This is genius." She propped her feet on her desk. She had more guests than chairs. Andy and Rose sat in the two she had. Duncan stood looking out her pitiful windows.

"Frigging amazing, Andy," she added. His rigged reception box looked like something a third grader put together, but it truly was amazing. "It sounds better and works better than the reception box that came with the audio bug. And I'm sitting at my desk."

"You're welcome."

Rose smacked him on the shoulder. "You're not leaving me out next time."

"Sorry, baby." Andy reached over to kiss her, but she smacked him on the arm again.

Nickie listened as she shared. "I have the first names for six voices, two male and four female."

"Julia is out of the picture for the time being." Duncan said it with venom.

He'd spent the last two nights pacing the floor and the last two mornings fighting the water, swimming more laps than she wanted to count.

And she got it. Julia had been beaten for Duncan's

distraction that led to Julia losing the girl she'd been grooming. He had a long way to go before he got over it.

"We're going to save her too, Duncan."

Andy squirmed in his chair. "Seems like she's part of it, Nick. She's grooming the kids, right? So they can be taken?"

"And she's beaten bloody if she fails," Duncan interrupted.

"Andy." Rose placed a hand on his forearm. The meaning was much different from the smack on the shoulder.

"I want to go undercover," Duncan said with his back to them. "Pose as a john."

Nickie closed her eyes and sighed. "It's the wrong venue, Duncan. You know this. They've seen you." She lifted from her chair and walked to him. Lowering her voice, she placed a hand on his back. "This is hard."

"I need to hurt them." He didn't say, 'Want.'

"It won't help the girls. It will just put you in jail."

His eyes said he thought otherwise.

"What about Rose?"

She turned to the sound of Andy's voice from her guest chair. "Rose what, Andy?"

"Rose. She's tiny." He turned to her. "No offense."

Rose shrugged. "I am."

"She buys her shoes from the children's department."

"Hey! Now, I'm offended."

"She could pass as a kid."

"No, she couldn't." All eyes turned to Nickie's office door. Just inside of it stood Nevaeh.

Oh right, Nevaeh. Nickie told her she could come by. "I can be with you in just a few minutes, Nevaeh. Lucinda there can show you to the—"

"She's not going to fool anyone," Nevaeh interrupted and gestured to Rose. "Sorry, ma'am. You are small and all that, but you don't look fifteen." She had the nerve to

walk farther into Nickie's office. She took hold of her
dreads and gathered them between the palms of her
hands like they were in a high ponytail. "But I can
totally make it as a fifteen-year-old."

Damn. She was right. "Nevaeh, honey—"

"Don't 'Nevaeh, honey' me. I can do this. I want to do
this."

Nickie's brows rose at her assertiveness. "You don't—"

"I totally do know what I'm getting myself into."

Nickie bit her lip at the rapid-fire interruptions in her
own damned office.

"I told you I wanted to do something. I *need* to do
something. It's why we were meeting today,
remember?"

She wasn't even whining like a college teenager.
Nevaeh was collected. Aggressive, but collected.

"Let me do this. Walk around a mall and pretend I'm a
teenager, right? I'm sorry, but I was listening. I can do
that. Let me do this, Detective Savage. Please. At least
think about it."

"Sheesh, Nick." It was Andy. She was thankful
someone finally stopped Nevaeh's tirade, because
Nickie was speechless with the possibilities. "At least
think about it."

"What about Bianca?" Duncan asked.

Rose shook her head. "Yep. Next time you're taking
me with. Who is Bianca?"

Nickie frowned. "No. No way. Bianca is the girl who
was originally abducted by this group. She's not ready
for anything like this. I doubt she ever will be. She's
working on survival right now."

"Okay, okay." Andy held up his arms in surrender. "If
Wednesday night is the deal, we have two more days to
decide."

"There is no we!" Nickie raised her arms in
exasperation. "I am going to Manhattan. I am going to
stake out. I am going to tail. I am going to take down."

She looked from one set of eyes to another. She knew she sounded stupid. It wasn't her juris-damned-diction. Again. She couldn't do this alone, and she really needed a decoy. "I have some friends I can call."

Duncan met eyes with her. He read her mind without giving away her connection with Special Agent Hurst. Did he know she also considered giving Child Rescue a call once more? Maybe the retired delta force members were back and willing to do some recon. Collapsing in her chair, she succumbed. "Okay. I'll think about it. Now, everybody out."

They complied. Everyone except Duncan, who was looking out her window again. She approached, wrapping her arms around his sides. "It's going to be okay."

"Two days. You'd better get calling."

Duncan sat, back straight, painting at the easel in the corner studio he'd created. It was well past midnight. He showed no signs of slowing.

Earbuds hung from Nickie's ears as she listened to the audio bug—like she'd been doing since they planted the bug last Saturday at the mall—for any pertinent information from the perps in Manhattan. Same old, same old. Booze, dope, slapping around girls. One girl would go into a potential list; another would be a wash. They were a patient and organized group. Disgust filled Nickie.

She wanted to ask Duncan what he was working on, but it was a moot point. His mind could not escape the Julia woman who'd been beaten. He blamed himself for it, as if his own hand had struck her.

She would never tell him she heard the beating through the audio bug. Nickie had a tough stomach, but the memories created from listening to the woman beg were nearly more than even she could take. She suspected that Duncan knew she'd heard, but like the particular painting he was working on, it was all a moot point by this time.

As her eyes peered over her reading glasses, her fingers hovered over her keyboard. She considered repeating her search for the john she killed, but instead did a search for any new information regarding the murder of Leslie Jacobsen. She needed to ask Duncan about plans to connect the dots and search for the mole in the department now that they had the Jacobsen files. Except now was not the time. The security camera pictures of Duncan and Andy sent pins and needles through her heart, as they had since they broke into Jacobsen's office. She understood the pictures they retrieved mostly held concealed faces, yet...Baltimore police combined the burglary and murder, understandably deciding the two were connected.

Murder. Andy. Duncan.

The john she killed.

Flipping the lid on the laptop, she changed gears and decided on her cello. He'd given her the sheet music for Allemande's Suite No. 1 in G Major. It had been a long time since she'd played other than from memory.

They stayed like that for nearly an hour, in the familiar cocoon that was their own. Duncan painted; she played. The concentration in his face grew in tandem as she learned the piece. As she worked the crescendo, her lids dropped and a bead of sweat fell down her temple, stopping where her glasses lay. Yes. This was where she needed to be, next to her lover, her husband. Next to her old wooden friend. The tips of her fingers burned against the thick strings as she pressed and slid them up and down the neck. It was a love/hate relationship, the cello and Nickie. The love was what poured through her body, escaping only through her hands and fingers. The hate came from where the cello originated. From her parents. She wouldn't let them take her down, not now. She reached the peak and shook the last note in a languid vibrato that lasted until her bow rested at the farthest length from the beast.

Her chest rose and fell again and again. A smile threatened her lips as she allowed her eyes to reopen to the reality of her evening.

"There you are." Sometime during her trance, Duncan had moved his stool and placed it in front of her. His forearms rested on his thighs.

She should have jumped at his proximity but fear was not the emotion that held her. His face was a complicated array of sadness, interest, love and desire. She saw each one clearly as she assessed his eyes, his lips, the way his jaw clenched and his lids remained only half opened. Methodically, she placed her cello and bow in the stand next to him before taking a leg and swinging it over his lap. He leaned back as she did, allowing his gaze to follow from head to toe. His love for her grew beneath the place she rested, making her lids betray her and try to close once more. She forced them open and watched as his grew dark. As she reached for her glasses, a hand wrapped around her wrist.

"Leave them on."

Her brows lifted, but she complied. Her hips rocked into the feel of him like they had a mind of their own. She grasped the buttons of her blouse as he worked the ones on his shirt. She watched as he watched. And wasn't sure which was sexier, the watching or the being watched. He slid his hands over her bare arms, down her back to the clasp that kept her hidden. The release sent waves of desire to her core.

Painfully slow, he slid a strap from her shoulder, kissing the trail it left in its wake.

She stood and reached for her reading glasses once more before repeating the process with her slacks.

"Don't." He smiled, making her nearly lose her balance. "They are like sexy librarian glasses. You're blushing," he added, and lifted her chin with his forefinger.

"I know," she said as he helped her remove the rest of her clothing. "How can I be blushing after all we've been through, all we've done?" But it was there, burning along her neck and face.

When she returned to her place on his lap, their bodies effortlessly joined. It was early for this, and her eyes flew open at the abruptness. His mouth was in the shape of a small O. The surprise in his gaze was as intense and awe-inspiring as what she felt. They began to move. She could go over in seconds like this. The warmth, the heat, the pace.

His Nickie was close to crossing over. It wasn't like her. He reached down and pressed his thumb against her. It was nearly instantaneous. Her forehead dug in his shoulder and her nails clenched his back. The cries that erupted from her penetrated his soul.

Her eyes. They lifted to him. He watched deep into the steel gray as she came down. Slowly, more, then up again. Her eyes said confusion. Confusion, then louder cries as her nails dug into muscle. Her hips moved against him, with him, around him. It was he who could scarcely hold on then. His Nickie. His wife. For always.

His hands gripped her backside as he hung on, clinging to her, clinging her to him. He held, moved, then held once more, releasing everything inside him. The good and the bad. She could do that to him, for him.

Her arms lay limp at her sides. He knew her legs would be like wet noodles as well, so using her backside he lifted and carried her to bed to find the sleep she so desperately needed.

CHAPTER 23

———◆ ◆ ◆ ◆◆———

Wednesday morning. Tonight would be the night she did what she could to help Bianca find closure as she healed at the safe house shelter. Tonight was the night she would save the women used to groom young teens. Tonight was the night she would save who she could from abduction and take down the perpetrators who schemed it all.

Eddy sat across from her in the break room, eating one of yesterday's donuts. "You're gonna get yourself fired."

She shrugged. "And leave all this?" She motioned her hand around the room. It was a risk. He was right. She'd decided not to tell her captain. Not to notify NYPD that she was going on their turf. There might be nothing to tell either of them. The whole afternoon and evening could be a bust.

"I'll miss you when you're gone, man," Eddy said.

His face followed hers as it jerked to the unmistakable suits that strutted through the center of the common area. Special Agent Hurst. She preferred him in his jeans but was relieved to see him nonetheless. And Special Agent Goodrich. Her relief turned to irritation. Parker followed them with Duncan on one arm and

Andy on the other. Officer Parker. Northridge Police Department Officer Parker. The relief evaporated and was replaced with goose bumps that erupted on her neck and arms. As they spotted her, they turned enough for Nickie to see the small body stuck in the center of all of them. Rose. The goose bumps turned into raw panic.

Eddy lifted from his chair and stepped between Nickie and the special agents. "What the hell?"

"Thanks, Lynx, but no need." She gave herself a moment to assess her options. It didn't take a rocket scientist to put it together.

He spun on his heels and looked down at her. "What happened? What didn't you tell me now?"

"Nothing." She inhaled, filling her lungs before letting it out. Rose. Not Rose. She had nothing to do with this. "I've got this." Not.

"What can I do? Who can I call? What's going on?"

She looked up at him. Why was he so pissed off? She kept something from him. She got that, but really? "Maybe let the captain know we've got company who will take up the interrogation rooms for a while."

"What?" he yelled.

Goodrich stepped into the room with them. He looked much too happy. "Detective Savage." He moved toward her as if Eddy wasn't standing between them. It was like a testosterone-infused game of chicken. Eddy lost.

"We'd like it if you'd remain right where you are," Goodrich said, then turned to Eddy. "If you'd excuse us, please?"

"Yeah, sure." Eddy's smile was evil, but he did not attempt to leave.

"No, sir. I'll need you to remove yourself from the area."

"Are you kidding me? This is our station."

"Do I need to get your captain, *sir*?" Goodrich said the last word with disdain.

Eddy left, giving Parker a shoulder shove as the group

passed. It wasn't Parker's fault. Andy and Duncan gave her looks clearly meant to reassure. Not gonna happen.

Rose stared forward with a classic pissed-off-ready-to-fight Rose glare. Be smart, Rose. Please be smart. Who had baby A.J.? Where was he? Her eyes turned to Goodrich. He stood, feet slightly spread, knees locked. He was facing the open door with his hands clasped behind his back. Was he getting ready for the National Anthem, or was he keeping an eye on a suspect while she waited her turn to be interrogated?

It wasn't five minutes before her captain stormed in. "Special Agent Goodrich, do you mind telling me why you have one of my detectives detained in my break room and both my interrogation rooms filled?"

Goodrich didn't move anything other than his lips. "Good morning, Captain Nolan. Detective Savage is waiting her turn for questioning."

"Did you read her her rights?" Dave turned to her. "Did he read you your rights?"

Goodrich rocked on the balls of his feet. "Detective Savage is not being detained. She is free to go anytime she pleases." He glanced down his nose and over his shoulder to her. "You are free to go any time you like; however, we would be back with warrants for your arrest in a few days."

"Okay. Well, okay, very well, then." Dave began to pace before adding, "Did he give you a phone call?"

Goodrich looked to her fully this time. "You can make a call any time you like, Detective."

The only person she would call was in an interrogation room at that moment. Goodrich knew that. Everyone knew that.

She kept focus on Goodrich's eyes, but noticed Dave from her peripheral vision as he made a mock telephone with his thumb and forefinger and placed it to the side of his face, mouthing the words, "Call me."

She allowed Dave plenty of time to get to his office,

then pulled out her phone and held it up to Goodrich, waving it back and forth in front of him. Before she dialed, she turned the ear volume down nearly completely.

"Nick," Dave answered. "What the hell is going on?"

She couldn't possibly answer that and pretended the phone was still ringing.

"No. Don't answer that," Dave said. "What can I get you? No. Not that either. Do you need me to pull rank?"

"Hello, Mom," Nickie said into the phone. "I'm going to be a little late for lunch. No, no. No need to worry. It won't take long," she lied.

"Can you use a diversion?"

"Aww. That's sweet. No, not that either."

"This is my frigging station."

"I know, and I'm sorry."

"That's not what I meant."

"I know that, too. I love you, Mom. You're the best. I'll call you later when we can talk more. Please don't worry." She hung up and folded her hands around her phone. No boot slung over a knee. No arm draped over the back of her chair.

"You know, I'm not going anywhere," she said to Goodrich. "This would go a lot faster if you left me and went and questioned one of the others yourself. I'll give you my phone. I can wait in the captain's office. Or the intel room, nothing in there."

He didn't answer.

"Or have Officer Parker babysit me. You chose him to help you with pick up."

How long could Goodrich stand like that? Her legs were stiff and might never move again, and she wasn't the one standing. Parker came around a corner, heading for the john. Goodrich flinched. At least she got to smile at that.

She checked the time on her phone. Eleven thirty.

Nevaeh expected to be picked up after lunch. Did she call and tell her she would be late because she was being detained by the FBI? Damn. Shit. Damn.

On Parker's way back, Goodrich stepped into the hallway. They spoke for only a few seconds before both turned to Nickie. She lifted her brows and forced her lips together.

"I won't ask for your phone, Detective."

No shit. "Thank you." She smiled.

"Sorry about this," Parker said, uncharacteristically out of his generally professional, by-the-book manner.

"No worries, Parker." She shrugged. "Better you than Vaughn."

His ears turned so red they were nearly purple.

It was only minutes before Special Agent Hurst came around the corner. "Nick, you're up."

With Hurst? This could be interesting. Did Goodrich know they had met and been communicating off the books? Did he know Hurst was doing recon for her about the department mole? Less was more and she kept her mouth shut.

The window of Interrogation 1 showed Andy and Duncan sitting at the metal table. She couldn't see who babysat them.

Interrogation 2 held Rose and Goodrich. Nickie could kick something. Or someone.

Hurst led her to Interrogation 3. They hardly ever used this room. It was piled with boxes and old swivel desk chairs that were no longer safe to sit in but no one took the time to part with.

"Have a seat, Detective."

She complied and kept to her less-is-more plan.

"I'd like to record this interview. As you know, you are under no obligation to comply. This is strictly a person of interest interview."

"I, Detective Nickie Savage, give you permission to record our conversation."

"Can you tell me where you were last Saturday between the hours of o'eight hundred and sixteen hundred?"

"I was with Duncan. We spent the day having sexy librarian glasses sex."

Hurst pressed his lips together. His eyes lit in a smile, but he kept them glued to his list of questions.

"A man matching Duncan's height and build was videotaped disarming an alarm, and breaking into a building and an office where a woman was found murdered. What do you have to say about this?"

"I'm truly sorry about any death. Truly. Duncan was with me. At home. All day."

"The deceased worked for your father."

Her blood pressure rose. She could feel it course through the veins in her head. No reason. It wasn't a secret. She would have asked the same thing. "Double ouch."

"Where were you on February 25?"

Ah. The date was familiar. The other time Duncan and Andy had broken into Leslie Jacobsen's office. "Excuse me?" She blinked. She wanted to be helpful, honestly she did. Hurst had been there for her. Gone out of his way for her. But, so had his two predecessors who went to the dark side.

"Check your home and station calendars and get back to me."

"I'm not a big dwell-on-the-past kind of girl." She pulled out her phone and opened the calendar app. "See? I erase everything as I complete it." It was true. There was nothing listed on her calendar before the present day. Well, except the yearly physical she was supposed to schedule weeks ago. "I'll look up the date in the station log and get the information to you ASAP."

He seemed to be changing his next question. "There was a break-in on that date by what looks to be the same two men."

She shrugged.

"Man number two matches the description of Duncan's brother."

"I wish I could help you." And she wished he could help her.

They went on like this for another half hour before he brought her to Interrogation 2 which they were using as a holding room.

Just outside, Goodrich waited for her. The smile on his face said cat with a canary. Shit. What did he have? Did Rose slip up? Andy? Her face fell and she waited for him to get it over with and rub it in her face.

"Nice interview, Detective. I heard nearly the entire thing. Can you follow me, please?"

Follow? He took her a whole fifteen feet until they hit Interrogation 1. "Wait right here, please." Goodrich entered the room but didn't shut the door. He must have wanted her to hear.

She *sort of* waited 'right here.' She was basically in the same spot, but if he was going to step away from her without a babysitter, she was going to lean over and see what was going on. Duncan was in the room. He looked as worn out as she was.

"Mr. Reed, sir. Your brother said he was home all day. With his wife. She said the same. You said you were with your wife as well. All day. Alone. At home. It's a bit too convenient, you see. I'd like to ask exactly what you were doing for that duration at your home."

Nickie ducked back around the corner. Why had she been so specific when asked that question? She knew better than to be that specific. She squeezed her eyes shut as she listened to Duncan's answer.

It was like she could hear the smile on his face. "Having sexy librarian glasses sex with my wife."

Her eyes opened. All she saw was the empty wall on the other side of the hallway, but it made her grin nonetheless. They had nothing. Could do nothing.

Interrogate all they wanted. They knew what they knew but had no proof. The grin turned into a smile that spread from ear to ear.

CHAPTER 24

Since Andy couldn't get Rose to stay home, they took a girl's car and a boy's car. Nevaeh rode shotgun in the latest sedan Duncan had rented using cash and a fake ID. A copy of *Seventeen Magazine* lay on the dash covering the serial number.

Glancing over to Nevaeh, she had to admit, the get up she wore was spot on. Her new extensions were crisp and smooth. A few slightly blonde and slightly red ones were braided in so well, they looked natural. All were pulled up in a high ponytail that swayed when Nevaeh walked. She'd gotten a professional manicure but no fake nails. Bright pink polish with fake pink sapphire inlays on the nail of a ring finger. A pair of dark blue jeans, boots and a designer laced hoodie. Classy, but young. With her naturally small frame, she looked absolutely fifteen.

It made Nickie nauseous with nerves.

She had wanted to make it to Manhattan by mid-afternoon. It was now early evening, and they still had a half hour of driving to go. Spilled milk.

In the earbud that was becoming a third arm for her, she could hear that the perps were there and didn't show signs of leaving anytime soon. They'd gathered intel on dozens of young girls in the past handful of days. A few had passed whatever tests had been deemed important. The voice. It was becoming all too familiar as well. Quick clip with a hint of Brooklyn.

Nickie checked the expression on Nevaeh's face. She looked pumped. This was bad. Her expressions should read cautious, smart and nervous. "You don't go anywhere with anyone," Nickie told her. "You're only there for stage one."

"Yes," Nevaeh said with way too much annoyance in her voice. "Share my contact information," she recited like an irritating required speech. "Say little else. Look interested and flattered. I've so got this."

"That shit is what bothers Nickie," Rose said from the backseat. "Just sayin', Nevaeh."

"I am Sabrina Watts. I'm fifteen and live in Queens. My phone number is 929-747-8213. This crazy awesome cell works for that number, and you have made up this ID for me. You gave me this secret cop bug thing in my pocket." She lifted the corner of her short jean jacket and spoke to the pocket. "I've so got this."

"ID practice is good," Rose said. "The cocky bullshit is stupid."

Nevaeh gave a great fifteen-year-old rebellious roll of her eyes, reminding Nickie that, even with what she'd been through, Nevaeh was a teenager. Maybe not fifteen, but a teenager.

Nickie was going rogue. Again. She hadn't called NYPD to notify them of her plan. On their turf. She hadn't told her captain. She'd used Duncan's illegal means to create an ID, driver's license and all. All with a teenage girl that didn't have her head completely on.

She was going to police officer hell. But Bianca deserved restitution. The girls already taken deserved to be saved. Future victims deserved to keep their lives. The risk was worth it. The audio bug that stuck to the perp's coat still worked. Did the guy ever wash his coat? It was like destiny.

Her cell buzzed in her pocket.

It was a text from Duncan. 'How is she?'

'Eh.'

'I'm worried about her.'

'Yeah. There is that.'

She followed Duncan's Audi into the parking garage. He chose a row on the second level that had a few empty spaces.

As they got out of the car, Nickie reminded Nevaeh, "You might be hanging out for a while."

"I know how to shop, Nickie." Nickie stopped, closed her eyes and took a deep breath. The sarcasm was truly going to make Nickie crazy. "Detective Savage," she corrected.

"I'm sorry, really I am," Nevaeh said. They made their way alongside the boys. "But it's like I'm getting a piece of good from all this bad. Making a difference. Sort of like I'm helping in some small way to make it so Caroline's death wasn't for nothing."

Everyone stopped at that.

"I'm sorry," Nevaeh said again. "Was that wrong?"

"No." Nickie closed her eyes even though her brows lifted. It was why she'd changed her name to Savage when she turned eighteen. In honor of the girls she'd left behind. It was the reason she was a cop. "It's perfect."

"Now that we're perfect," Duncan said as he joined them, "let's go over this again."

As they walked, Duncan made Nevaeh recite her false credentials again. Much to Nevaeh's annoyance, he also had her go over what information she was and was not allowed to share with any potential perps, and look at the sketches he'd drawn of the male and female he interacted with. Nickie had just made her do all that.

"Patience, Nevaeh," Nickie reminded her. "There are plenty of shops around the central location to keep you busy for the duration."

"Duncan cannot be seen but he will cover the nearest exit. Rose, Andy and I will keep you in our sights at all times. Each of us has a receiver. We can hear everything. Please know this. Even if you can't see us, you are safe."

Most likely.

"Everyone remember, at all times, there will be a lookout. They will be good at this; they've done it for months, maybe years. This is our first time. Let's not forget that." Nevaeh's expression didn't ease Nickie's fears. "What do you do if someone tries to lead you away from the proximity of the designated hallway? Anywhere away. A nice shop they want to show you. A pretzel they want to buy you. Anything?"

"I tell them I'm waiting for a friend and Rose shows up."

Nickie handed her the keys to the rental.

"Where is the meeting point?"

"The fast food joint down the street. I've got this already."

Moderately satisfied, Nickie nodded. The five of them entered in intervals. Nickie and Rose went first. They were to play the role of girlfriends shopping. Irony. Neither had much experience with shopping, let alone hanging with girls in general. It was why they'd become so close.

Duncan was next. He would keep his distance but gesture, pointing out the direction to the smoothie shop where he'd spotted the female groomer the last time they were here.

Andy took caboose. It was his job to hide, but keep Nevaeh within eyeshot. He would blend in easily. He loved to shop and was made for this mall shit.

A pair of new boots and a cell phone case later, Nickie could see the impatience in Nevaeh's posture. She wished the bug in Nevaeh's pocket went two ways.

Nevaeh said something inaudible into the air.

"Who is that you're talking to," a strange voice asked.

Nickie didn't recognize the voice or the face. The woman looked like she'd just left the catwalk at a fashion expo. She was black like Nevaeh. Did they do that on purpose? Don't get ahead of yourself, Nickie.

"I'm singing, actually." Nevaeh looked down and blushed.

It might have been nerves but it seemed to have worked.

"Stevie Nicks. My mom says she's a classic. I just think she rocks."

Not too much talking, Nevaeh. Just smile and listen. Answer questions.

"Oh, I adore Stevie Nicks. Do you mind?" The woman gestured to the seat next to Nevaeh at the Formica table.

Nevaeh shook her head and smiled.

"I was just noticing your beautiful hair. Do you mind if I ask where you got it done?"

Oh shit. Already? The kid wasn't prepped for this. She wasn't an undercover cop.

"I did it!" Nevaeh squealed. "It took forever since I did it myself, but it was worth it."

"Wow." The woman tucked her folded hands beneath her chin. "You're good. And I know good. I'm part of a traveling modeling team."

There it was. They were a go.

Rose picked up two bandanas and pretended to ask Nickie which one she preferred as she rotated to give Nickie full view of what transpired. Nickie held a green one against her hair and glanced in a tiny sunglasses mirror as she watched.

"Wow," Nevaeh said like she was watching a fireworks finale.

"Your nails, your hair. Natural yet classic. My name is Emma." The woman held out a hand. Nevaeh took it.

"And yours?"

Nevaeh had to look down and to the side to retrieve that information. Bad. Very bad. "S-S-Sabrina."

"It's nice to meet you, Sabrina. You're very good," the Emma person repeated. "Do you work professionally?"

Nevaeh blinked several times. Keep it together. You can do this.

"You mean model? Oh, no."

The woman placed her hand on Nevaeh's forearm. "Oh no, honey. I'm sorry. I meant the hair. You have real talent. The people I work for mostly use adult models. But they've been known to give internships to promising high school students. You are in high school, right?"

Nevaeh's chin bobbed up and down quickly.

"How old are you, may I ask?"

Again with the pause. "Fifteen," Nevaeh answered.

The Emma woman sat back like she was assessing Nevaeh. Her head tilted one way, then the other. Nevaeh looked at her hands nervously, which was completely perfect. Finally, the woman nodded and spoke. "Yes. Look at you. I think you would be perfect. Let me give you my card. I will say something to my boss. I can't make any promises, but if you're interested, talk to your parents. Have them call if they have any questions."

A large and confident smile spread across Nevaeh's face as she took the business card from the Emma person. "Thank you. I will. I really will."

Now came the part Nickie didn't like. Nevaeh would absolutely be followed. And she couldn't be seen with four adults following her.

Duncan would already be taking the stairwell to the second floor of the parking garage. He could get to his Audi before Nevaeh reached the rental and would keep an eye on her. Andy used the elevator. She and Rose would head for the door after Nevaeh but would need to put plenty of time between them.

Nickie refused to let her out of her sight, which meant that their identities would be noted. As instructed, Nevaeh bought more almonds before she left.

Nickie spotted the perp. The one Duncan had identified previously. The one she'd been listening to for days in the damned earbud. She hadn't heard him in nearly an hour. He leaned a shoulder against a mirrored post with no attempt to follow.

Nickie bought both bandanas, sticking the bag inside her box of boots. She tucked an arm around Rose, pressed the sides of their heads together and whispered, "No matter what, we walk at a normal pace, even if it means running into Nevaeh."

Nevaeh seemed somewhat apprehensive. She walked fast and with too much purpose. Her head turned from one side to another, and she ignored her almonds. "I'm in the parking garage. I don't see anyone. It's freaking me out."

It's okay, honey. We can see you. Just a few more yards. Pretending her bags occupied both arms, Nickie rotated and used her back to push open the door to the parking garage. She didn't mean to look up, but it was natural. So was the unfortunate stare she received from the perp. Although it was only for a fraction of a second, his lifeless eyes fixed on Nickie's. The hair on the back of her neck prickled but she was able to keep forward movement without pause.

Duncan pulled into the place set as the designated meeting spot that was next to the rental Nevaeh had driven. Impatience buzzed through Nickie's veins, and she opened his car door before he'd completely stopped. Nevaeh was safe, of course she was, but her reaction in the parking garage worried Nickie and she needed to see her for herself.

"You were great," she said as she approached the

driver's side of the rental. Golden arches towered over both of them.

Nevaeh was nearly out of the car. The look on her face confused Nickie.

"Sorry it didn't work out. Can we try again tomorrow?"

Nickie looked to the other three, who were within earshot by that time. The looks on their faces said they weren't following Nevaeh's line of thought either. "What are you talking about? It was perfect. You were perfect." A few stutters. A few near mishaps, but she'd pulled it off.

Nevaeh's brows dropped low. Methodically, she looked from Duncan to Andy to Rose and ended back at Nickie.

"We didn't find the bad guys."

"I'm sorry, honey. I don't know what you're talking about. Emma. She is one of the bad guys."

"But." Nevaeh dug in the pocket of her hoodie. "She gave me a business card." She held it out.

Nickie dug in the pocket of her jacket and pulled out one of the evidence bags she carried with her everywhere.

"It has a phone number. She said to tell my parents. I thought she was really interested in me for me." Tears welled in Nevaeh's eyes.

It made Nickie realize how much Nevaeh truly was just a kid. More so than Nickie ever was at her age. Nickie turned the bag inside out and maneuvered the business card into it. She pinched the card between her thumb and forefinger, then turned the bag right side out and smiled warmly. "You were great. And you look positively beautiful. These people are very good."

"How can they talk to my parents and give me a phone number and still be able to take children? They didn't try to lure me."

Nickie led her to the backseat of the rental. Rose climbed in to drive. Duncan and Andy slithered away into the Audi.

"This is how they lure you, honey. It's okay. You were amazing. I can hear them talking about you now." It wasn't true. The receiver feed pumped through the earbud in Nickie's ear, but only carried the sound of the perp's jacket rustling at the moment. "It's their job to be believable. They are gaining your trust. We call it grooming. The girl who told you her name was Emma is a groomer."

As Rose pulled away from the parking spot, Nevaeh drew her knees into her body and hugged herself. "I was stupid. I almost told her my real name. The only reason I didn't was because I thought the real bad guys might have been watching or listening. I could have been taken."

"No. Your intuition would have woken long before they could have gotten you. And I was with you. You were amazing. Here." Nickie handed her a soda. "You're shutting down. Don't be scared. Drink this. The sugar will help keep you from going into shock."

Tears streamed down her beautiful brown cheeks. "They would have taken me. They think I'm fifteen and they would have taken me. Made me do things again and again that I only had happen once."

"Don't." Nickie turned Nevaeh's chin so their eyes met. "Don't minimize what happened to you. You wanted to help, and you did. More than I can say."

"I want to go back."

"No. No way. We're on our way home."

"I know." She took a deep breath, setting her legs down and wiping the tears from her face. "I mean next time. You need me, right? They want me. They're going to want me next time. You need me," she repeated.

It all depended on if they deemed her a safe target. "We'll see."

"I have the number on the card memorized. I can call them myself."

Nickie's brows lifted at the threat. "Drink the soda, little girl. We'll talk about Plan B after that."

CHAPTER 25

◆ ◆ ◆ ◆

Nickie sat at her home desk computer sorting through her spreadsheet of johns. She used the information gained from her interrogations to piece together probable groups of the girls and boys used in trafficking.

Her columns of data included location and preference, but she was nowhere near to the ten to twelve groups she'd been told were connected to Zheng and Fu Haizi across the nation.

She was too distracted and anxious to call Bianca and tell her about the progress she'd made in capturing the men who took her. She'd listened in as the perp she now knew as Anthony connected with the ones who watched over the street use of the girls already taken. He mentioned to the men he worked with that he thought he had two new girls ready to take. Nevaeh's alias, Sabrina, wasn't one of them.

Nevaeh had threatened her way into the next stage of the op like a pro, or maybe a tantrum-throwing teenager. They were nearing the time to make the call to Emma.

Duncan didn't paint that night. He sat in the cushioned office chair at the other end of the ridiculously large desk his uncle had made for him. He was deep in whatever work he was doing, so she took a short mental break. Xena lay on her back, feet in the air, snoring like a hibernating bear. The area seemed to morph more and more into a studio apartment rather than a master bedroom. Said ridiculously large desk took up a large part of one side of the room. Duncan's painting studio, the master bed and the master bath, which were bigger than Nickie's entire last apartment. She'd added a microwave behind the wet bar, along with a smoothie machine for the mornings she had time to make one.

"I'm afraid I'm at a loss." Duncan spoke but didn't take his eyes from the monitor on his laptop.

"Hmm?" Nickie asked.

"The mole."

Ah. He was working on that again.

"His source was murdered. It seems he hadn't gotten a replacement contact as of yet. Plus, he is aware someone is illegally keeping an eye on him. I fear we've lost our lead, our edge."

"Hurst didn't have any more for me either." It bothered her, but bothered Duncan more. She was used to being stabbed in the back by the force and political figures, used to betrayal by the people she trusted. It took a lot to shake her. Duncan was another story. He was all about taking care of her and loving her. "I love you back."

His head turned, and his eyes met hers as if he just noticed she was in the room. Pushing away from the desk, he stood and walked to her. "And I you." He took her hand. "What are you working on?"

"I think I'm going to bring what I have to Zheng. He knows more. I've been spinning my wheels with this list of johns and Fu Haizi. I might be able to make him slip up and give me some morsel of something I can use." She adjusted her monitor so Duncan could see from his standing position. "I have a file of eleven photos of registered sex offenders and inmates who admitted to or suck at lying about whether they know Zheng. I think I'm going to bring the list to Zheng in the morning. Nevaeh is coming in over my lunch hour to make the call to the mall perps. I can hit him up before then."

The muscles in his jaw flexed and released. "Shall we go for a midnight swim?"

Change of subject distraction. She truly loved this man. "Mmm. That's sounds yummy."

Nickie pressed send, shooting her latest report to the captain with a half hour to spare before Nevaeh was due. This was bad since it meant she had time to dwell on the fact that she hadn't yet contacted the NYPD captain about her leads with the mall grooming scam going on in his jurisdiction. Was it awful that she was simply tired of the testosterone bullshit and red tape that came with the job? The levels of corruption added to the sick and tired, making her wonder how she ended up in this position. Oh right. The honor of the nearly dozen girls she'd left behind when she escaped captivity. The ones that were likely falsely suspected of helping or at least having knowledge of her escape. And then beaten for it.

She could easily dwell on it. And dwell on not calling NYPD. And dwell on it all as easily in the break room with a Diet Coke as she could at her desk. She grabbed a handful of quarters from her drawer and made her way to the pop machine. Eddy was at his desk as she passed. He'd been quiet lately. Ever since the kiss on the forehead thing. Ugh. She smiled, nodded and didn't stop.

The first two quarters dinked into the machine but made a noise that didn't sound like quarters dinking into a machine. Her fingers grasped the next quarter near the coin slot and held. It was a voice. Pulling her hand away, she turned her head to hear better.

Her eyes flew open. She moved toward the distinct sound of distress, her mind spinning with possibilities.

Zheng had infiltrated the station once before. He was in custody but had plenty of people on the outside.

She stopped in front of the utility room, pulling out her Smith and Wesson and taking it off safety. Slowly turning the knob, she pressed a hip on the door, and then sprang.

This was something she would never be able to unsee.

Officer Parker's bare ass, pants around his ankles.

Or unhear.

ADA Miranda Vaughn's last sex whimper before they noticed Nickie standing with a gun pointing at the two of them. Vaughn turned to a place in the closet somewhere behind Parker.

Nickie's brows lifted as the two of them scrambled apart.

"No!" Nickie yelled, but it was too late. Escaping body parts. "I need therapy."

She turned her back to them, not so much to give them privacy but to keep herself from having any more nightmare ammunition.

"It's not what you think," Parker's breathy voice huffed.

"Right. Because your white ass didn't just tell its own story. There are cameras in here, ya know." The audible male/female gasps were worth it. A large grin spread over Nickie's face. "It would be so much more fun if I was kidding. It would almost make it worth turning back around to see the looks on your faces. But then, no."

"What?" Miranda almost cried. "Where? How?"

Nickie didn't need to answer. Parker and Miranda both knew what the cameras looked like. "How did you not know this?" Nickie assumed Miranda wasn't asking her.

Parker begged, "I'm truly very sorry."

"A round of drinks at The Pint and I'll tell you how to get the disc," Nickie said. "Although I will rub this in forever, blackmail you and tell Lynx so he can do the same. It's only fair I tell you this ahead of time."

"You can do that?" Parker said before an audible zip. "I am referring to obtaining the disc, of course."

"What if this, um," Miranda whined, "wasn't the first—?"

Eww. "Two rounds of drinks and a fifty will do. You owe me so big."

Nickie almost forgot about her Diet Coke. That would have made all bets off on her agreement with the horny cougar ADA and her boy toy. She nearly snorted carbonated soda through her nose at the thought.

Nosy desk clerk Lucinda came around the corner, escorting Jimbo. Jimbo? No. She was supposed to have Nevaeh. Nickie nearly stomped her foot. She did not have time for this.

"Stop," she said to Lucinda, not Jimbo. "Do not let this man in the building. Ever. Do you understand?"

"He said he's an official police informant."

"Not ever," she repeated.

"You've had him in here before."

Nickie got in her face this time. "Not. Ever."

Lucinda shrugged. "Come." She guided Jimbo around and toward the elevator.

This was not happening. "Stop. Come back. You." She pointed to Lucinda. "You might want to go look in the want ads for a new job."

"Bite me," Lucinda said as she shuffled back to her desk.

"My office," she said to Jimbo. "You have three minutes."

Jimbo followed. "I got a haircut," he said as he plopped into her guest chair and set his feet on her desk.

She smacked his feet down to the floor. "So?"

His face looked pained. "You told me to get a haircut. I did. I did my official police informant thing and spied on Phil."

"Not official. No spied." He started to lift his foot to her desk again, but she pointed at him and shook her head.

"He has a new tat."

A new tat? Setting her elbows on her desk, she rested her face in the palms of her hands.

"I don't know what it is. It's covered. Ya know. New one?"

"A new tat that is unidentifiable. Not so helpful, Jimbo."

"He's packing."

She lifted her head. Did he say what she thought he said? "Packing?"

He rolled his eyes and swayed his head from side to side like she was in junior high. "Um, are you for real, Detective Dude? Packing? Ya know, you might not be the sharpest icing on the cake."

"Jimbo, if you don't answer my question, I'm going to break your arm, then call your woman and tell her which titty bars you go to."

"Damn, that's low. This informant shit is shit. He's packing a gun." He used his thumb and forefinger to demonstrate like she might not know what he was talking about. "In the back of his pants. It looks like it might be a glock."

Her brows drew together. "And you thought an unidentifiable possible tattoo was more important to tell me first?"

Jimbo shrugged, leaned back and lifted a foot like he was going to try and set it on her desk again.

"Don't even think about it."

"The door to his back room was locked."

"You tried it?" Phil would notice something like that.

"No, but one of the worker dudes did."

"Did you happen to get a look behind the reception desk?"

He smiled. "Yep. Clean."

She nodded. Oh, Phil. What the hell are you up to?
Keep your eyes open. That was what he'd said to her.
"Okay. Okay, Jimbo." She pulled some money from the
left back pocket of her slacks and tossed a bill at him.

"Whoa." He snatched it before it could blow to the
floor. "Really?"

"Spend it on your woman and not a titty bar."

"Sure thing. Will do." He stuffed it in a front pocket
of his worn jeans. As he reached the elevator, Nickie
saw Lucinda with Nevaeh on her arm this time. Nickie
stood. "Nevaeh. Welcome. Let's meet in my office. Can
I get you anything first? Soda? Coffee? Greasy stale
donut that will be sure to rot your stomach?"

Ice breaker. Nevaeh shook her head and smiled.

"Come sit, then. It's good to see you."

"Do you have the cell phone?" Nevaeh asked. "Did
anyone try and call it?"

Who was the cop here? "Their MO is to call two
weeks after initial contact if no attempt has been made
to connect from the child."

Nevaeh winced at the term child. Nickie would have
to watch how she spoke around her.

"And to answer your question, no. There has been no
activity on this phone. Do you feel ready?"

"I do, but you're going to make me go over everything
again anyway." Nevaeh wasn't asking. Good girl.

They turned the corner to Nickie's office, and she
gestured for Nevaeh to have a seat in one of her guest
chairs. Purposely, Nickie made sure to have both of
them cleared so she could sit with her instead of across
her desk. Sinking down next to her, Nickie said, "So,
how about that going over everything anyway?"

Nevaeh rolled her eyes. Was this what it was like to
be the mom of a teenager, because it didn't suck.

"I call and ask for Emma. I tell her I talked to my
mom, and that I want more information about the
internship."

"That's good. What if they ask to talk to your mom?"

"I give the phone to you, Mom." Nevaeh smiled at that. It made Nickie laugh. Shiver from head to toe, but laugh.

"What if she asks you more questions?"

"Keep to the mall plan. Name, address, phone number, high school. Did you really get me an ID at a high school in Queens?"

Duncan had managed that. "Yes. Take your time. Don't rush. Tell me when you're ready."

"I've been ready. Give me the phone!"

Nickie took out the business card. The prints they lifted from it were partials and didn't come up as a match in the NCIC database. She placed a tracing device on the cell, then dialed the number.

"Hello?"

"Oh, hello. This is Sabrina Watts. Is this Emma?"

"No, but I can get her for you."

The voice was dripping with friendly. It pissed Nickie off.

"Hi, Sabrina. I'm so thrilled you called. Oh my gosh, I was just talking about you. How have you been?"

The rate of the rise and fall of Nevaeh's chest increased. Nickie lifted the corners of her mouth, trying her best to reassure her.

"I've been great. Thanks. I'm calling about that internship thing you mentioned. Is that still—?"

"Oh yes! Of course it is. Did you talk to your parents about it?"

"Yeah. That's sort of what I'm calling about. Like, I'm super interested, but they wanted to know more stuff about it."

"Right, of course."

"They wanted to know dates and everything. And they want to talk to your boss. I'm so sorry. They are stupid. It's embarrassing."

"No, they're smart."

Too smart?

"My boss is free right now. Is now okay?"

"Yes. Mom!" Nevaeh yelled in the phone, making the few people in the commons area who weren't taking their lunch hour turn their heads.

Nickie shook the noise from her head and took the phone. "Hello, this is Mrs. Watts. Sabrina and I are so thankful for this opportunity. A real internship. Wow." It was Nickie's turn to roll her eyes.

"You're welcome. Emma speaks very highly of your Sabrina."

It was him. She was hearing him in each ear. One from the audio bug and one from the cell. She hadn't heard him make a parent or victim phone call before. This was a whole different tone.

"Oh, Emma must be the sweetest thing. Thank you so much. The opportunity sounds amazing. I can't thank you enough for this chance for Sabrina. Can you tell me about the dates? How does she get where she's going?"

"We take care of that. You'll have a phone number where you can contact your daughter at any time." He went on with bogus dates, times and locations. They were sooner than the MO led Nickie to believe. "You know, give it a few weeks or months if you need to. We have another trip in the fall."

Ah, leave options.

"We'll need copies of her insurance card and need you to fill out an emergency contact form. Give me your email and I'll send you a copy."

Nickie looked up to Nevaeh. An innocent teenager making her way in this world. Not hurting anyone. Trying to help, in fact.

This crime ring was a well-oiled machine, and Nickie was more than ready to disassemble it.

CHAPTER 26

Nickie grabbed her file and made her way down to the county pen. She had just enough time to badger Zheng before lunch. The prospect of getting Zheng to slip up always gave her a lift.

She set her holster on the check-in desk and signed in.

Grabbing a folding chair on the way, she parked herself in front of his cell. She'd interrupted a set of pushups. He didn't pause for long at the sight of her before he turned over and started with crunches.

"Good day, Zheng. How's it going?"

"Very well, and you?"

"It's an excellent day. Excellent. I have some pictures I was hoping you might enlighten me about."

"I'll do what I can," he said between lifts.

She held up the first photo. He squinted as he lifted but didn't pause long enough to get a good look at it.

"You know, Zheng. I read faces." She held up the next one. "There is all sorts of research on where a suspect's gaze turns. Right? Left? Down? Up? Each tells a story."

He smiled and curled, this time twisting at the waist as he lifted.

"There is also the blinking. The number of blinks tells if a person is lying, if they are uncomfortable and all that. Did you know that?"

His eyes glanced to the pictures as she held each up for him. No blinks or traveling eye focus.

"And then there is the monster. This is the person described to have no conscience."

Lazily, his gaze turned to her.

"This person kills lie detector stats and is nearly impossible to read regarding facial expression for signs of dishonesty or emotions that include guilt, fear or pain."

He sat up completely now, crossed his legs and rested his forearms on his knees. His smile was evil. She knew it well.

She leaned in, mimicking his pose. "The textbooks don't take into account those of us who read monster like it was a second language. I like to think of myself as a professional."

Taking the stack of photos, she returned them to the file folder. "Thank you for your time, Zheng, and the knowledge that you recognize each and every one of these men."

The way his face morphed from snarky to concerned to dangerous should have created fear inside of her. After all, this man had abused her for eighteen months of her childhood. But it didn't. Her background and circumstances might influence who she was, but she was responsible for who she had become.

"I truly appreciate your cooperation. I am learning how you organize groups of children, where and how many. I am always grateful for your assistance."

"You will regret the day you were born."

"I like how your accent comes out when you're angry. It helps as I work to learn, piece together and analyze your reactions."

She hadn't been sure if it was going to work, but she had Zheng tripped off his game. Keeping her sarcastic face on, she slid the last photo from her file. The john she killed. It was the mug shot from one of his previous arrests for soliciting sex from a minor. She still hadn't found the obit.

Zheng didn't attempt to conceal his expression this time. "Is my Savage becoming nostalgic?"

Damn him if that didn't send a brutal wave of nausea beating through her heart.

"Ah, yes, my Nicole. My Nicole who became the detective. There is no statute of limitations for murder."

"How can there be a murder? There is no body."

"What if there is a body?"

He knows. Of course he knows. "Prove it," she spat before leaning back. The phrase was getting easier and easier to use. "Is there anything else you would like to say," she added. "Not say? Threaten?" She waved her hand in front of her like she was waving him over to the cell door. Leaning toward it, she worked to appear as if she was providing him better access to her ear.

The look on his face was all she needed.

She'd gotten a helpful tip from Jimbo, completed a successful call for Nevaeh and gotten intel from Zheng. Life was good.

Duncan heard the click of Nickie's boots along the concrete walk leading to the stalls. Abigail did as well. Her blonde tail swished from side to side, slapping Duncan's back as he adjusted her saddle.

"Hey, girl," Nickie said and walked to nuzzle his horse.

Abigail snorted and moved into her.

"I was not provided nearly the same greeting," he said.

"It's a girl thing." Then, she turned her steel-gray eyes to him and stepped forward. "Hey, sexy." Her soft, full lips rested on his. He laced his fingers through her hair, pulling her in deeper. "Mmm. There you are." He pulled away to assess. Blue jeans, snug. Brown, low, thick-heeled boots, which for Nickie meant two-inch rather than three or four. Long-sleeved, cotton flannel, buttoned-down shirt with lace at the cuffs and hips. "You're beautiful."

"I'm flattered."

He took hold of the side of her face and ran a thumb over her lips. "You have a lot on your mind."

She moved her head back and forth in agreement. "We both do."

"Tell me."

Abigail bumped Nickie hard enough that he needed to catch her from falling. "Abigail seems to say that we need to ride as we talk."

He handed her the reins. Abigail would never allow him to ride her with Nickie around. Nickie pulled a carrot from a back pocket. How had he missed a carrot back there? He truly needed to spend more time with his hands on her backside. Abigail ate as Nickie led her out of the stall and down the walkway to the barn door.

Duncan stopped in the next stall to get Andy's horse. He was one of the few horses Abigail would tolerate. He and Nickie mounted as they reached the exit, then took off in a trot for the few open acres before they reached the trees.

Andy and Rose lived on the other side of Duncan's property. The air out here seemed cleaner.

Inhaling deeply, he noticed how the wooden fence surrounding the acres' perimeter was aging. They were all aging. "Andy Jr. is growing."

"Yes," she said from next to him. "He is alert and seems to know what everyone is talking about."

The muscles along the back of Andy's horse flexed and released beneath Duncan's legs. "What are your thoughts on children?"

"I like them and all that."

"I mean for us."

Pulling back on Abigail's reins, she stopped the horse.

She didn't yell or snort or run away. That was something. The sigh that came from deep in her chest could have proven to be worse.

"We've talked about this."

"We have not talked about this," he argued. "We've talked about talking about it after the Zheng case is over. Let's talk about what we'll talk about."

At least he made her smile. "I have no parenting skills. No experience. No role modeling."

"You had no training skills or experience with Xena."

"You did not just compare raising a kid to raising a dog." She pressed her heels into Abigail enough to let her know she was carrying on.

"You had no training in how to be a spouse."

"Right, because I'm killing that job. Maybe literally."

This time he reached out a hand and took her arm. She looked down at his hand then up to him. Her expression was confused.

"Don't say that. I am happy we're married more today than I was yesterday and less than I will be tomorrow."

"I nearly lost you from pushing you away. I did it again with these cases I've been working on. I'm not getting much better."

He slowed as they approached the trees and allowed her to go first. "Your instincts took you back to singular autopilot. You reached out for assistance and changed. I say it's much better. As am I with refraining from keeping things from you."

He pondered this as they rode. The late spring ground was still soft but hardening with the turn into summer. The leaves on the trees were full yet clung to spring with their bright green color. A group of baby squirrels ran dangerously close, spooking the horse Duncan rode but not Abigail. Never Abigail.

He scratched the side head of the horse she rode. "It's okay. They are smaller than you."

"So is a mouse," Nickie said from in front. "But I

would be just as jittery if one came running around my feet while I was trying to walk in the woods. I went and saw Zheng today."

Interesting how a subject change could morph his body from serene to anxious in seconds.

"I showed him the photos of the perps who admitted or showed signs of knowing him. He's getting easier to spook. He solidified my suspicions. He knew each of them. My spreadsheet is coming together. I've been able to come up with eight probable groups."

"Yes, your data is quite specific. There is much more I feel you could assume in order to expand your lists."

"I don't work well with assumptions."

As he well knew.

"Nevaeh made her next call. She was awesome. Now, we wait. You know how I love waiting."

"And patiently," he said sarcastically.

"And Jimbo thinks Phil is packing again."

"You say that as if he was a drug addict."

"Same difference. And that back room was locked."

"Did he try to open it? Phil wouldn't have liked that. He's not a warm creature."

"Ha. I asked the same thing. Jimbo said one of the barber dudes tried it."

Duncan knew the place well. He'd already broken into it once. Another time would be just as simple, possibly more so. "This is the same man who allowed Jun Zheng to use said room as a meeting place."

"Duncan." A useless warning call.

His words this time were more of thinking out loud. "This is the place of a man who is on probation for aiding and abetting in said room."

"I know where you're going with this. I can't use what you find."

"It will do nothing more than to serve my curiosity, then."

"Don't get caught."

"Never."

Duncan departed before the sun came up. He left a note for Nickie, but he didn't tell her and would get hell for it. Deservedly. But he had to find out what was going on at Phil's place. This was the guy who aided and abetted Jun Zheng. Here. In Northridge. The fact that he was breaking probation by carrying a gun and needed a lock for a break room at a barber shop was enough reason for Duncan to need to take a look around.

He drove his SUV and parked several blocks away. Andy would have his head if he knew as well. After the scare with Leslie Jacobsen, it was difficult enough to ask for his assistance with the Uptowne River Shoppes stakeout. Duncan was in no mood to put Andy in danger with this as well.

The sun wouldn't come up for another hour and the barbershop wouldn't open for another three. The street was empty. Cigarette butts littered the sidewalk as he passed Lucky's and T & As. He approached Phil's place, then dug in his pocket for one of the two pinches of C4 gum he'd taken from his rifle cabinet. Looking up and down the street, he didn't see any new security cameras, private or public. And nothing in the store as far as he could tell.

He began stuffing the C4 in the dead bolt before noticing a new lock near the ground. He needed the other pinch for the door inside the shop that led to the former break room, so he broke the pliable substance in two and hoped it would be enough for both. He pulled out his phone, pretending to check his messages as he glanced around and reached for his lighter.

He lit one, then the other, and watched as the door moved outward a few inches. Pushing through, he went right to the two spots he'd decided on. First was the reception cabinet. It was more of a lectern but had been used to conceal firearms in the past. Jimbo was right. It contained only papers and ink pens now.

His feet moved to the room in the back. The door had been changed. It was paneled, not flat as before; a different material. And there was a dead bolt. Why hadn't he brought more explosives? He ducked behind the wall of the meeting room as he pulled the next pinch of explosives in half. Again, he metaphorically crossed his fingers as he slipped around to the door and pressed some in the door handle lock and the rest in the dead bolt.

He lit the dead bolt first but didn't get to the second lock. The door flew open before he could reach it. There were two of them. A man with a liquor-red nose stood facing Duncan, gun drawn. The other loosened his tie as he maneuvered his gun around the opening door.

Duncan grabbed the gun arm of the closest one who was unlucky enough to be in front and flipped him around, using him as a shield from the line of fire. Twisting the man's arm as he did, the gun flew to the tile floor, stopping when it hit a plywood box.

"Don't move," the man with the red nose said as he aimed at Duncan's head.

"No one needs to die," Duncan said. He held tight to the one with the loose tie as his eyes roamed the room. The box. There were several of them lining the walls. Guns. They were gun boxes. Big gun boxes.

"I was only looking for a little cash," Duncan added as he crept toward a stepping stool that reached more boxes above a wall of cabinets. "I'll leave. No one has to die," he repeated.

He placed a foot on the stool. Red Nose, who still had a gun, looked down at the movement of Duncan's foot long enough for Duncan to shove Loose Tie into the line of fire. Three gunshots echoed in the small room. Loose Tie stumbled, but Duncan wasn't sure if it was from the push or a bullet.

Using his entire frame, Duncan swung his left arm over Loose Tie as he stumbled to his knees. The closed fist connected with Red Nose's face. Cheeky flesh molded around Duncan's knuckles, toppling Red Nose's entire frame from the impact. The skin on Duncan's knuckles peeled from the force it took. The guy rocked and fell to the floor as Loose Tie lifted from his knees and gained his balance. He elbowed Duncan in his chest, barely missing his diaphragm but catching the bottom of his rib cage.

Duncan heard a crack but willed himself to ignore it for now. Loose Tie glanced over at his gun as it lay on the floor. Instead of the gun, he went for Duncan. The forward momentum was welcomed as Duncan sidestepped as he planted a quick jab toward the center of his approaching face. The crack he heard this time was the distinct crush of nose cartilage.

Red Nose lifted to one knee, then the other. Loose Tie barely had time to start bleeding from his nose before he rounded on Duncan. Fists flew. A knee landed on Duncan's broken rib. The pain was too much to ignore this time. A blow to the side of his head added stars to the darkness, and he leaned over and grabbed the counter next to him.

In the darkness, he flung his head backward, gambling that one of them was there. Bone hit bone as skulls made contact. Instead of letting the man fall where he stood, Duncan grabbed hold of him by the shirt and swung him around for a large sweep in the direction of the other one. Bodies mingled until Duncan heard the cock of a gun.

His vision cleared instantly. Pulling Loose Tie close, Duncan used him as a shield and rotated, tucked a knee, then kicked out, striking the gun with a foot. A shot rang out just before Duncan made contact. Loose Tie dropped to the floor and rolled in pain. Lethargically, Duncan cocked his fist and swung, hitting a gunless Red

Nose directly on the spot in the temple that should knock him out. Duncan took a breath, placing his hands on his thighs before making his way to Loose Tie who rolled around clutching his right arm with one hand and nose with the other. Placing a foot on the man's chest, he repeated the blow once, twice, three times to the man's temple before both lay still on the floor.

Blood dripped from the corner of Duncan's eye and lip. His phone rang. Cradling his broken rib, he reached in his pocket to answer. No. It wasn't his phone. A light flashed from the pocket of Loose Tie as he lay unconscious. Duncan dug out the ringing phone, pocketed it, then decided to take Red Nose's as well.

Whoever was calling would likely show up soon. Duncan didn't give himself a break before cleaning up his tracks. If he did, he feared he wouldn't be able to get moving again. And time was ticking.

CHAPTER 27

———◆ ◆ ◆———

Nickie stared at her cell. Her fingers tapped her desk in front of her. She'd already swum a mile and sorted through the spreadsheet of Zheng's probable groups of trafficked children. Her inbox was down to a single page. She'd copied her schedule for the day into her phone and even set reminder alerts for two of the meetings she had to show up to.

Unfortunately, she was long overdue with her call to the NYPD captain. This wasn't the first time she had to admit to a police captain that she'd been working on his turf without permission or notification. Last time was ugly as hell and left her with pitiful support. And it all made sense. If the tables were turned, her captain would be pissed as hell. She would, too.

But, the set up with the modeling internship façade came together faster than she'd expected. The perps had two other girls they'd tagged and wanted to take the three of them at the same time. None knew about the others. The only reason Nickie knew was because the Anthony dude never threw his jacket in the wash. The audio bug was strong as ever. She knew this guy like he was an evil brother.

It wouldn't be smart of him to alert the girls to each

other beforehand. They might talk and share notes. It could cause suspicion. How many girls had they taken over the months? Years? How many malls? Public locations? Oh, how she wanted to get her hands on the computer or laptop she'd heard his partners in crime pound away on time and time again.

Time to man up. She rubbed her hands over her face, then dialed the number to the NYPD captain's secretary.

"This is Darlene, Captain Johnson's assistant."

"Good morning, Darlene. This is Detective Nickie Savage from the Northridge Police Department. May I speak with your boss, please?"

"Can I ask what this is about?"

"An undercover op." Sort of.

"One minute, please."

Nickie tapped her fingers and winced.

"Captain Johnson."

"Good day, Captain. This is Detective Nickie Savage from the Northridge Police Department. I'd like to alert you to a possible trafficking scam I've detected in your jurisdiction." She paused, expecting some questions regarding how she knew and what she was doing on his turf. He didn't jump, so she did. "I got a hit about an organized system that brings in young teens." She couldn't say too much…that would let on that she'd been nosing around his turf for, well, as long as she had been. Couldn't say too little. The scenario would seem unfounded. Rock. Hard place.

"They've set their sights on a nineteen-year-old I know. They think she's fifteen."

"Why didn't you call earlier, Detective?"

She had. The Detective Berkley who answered the phone may have blown off her request for assistance, but she wasn't into throwing another cop under the bus. The nosy desk clerk Lucinda absolutely, but not another cop who showed no signs of corruption. Stupidity maybe, but not corruption.

"I did. I spoke with someone in your department. The initial situation was illusive. I understand and support his reservations." Not.

"Berkley?"

Oh boy. "I honestly don't remember the name, sir." Lie.

"Mmm hmm."

"I'm going over his head now, because the perps are ready for this girl to come out with her suitcase tomorrow night."

Awkward silence. Nickie squinted one eye, waiting for the tirade. More awkward silence.

"Give me the details. I'll consider your plan and am willing to offer some muscle if I think it seems sound."

That was it? "Sir?"

"I've had trouble with my men and vice arrests involving minors. They honestly don't get it and don't know what to do when presented with it. I have training scheduled, but until then, I appreciate the call, and as long as it sounds reasonable, will offer backup."

She was speechless but found her voice enough to explain her plan. Over the next twenty minutes, they went back and forth. He provided insight on the mall layout and another op he'd performed there.

"I have a meeting, Detective, but I'd like to continue this conversation later this afternoon. When are you available?"

"I can rearrange my schedule any time after 2:30 p.m. I am truly grateful, sir. I'll wait for your call. Thank you."

This was going to be a good day. Her captain decided the work she was doing with Fu Haizi was worth station time since they had Zheng in their basement. The NYPD captain had her back. Yes, a very good day.

She grabbed her phone from her desk and headed for the pop machine.

She checked her messages as she walked. Four missed calls from Duncan. Her adrenaline level rose as she dialed. The note he'd left her that morning said he was going into work early. It seemed normal at the time.

"Nickie." He answered on the second ring.

"Why do you sound stuffy? Are you sick?"

"Phil the barber."

No. He didn't sound sick. He sounded near death. "Where are you? What happened? Are you hurt?"

"I am home. I've been in a fight. I won."

"I didn't ask if you won. I asked if you're hurt." She stood and grabbed her coat.

"Nothing I can't take care of myself."

She passed by Eddy's office. He didn't look up. Dave's office door was open. He was pacing behind his desk with his phone against his ear.

"I'm on my way," she said as she neared her captain's office.

"Phil the barber," he repeated.

His definition of a fight was not an average definition. He sounded like he had a cold. Broken nose? "Hang on a second."

She knocked on the door below the plastic plaque that read: Captain Dave Nolan.

"Hold on," Dave said and pressed his cell against his chest.

"I'm taking an hour. I'll keep my phone on."

"Is everything okay?"

"Yeah, yeah. I'll be in touch."

His expression said he didn't believe her.

She took the shortcut from Dave's office to the stairs. "Is anything broken?" she asked Duncan.

"He's got a stash, Nickie."

Phil? "Damn it, Duncan, is anything broken?"

"A rib. I wrapped it. I broke into the back room." His voice was throaty like he was nearly asleep.

"You searched Phil's place already? We just talked

about it last night."

"There are boxes of what I suspect to be guns. Big guns. I didn't get a chance to open any of them. I ran into two men there who served as overnight guards. I surprised and woke them."

She would forego her siren but turned on her lights as she took off out of the station parking lot. "Phil has guards? You went with Andy? Without telling me?"

"I went alone. I left them unconscious and bleeding. I have their cells. Someone called. I didn't answer. They will be checking on the men any time now. You need to get someone out there." The last part was barely a mumble.

The highway came too slow. She didn't know a Camry could fishtail before then.

"Are you bleeding?" He certainly was nearly unconscious.

"Not on our sheets."

"Not helping."

"Don't come home. Call Lynx. Get backup. Get out there."

Like hell. "I'll call Eddy. And I'm coming home." She hung up and pressed Eddy's speed dial. It rang eight times and he didn't answer. Damn him. She chose her captain's number this time.

"Nickie, what's going on? Is everything okay?"

"Duncan's hurt. I'm going to him now." Oops. He would assume the next part was related. "Phil the barber has a large stash of guns."

"He's on probation for that."

"Exactly. Can you send Lynx and some guys? It's sort of time sensitive."

"I can do that, yes."

She hung up and spun onto her drive. She didn't mess with the garage door opener and parked by the front steps. She took two at a time, unlocked the door and assumed Duncan didn't have time to reset the alarm.

Puppy whining came from the back of the kitchen. Nickie was halfway up the first set of stairs when she noticed Duncan lying on the couch in the front room. He was shirtless. It took her a moment to catch the air that sucked into her lungs. Her feet seemed to thrum back down the stairs on their own as she assessed him. He'd placed a piece of gauze above his eye. It was drenched in blood. The eye was swollen completely shut with bright red flesh surrounding it. It took more than one blow to make that much damage.

"Holy, what the hell? Duncan. We need to get you to the ER."

He shook his head. "I need to lie here."

His lip swelled on the same side of his face as the eye. A drip of dried blood crusted on his chin. When she got to him, she noticed the bandages that were wrapped in a mess around his chest. "How? When? How?"

"It looks worse than it is."

"Where's Andy?"

He shook his head.

"What does that mean?"

"I told you. I didn't take him."

She closed her eyes for enough time to get her thoughts together, then made her way to the kitchen. "You went alone." She wasn't sure who she was talking to. She pulled open the freezer and dug for a bag of peas. When she came back, he was sleeping. Gently, she placed the peas on his face, making him jump. "I'm sorry. Be still. Rest."

"Do you have someone going out to Phil's?" Okay. Not sleeping.

She nodded before she realized his good eye was shut, too. "Yes." Her voice caught, so she repeated. "Yes. Dave has Eddy going out with some beat patrols."

He nodded. She thought he might have fallen back to sleep already but he added, "You need to get out there yourself. One of them got a call while he was unconscious."

Dipping her head closer, she checked on his cut lip. The scar on his shoulder caught her peripheral vision. She rested the tips of her fingers on it. He'd taken a bullet for her. Now, this. Pulling the blanket from the back of the couch, she covered him up as his breathing slowed into deep, constant steps.

She wanted to get a look at the wound beneath the gauze on his eye but didn't dare. Not yet. Instead, she picked up her cell.

"Hello, Nickie." It was his aunt.

"Hello, Brie. Are you busy? It's no emergency, but there's been an accident."

It took every piece of her to leave Duncan with his aunt, but he would have her head if she weren't there for the Phil the barber mess. And she had a score to settle. 'Keep your eyes open.' That was what Phil had said to her.

Regardless of the rise of the sun, siren lights spun circles down the street before she reached Phil's shop. Three black and whites, a fire engine, two rescues, and her captain's vehicle sat in front. Officer Parker was stringing crime tape. Dave wore gloves and carried a handful of evidence bags.

She parked at the edge of the mess, then made her way to the center of everything while looking for her partner. Reaching her captain first, she assessed the area as she spoke. "Where's Lynx?"

"I was going to ask you the same thing," Dave said, placing an evidence marker with the number twelve on it next to a shell casing on the sidewalk.

"What are you talking about?"

"He's MIA. Not answering his phone or in his office."

She pulled out her cell and dialed his number again. As it rang, she spoke. "Phil get here yet?"

For the first time since she showed up, her captain

stopped what he was doing and looked at her. "Isn't that why you called?"

"Yeah. Catch the bastard. Guns? Locked rooms? Some people never learn."

"You should go inside, Nick. Then, we need to talk."

She gave herself time to read the expression on his face. None of it fit, so she went inside. She hoped the perps were as bloody as Duncan and sitting in a chair waiting for her to interrogate them.

She entered the room Phil had used time and time again as a meeting place for Zheng and who knows what else. Two beat cops. Evidence markers already placed. But no boxes of guns. Duncan described boxes...plural. Several and large. Someone had come in and emptied the place of the boxes and the two beat up guards.

But most importantly, there was Phil. In a large pool of blood with a single gunshot to his chest.

CHAPTER 28

Of course Duncan came first, but Nickie was beyond worried about Eddy. And why hadn't she thought to call Duncan's aunt every other time he needed to see a doctor? She was like the boss, the principal. She had him in the ER faster than Nickie could have gotten him to take ibuprofen or let her change his dressing.

Two cracked ribs and stitch glue above his eye. Although they might not have wrapped his ribs any better than he had himself. And with Duncan's Army field experience, he probably could have glued his own eye, but it made Nickie feel better anyway.

Not so much with Eddy. It was mid-afternoon and no one had heard from him. She'd been tied up at Phil the barber's shop nearly all day. Trying to explain the missing guns and perps to her captain without ratting out Duncan would have been a challenge if not for all the evidence that was left behind. Scratches from large boxes that had been dragged along the floor; leftover strands of packing paper; spatters of blood that didn't come up as a match in the NCIS DNA database that were left everywhere. Whoever followed Duncan was in a hurry. It was evident there had been cleaning up, but no one knew much of it had been done by Duncan.

She beeped her Camry lock and jogged toward the
station parking stairwell. She didn't hit each step like
she usually made herself do. She skipped two at a time
all the way to the fourth floor. Opening the door, she
stopped and looked around. Same old, same old.
Lucinda nosing around instead of working. The lights
off in her office. Lights on in Dave's.

She made her way around the commons area to reach
Eddy's office. She took a walk through although it was
dark and seemed like a waste of time. He'd been there
that morning. They had made eye contact. No, they
hadn't. She had walked past. He had never looked up.

His computer was shut down. No papers or pens lying
out. Drawers shut. Printer off. She walked toward the break
room and decided to check on Parker and Vaughn's sex
closet. Nothing. She walked past Interrogation 1 and 2, and
even number 3 that was never used looking in through the
rectangle of glass at the empty rooms.

She came back to the commons area. The few desks
that were occupied at this time of day held beat cops
typing reports on their PCs and desk clerks answering
phones. She headed toward the stairs. She would search
every space in the parking garage for his car, call every
friend and family member he had. Who were his
friends? His family? How did she not know these
things?

Guilt sagged her shoulders and made her feet drag
along the concrete stairwell steps. She made it to ground
level and almost exited out the parking lot door when
she noticed something. Feet something. Jogging down
the last flight of stairs that led to the basement and the
walkway to the county jail, she found him.

"Somebody help!" she yelled at the top of her lungs.
"No." Tears burned the backs of her eyes. "No, no, no."
A large puddle of blood lay beneath Lynx's still body.
His skin was gray. She could hardly breathe. "Someone
help!" she yelled louder.

Dropping to her knees, she took his hand as the tears began to spill. But his hand wasn't cold. She dug her fingers beneath his neck and found a pulse just as the ME came through the door. "Call 9-1-1! Get me a first aid kid. And the AED kit."

One of the probation officers came into the stairwell as the ME ran out. "Detective…"

"No, you don't," she yelled at the lifeless body of her partner. She pulled his shirt apart, ripping the buttons to expose the wounds. Dried blood caked around a gunshot to his stomach. "Give me your shirt," she yelled to whoever was behind her. The officer took off his shirt and ripped it in half, then gave her a piece. Together they tore strips. "You die and I will kick your ass," she mumbled as she ran the strips beneath his back, tying them in the front. In no time her hands were covered to her wrists with his blood. Salty tears dripped on his stomach as his limp arms flopped to the floor like magnets each time she moved him.

When she finished her field dressing, she checked his pulse again. Somewhere she noticed a silent crowd had gathered. "His pulse. It's barely forty bpm. What do I do?"

Nickie sat at Eddy's desk in the dark. She wore latex gloves but still didn't touch anything. Her phone rested between her ear and shoulder. On the other end of the line, Duncan tried to console her. Her tears ran dry, making her cheeks stiff from the salt.

Phil was in the morgue. Eddy lay in ICU.

His gun holster, she thought. "His gun holster," she repeated. It was empty. She stood, banging her thighs on his desk drawer. "It was empty." His gun was missing. His gun was missing. Her feet thought before her brain did. They took off past Lucinda, down the stairs, through the basement walkway, and right to the county jail. The officer at check-in did a double take as she passed and ordered him to unlock the entrance.

"Detective, I need you to—"

"Bite me. Open it."

He looked at her like she was crazy but did it. Her feet kept moving to Zheng's cell. A few catcalls came from bored inmates, but nothing from Zheng. When she stood in front of it, she saw a head with short, black hair resting on his pillow. The clear shape of a body was tucked beneath a flimsy blanket.

But she knew. She knew. Pillows or mattress stuffing were all that was under the sheets and beneath the hair that was fake. "Guard!" she called.

The same guard from check-in came running. "What is it, Detective?"

"Open this cell."

He stood and stared like he was looking at a ghost. Slowly, his eyes turned until they met hers. "Detective Lynx took him out for questioning hours ago."

Her head started to spin. The guard was babbling something about thinking Zheng had been returned when he did his latest rounds, but Nickie couldn't really hear much of anything over the swirling in her head.

The drive to Manhattan gave her too much time to think. She ignored the pulse in her head caused from each beat of her heart. She sat still as she stared out the passenger window. The mission. It was all about the mission. Duncan's hand reached for hers, making her fingers shudder. The warmth was appreciated but did little to temper the fact that he had a large bandage taped above his eye and beneath his shirt his ribs were wrapped. She wouldn't let him come with unless he agreed to let her wrap them twice.

Eddy lay unconscious in a hospital. Zheng ran free. He shot her partner and took his gun. She had to listen to a perp in her earbud as he spoke about the three girls he planned to abduct that afternoon, and one of them was a girl under Nickie's care.

Nevaeh sat, tapping her heel, in the back of Duncan's SUV. "As long as we're driving, can we go over this again, please?"

Nickie lowered her chin and closed her eyes. Nevaeh sensed Nickie's disturbance. She turned to give Nevaeh her undivided attention, but was beyond the ability to offer a warm expression. "Yes. That's a good idea."

Her leg stopped shaking and her shoulder relaxed, but Nevaeh watched Nickie's face with a guarded reservation. "So, I've got this suitcase. Are you sure I need to have all this stuff in it? Did you put surveillance stuff in it?"

"Someone might offer to carry it for you. Heavy is normal for a teenage girl. It's okay if someone opens it. They might want to check for electronics or wires. You're clean."

She nodded. "Right. I am here to help capture the people involved in taking innocent girls. All you need is for me to let them lead me to the meeting room where they have the other girls." She swallowed hard. It was one of the first normal reactions Nickie had seen her give. Caution is good. It's smart. "There will be officers watching and following me at all times."

"Yes, honey. Undercover officers. At all times. They are good at hiding. Duncan and I can't be visible either. The perpetrators have already seen us."

She nodded again. It seemed she was reassuring herself more than Nickie. "There is nothing I need to say or do," she said. "You will hear this Anthony person in your earbud." She pointed to the white wire that hung from Nickie's hair. "I just need to be quiet and seem nervous. No problem there."

Sarcasm. Nickie liked this girl more and more every day.

Duncan pulled to a curb three blocks from The

Grande Chateau. This was it. Beads of sweat lined the hair on Nickie's scalp. Her eyes seemed to scan the area without looking at anything or anyone straight on. A woman about her age leaned against a light post, reading a newspaper. NYPD undercover. He spotted another, a male, a few buildings down as he checked his phone.

Nickie rotated her body and faced Nevaeh fully. "You will be followed by the police. It's okay. Even if a suspect follows you. It's okay. You'll have undercover officers everywhere. They do this all the time. You are not alone."

Nevaeh's eyes went to the closest undercover female.

"That's right, honey," Nickie said. "She's here for you. Try not to look at her. The girl you know as Emma is already in place." Nickie tapped the black earbud in her right ear, showing how she knew. "Straight to the coffee shop, Nevaeh. To the right as you enter the lobby. You're going to do great."

They watched in silence as the girl walked away. Duncan drove the three blocks to the hotel parking garage. He counted four unmarked police-issued cars as he made his way up to the level NYPD had instructed him. The cars were ordinary sedans, but the all-numeral license plate numbers and bland hubcaps would likely be as easy for perps to spot as they were for him.

His eyes met Nickie's. She checked the gun beneath her brown leather jacket, then the one under the cuff of her pants. He did the same before locking the SUV.

They didn't walk far before an average-built man with salt and pepper hair approached them. "Detective Savage?"

"That's right." Her feet stopped. She stood and locked her knees but didn't offer her badge.

The man held out his hand. "I'm Captain Johnson, Detective."

Nickie's brows furrowed, then dropped. She didn't

offer hers to shake in return.

"May I see your identification, please?" She pulled back her coat, showing the badge she had pinned to her belt.

He complied as well. "Are there any last minute changes in the plan?"

Nickie shook her head, then held up a finger and cupped her hand over the ear with the black earbud. "The female spotted our girl," she said and started walking toward the elevators.

The chief spoke into his walkie. "The girl has been spotted. All eyes open."

Nickie stopped before she reached the door, causing both Duncan and the NYPD captain to nearly run into her. She cupped her ear to hear better, then said, "Tell your men to stand down. They are waiting to approach our girl. The perp already has one of the other girls in room 2025." She turned and looked to the captain. "There is no twentieth floor."

The captain barked orders into his walkie, but for Duncan the only decipherable sound was the pounding of his shoes as he limped to the stairs of the parking garage. He ignored the pain that shot through his ribcage with every step. Nickie stayed with the captain. She would want to whip together a Plan B. Duncan's focus was finding which building they planned to take the girls.

He reached ground level and ran through the exit meant for cars. Amid honking vehicles, he maneuvered to the center of the street and looked up. Two of the buildings were taller than twenty stories. Both were on the north side of the street. Ignoring the fingers lifted on his behalf, he walked to the south side. Which building? The one on the left had valet parking and a doorman. Surveillance. He decided to gamble on the right and walked at a clipped pace toward the entrance.

No sign of the perp he recognized or the Emma

woman Nevaeh described. Most importantly, no Nevaeh.

He made his way through the lobby to the elevator. He pressed the button for the floor below room 2025. As he rode, he texted Nickie. 'I'm in the Esquire. Three buildings west of you. I'll wait next to the stairwell on the nineteenth floor.'

She answered almost immediately. 'I have no word the other girls are there.'

'I know. It's a hunch. Keep me informed.'

A guest entered the elevator from the fourth floor. Going up? He was short and wore a cloth, hip-length trench coat and hoop earrings in both ears. He gave Duncan a once-over before stepping in. Duncan didn't ask which floor the man wanted, and instead of offering to accommodate, stepped away from the elevator buttons. The man reached over but pressed the button that opened the door instead of choosing a floor.

A woman Duncan didn't recognize came in with a young teen carrying a suitcase. Duncan's heart jumped into his throat. The woman pressed the button for the twentieth floor. The man didn't choose another.

Duncan checked his phone for nothing, then straightened his jacket. He fought against his lungs, forcing his breathing to remain slow. The child looked to be about sixteen. Blonde with short hair and designer jeans. "There are other girls?" she asked in a squeaky voice.

"Oh yes. There will be three of you. Elizabeth is already waiting for us in the meeting room. Sabrina is on her way." The woman tucked her arm through the child's. "This is going to be so much fun." He'd never wanted to actually strike a woman before now.

Duncan's cell buzzed in his hand and nearly made him jump. None of the trio acknowledged the noise, so he slipped it into the pocket of his coat as they reached the nineteenth floor. He stepped out without looking back.

The door closed behind him and he stopped, placed his hands on his thighs and caught his breath. Pulling out his phone, he dialed without reading the incoming text.

Nickie answered on the first ring. "Duncan, they have her. They are leaving with her. The only NYPD tails close by are the ones we spotted on the street."

"They're here," he said.

"Who? Where?"

"The Esquire. They have a girl named Elizabeth already in the room."

"I heard that part in the audio bug."

"I ran into another girl on the elevator. Maybe sixteen and mousey. She's with a female. Black hair. No coat. Floral blouse. Short, equally as mousey. And there's a man." Duncan noted a love seat and chair next to the elevator and assumed there would be one on each floor. "The man is short as well, wearing a worn cloth jacket. His hair is buzzed and brown. He has gold hoop earrings." Duncan found a short hallway that led to the floor's linen closet.

"We're on our way," she said to him.

CHAPTER 29

———— ◆◆◆ ————

"I'm not comfortable with this, Detective."

She didn't have time to explain her use of Duncan's eidetic memory or his history as a civilian consultant. She hadn't even introduced him as her husband let alone any kind of personal acquaintance.

With two of his guys following him, the captain headed toward the door leading to the lobby. "How did this guy of yours end up at the right hotel?" he asked her.

Less was more, and she couldn't afford to be spotted. "He's ex-military, Captain. And he's good. We've used him before. I can't afford to be seen, sir. They know me. I'm taking the parking deck exit." A set of soft shoes followed her. Was he having her followed or offering support? It didn't matter. Nothing mattered except keeping track of Nevaeh.

Flipping up the collar of her jacket, she jogged down to the building Duncan had directed her to. "I'm looking for a side entrance," she said to the undercover officer at her heels. The door led to a set of service stairs next to a worn elevator. She chose the stairs. Less likely to get trapped.

"Detective?" he asked and gestured to the elevator.

She couldn't take the risk that one or more of the perps would use it. "You take it if you want," she said behind her as she opened the door and checked her surroundings, then started the climb. Either the undercover was told to keep her in his sight or wasn't willing to be shown up by a woman. "What's your name?" she asked as they climbed.

"Officer Maple, ma'am."

"It's a long way up, Maple. Call me Detective Savage or Nick." She took the stairs two at a time and ignored the panting man behind her. "I'm not sure how much your captain told you. I can't be seen. I have a man on the nineteenth. The perps are on the twentieth. They have two underage girls in captivity as we speak." Or as she speaks and he gasps for air. "I hear two men with them." She faced him as they turned the next corner, tapping the black earbud in her ear. "There may be more. Our mission includes the girl I brought and the two they already have, but also the perps. I want to take them down and find out whoever it is they work for. The women they have with them are likely victims as well."

"With all due respect, ma—Detective." He was panting like a dog in heat. "But how can you assume adult women are captives?"

She wanted to kick his ass. Either that or tell him to invest in a treadmill. Instead, she ignored him and climbed the last few steps to the nineteenth floor. The service elevator was next to the stairs. The linen closet Duncan had mentioned was next to the elevator, and Duncan was next to it. He nodded an acknowledgement to her as he surveyed the officer.

"Nevaeh is en route to the building." She was talking to both of them now. "Captain Johnson has two men following at a distance. The rest of the officers are still at the first hotel. They're regrouping. There are three youth and a minimum of three adult women and two male perpetrators. As soon as they have Nevaeh in the elevators, we're on." She turned to the officer. "You go up and cover the service stairs and elevator."

He hesitated. So, he was sent to babysit her after all.

"There are no police up there, Officer Maple. We're making this up as we go." She gestured between Duncan and herself. "We've been IDed on previous ops. Your captain's men aren't even in the building yet."

"I, um—"

"Yeah, yeah," she said. "I get it. Whatever." It wasn't Maple's fault, but she was in no mood for well-placed aggression.

"I'm going to head up," Duncan said, ignoring Maple. "I'll be just inside the service stairs door that leads to the twentieth floor."

"I'll take the public stairs," she said as he disappeared into the stairwell. The waiting was going to kill her. She paced. Then, paced some more. Her feet stopped as her hand flew to cup the black earbud in her ear.

'Get them out of here. One of them is undercover.'

The girls. No. She looked at Maple. "Abort. We've been made."

He stood as if he wanted her to tell him what to do.

"I'm taking the public stairs," she said to Maple. "Follow me or not."

She made her way across the hallway, the officer following on her heels. She had to get to the lobby before the perps did. Pulling out her cell, she began to call her captain when a loud whooshing sound came from the earbud that gave her the perp's audio feed. "Damn it." She ripped it from her ear. Water. A toilet or a laundry machine. They found the bug and flushed it.

Her fingers dialed faster. She'd barely made it to the next landing before it hit her. The timing wasn't a coincidence. She turned as the sound of Maple's gun cocked.

"I need you to stop, Detective."

Of course. Why not? Her fingers wanted to rub her temples. Officer Maple stood with his gun pointed at her chest. "You've got to be kidding me. You tipped them off. Your captain, too? Who isn't crooked in this frigging business?"

Oh no, Nevaeh. She needed to get to her.

"Not my captain, no. He's as squeaky clean as they come."

Familiar movement came from above. Duncan. She made sure not to take her eyes from Maple as he justified his corruption.

"And he has three kids and lives in a two-bedroom flat."

Duncan carried what looked like two laptops in one arm.

"Cap would have been okay if I'd left you alone."

Was that blood on Duncan's shoulder? Concern and curiosity took her, but she wouldn't let herself look at him straight on and give away his presence.

"My real boss, on the other hand. Not so much."

At the top of the set of stairs, Duncan set down the laptops.

"Your captain is going to wonder why I'm not contacting him," she said.

"I agree. You're going to take care of that right—"

She tried not to show her relief as Duncan leapt into the air. Timing his descent, she ducked out of the way of Maple's line of gunfire as Duncan slapped it from his hand and jumped on his back. She flew down sets of stairs as she heard the distinct sound of fist to flesh.

She raced against the elevator that carried the girls.

When she reached the lobby, she didn't find the captain. Or the suspects. She turned in obvious circles, trying to spot anything worth spotting. The captain stepped out from behind a square, mirrored pillar. His face said it all. He knew nothing.

"Surround the building," she said. "They're on the

move."

"What?"

He didn't believe her.

"You have a mole!" she yelled and ran from the elevator.

Carrying the laptops was cumbersome enough that Duncan decided on the elevator. Maple must have been the one who tipped off the kidnappers. Duncan left the one who he found wiping down room 2025 unconscious.

His phone buzzed. He pressed the first floor button as he read.

'They're not down here. Nevaeh's missing. We're searching the perimeter.'

The captain was in the lobby? He had men out front? How could they have missed men with the girls?

The fourth floor. It was the one the suspects had used in the first place. He pressed button number four, then decided he would be spotted and pressed number five.

He texted Nickie as he finished the ride. 'When I arrived, three of them entered from the fourth floor.'

He exited and turned for the stairs. Creeping into the stairwell, he noted it was empty, then took off. He nearly ran into them. Two girls. Two women. No Nevaeh. Three men. He recognized two of them. One was the man he knew as Anthony. The other was Jun Zheng.

Zheng looked as surprised as Duncan was. Duncan may be injured, but he had rage on his side.

"Take these two girls. Forget about the third one. She will be an undercover agent. I've got this," Zheng spoke as he tilted his head from side to side in Duncan's direction.

The men moved to expose Zheng's gun as it pointed at Duncan's head. Duncan slipped the laptops around and used them as a shield, stumbling back as the force of the bullets hit the metal. He took advantage of Zheng's confident reprieve and used the laptops as Frisbees, sending them into Zheng's rib cage. The gun flew down the hall.

Duncan had his guns—both of them—but chose not to use them. Hand-to-hand combat was what he needed. Zheng held his side and kicked the laptops out of the way.

"You're in good shape for someone who's been in a pen for months."

"Weeks."

"Who let you out?"

"It wasn't difficult," Zheng said as he tried an upper cut, followed by a crescent kick.

Duncan dodged the first and grabbed Zheng's foot as it spun toward his face, then used it to flip him on his back. "Out of shape amateur."

Flinging his legs in the air, Zheng used his momentum to kick upright. The flashy shit gave Duncan ample time to ready for him. Duncan began his swing, and just as Zheng landed on his feet, Duncan planted his knuckles to the side of his temple. The wounds from the fight with the boys from Phil's place opened instantly, but the pain was obsolete. He followed with two jabs before Zheng swept Duncan's feet from beneath him. The fall was enough for Zheng to step into a kick in Duncan's side. The loss of air was instant, but the pain on his freshly cracked ribs was blinding. He had the image of his Nickie to make all of it meaningless.

At the next attempted drop kick, Duncan grabbed Zheng's leg and returned the favor, kicking his foot in the air and into the soft flesh of Zheng's side. They rolled for a few rotations before Zheng landed on top, throwing one, two, three punches to Duncan's bad eye.

Using the sides of his hands, Duncan brought his arms together and clapped Zheng's ears. His eyes blinked, then he fell, getting in one last punch on the way down. They lay panting before Zheng's gaze landed on his gun. Using his arms, Duncan pulled along the floor toward it.

As he reached, Duncan realized Zheng wasn't moving for it any longer. He was on his feet, stumbling through the door to the stairwell.

Duncan's head fell back, and he texted Nickie. As his vision blurred and his chest pounded, he punched the numbers and letters on his phone.

"Mole?" The look of disbelief on the NYPD captain's face was something Nickie had no time for. She kept her feet running to the front doors. Finding Nevaeh. It was her only purpose.

"We think they got off on the fourth floor," she yelled as she passed reception.

"Fourth floor?" he asked. "The gym is on the fourth floor. There's an outside customer entrance."

She didn't hear the rest. She was on the street. No perps. No girls. She clipped her way toward the first hotel. Cars. Distant sirens. Businessmen. A woman with impeccably smooth, dark brown hair, ice pick heels and a faux fur boa.

Emma.

She came from around the back of a parked yellow cab. Their eyes met and she spun on her four-inch heels around the back of the cab like a pro. Nickie sprinted. She stepped on the front of the cab with one foot then sprang from it with the other. As she flew to the Emma woman, she noticed the cab driver slumped over his steering wheel.

Nickie barely reached the Emma woman's back and clasped a chunk of the leather jacket. Emma's feet came up from beneath her, and she landed on the concrete. Cars honked and swerved around them.

Nickie expected a junior high girl catfight, but Emma was far from the hair-pulling and scratching type. She lifted to her feet and planted two quick jabs to Nickie's nose. Nickie felt the cartilage crush and tasted blood as she tried to block the following hook. It landed at the side of Nickie's head with enough force to knock her to the street.

A quick shake of the head and Nickie was back on her feet, fists clenched and ready to take this bitch down.

But what she saw and what she heard scared her more than any bloody nose or punched skull. Emma was pushing the limp driver to the passenger seat as teenage screams came from the trunk of the cab. Nickie dove for the car only to spin back to the concrete as it pulled away.

She stepped in front of the next cab and held out her badge with one hand and her gun with the other. "Get out."

"Okay, okay," the driver yelled and got out with his hands up. She threw the car into drive and pressed the gas pedal to the floor as she saw the Emma woman's cab turn two blocks down.

Nevaeh. It was Nevaeh Nickie had heard. She was in the trunk.

The light at the corner Emma took had turned red. Nickie ran it, swerving around a bus and a white box truck. As Nickie made the corner, she noticed a three-car pileup that must have been courtesy of Emma. It slowed her down enough for Nickie to see her turn down the next block. Nickie sped around the pileup and swerved behind Emma. Nevaeh. Her fear was so close, Nickie could taste it. Emma's cab drove faster and faster. The light she headed for wasn't turning red; it was red. Cars drove back and forth down the busy Manhattan intersection. Emma sped for it as Nickie yelled, "No!" but followed just as quickly. Cars laid on their horns, screeched their tires and spun out of the way, but Emma made it. She left an impassable maze of metal in her wake as she turned down an exit ramp.

Nickie slammed on the brakes of her stolen car, skidding into the side of a Mercedes limo. She shook her head and took off on foot. The ramp, the ramp, the ramp. Nickie jumped over two cars and dodged the rest as she pumped every ounce of force into her thighs. She ran for the bridge that went over the ramp's crossroad, then jumped. Her legs and arms moved in big circles, launching her so she landed squarely on the hood of Emma's stolen cab.

Her body broke the windshield and dented the hood. Emma swerved into a guardrail, the sudden turn tossing Nickie onto the road.

Her clothes were torn. She had blood coming from both knees, elbows and her nose. She staggered to her feet, squatting with her left hand in gravel as she drew her gun, then stood. Wiping the blood that dripped into her mouth, she took her Smith and Wesson off safety and pointed it at Emma. Her body was lifeless. Her head rested in the hole it had made in the driver's side window.

Cries came from the trunk. Nickie limped toward it, stuffing her gun in the back of her pants. It popped open before she reached it, a terrified Nevaeh kicking and flailing her arms and legs like she had scorpions covering her.

"It's okay. It's okay. You're safe. It's me." Nickie grabbed whatever body part she could reach. "I'm here. It's Nickie. See? Look at me. It's over."

Her beautiful brown eyes latched onto Nickie's. Her body stilled and tears began to fall. Nevaeh's hands covered her mouth as she sat in the trunk. Sirens came maneuvering through the traffic. "Did we catch them?" she asked.

Nickie scrunched her brows, cocked her head, then smiled. She took the dangling black earbud from her waist and stuck it in the only part of her body that didn't ache. She smiled and nodded. "Yes. Yes, honey. Yes, we did." She tapped the earbud with her fingers, then sat at the edge of the trunk and took Nevaeh in her arms.

Today was the day of the upstate New York police

training Nickie had coordinated with precincts from three counties to join in, learning how to handle a vice bust when it involved underage prostitutes. She was pumped. The CEO from Child Rescue said he had an anonymous donation to fund the training. Duncan still refused to fess up about it.

She pulled into the station lot to find someone parked in her spot. It was too early for other officers and detectives to arrive. Who would dare? It was okay. She'd captured thugs and saved girls. It was what she lived for.

The fact that it was one of Zheng's trafficking rings was more icing than she could spread on her cake. The ten to twelve groups of Fu Haizi had turned into eight to ten. Bianca was back with her family and rested a little easier at night knowing the men who took her were locked up behind bars.

A car parked in Nickie's spot wasn't going to ruin this day.

The next thing she noticed was her captain standing next to her taken parking spot. And Vaughn? And Parker? Did someone die? Wait, that could be real. She parked where she could and walked toward them.

"You decided to show up?" Dave asked as she approached.

She pulled out her phone and checked the time. She was early. It was a warm summer morning; she was holding a training that day and they weren't going to mess with her happy.

"What are you doing here?" she asked. So early. In the parking lot.

Dave handed her a set of keys.

Every muscle in her face fell. "No." She looked to the car in her spot. It was a dented, ancient Cadillac Eldorado. She could squeal.

Nickie drove home in the dark that night in her new

unmarked police issue. New, as in thirty years old. Gear shift that was actually a gear. Knobs for tuning the radio. The rumble was an aphrodisiac.

Nevaeh was working with Child Rescue on becoming a trainer to teach high school and college-aged girls how to keep themselves safe. Bianca initiated interest in testifying against the pimp that sat in Manhattan County that moment.

Duncan had known to check room 2025 at the Esquire hotel even though the perps had left with the girls, and he knew to take their laptops. He and Andy were working on digging around bullet holes to retrieve the information from the Internet history and the hard drive. Also an aphrodisiac.

Zheng was free. He had enough connections that, even from jail, he'd been able to stock pile guns at the barbershop. He killed Phil the barber. Eddy was still in a doctor-ordered, drug-induced coma but healing and scheduled to be woken in the morning.

She turned up the asphalt drive that led to her house. For tonight, she was going to celebrate with a quiet evening at home that included working with her dog, drinking wine and having marathon sex with her husband.

She stopped before entering the garage. Soon, they would spend Independence Day at Duncan's aunt and uncle's home. Eddy would be well enough to come. She had to believe that. Duncan and Andy would shoot off ridiculous amounts of fireworks. Illegal fireworks in front of not only her but her captain. If she closed her eyes, she could smell the gunpowder.

Pulling into the garage, she made sure to center her car over the large piece of cardboard Duncan had placed on the concrete floor meant to absorb her oil leak from her beautiful piece of shit car.

She heard Xena whine on the other side of the door leading from the garage to the house. As she walked in, she greeted the pup. Duncan stood at the kitchen counter, slicing onions and mincing garlic.

"Are you hungry?" he asked.

She was, just not for food. "I am. What can I do to help?"

She didn't hear his response, because her eyes stopped on the center of the kitchen table. A large bouquet of red roses sat in the center. There must have been two dozen of them. She was flattered and appreciative, but it wasn't the flowers that stopped her gaze. Her eyes stared at the spot on the table they seemed to use whenever they wanted to send a special signal to each other about something they needed to talk about. An email. A folded Jets apron. It was her birth control pills. And she knew just why Duncan would want to discuss them.

THE NICKIE SAVAGE SERIES

Turn the page for an

excerpt from

SAVAGE
BETRAYAL
The Nickie Savage Series
Book Four

R.T. Wolfe

Nickie stood in the bedroom door of the empty apartment. Unmade bed, clothes strewn on the floor. A few live shells and a magazine clip were tossed on the only dresser in the room. The clip was full. She could see the neatly lined bullets inside from where she stood.

The search felt like betrayal. Maybe because it was. This was her partner, her friend, her ex lover. And possibly the department mole who had been stabbing her in the back for weeks, months, possibly even years.

Like a search beam had been flipped on, light poured from the hallway behind her. Without turning to look, she took one large step and pressed herself against the wall just inside the bedroom door.

No. It was probably the wind opening the front door wider. Then, why weren't her feet moving? Because she was executing a search without back up. Because there was nothing standing between her and the front door other than a short apartment hallway. She leaned her ear closer toward the hallway, stopping at the trim around the door. She wasn't just searching for a department mole, she was searching for a person who may very well be involved with a murder. Or else, she was wrong about the whole damned thing.

Sliding her Smith and Wesson out of her holster, she took it off safety and aimed at the opening of the doorway. This was stupid. There were no footsteps. No moving shadows. She leaned over to take a look. The hallway was clear. It did little to soothe her tension. With gun drawn, arms extended, and elbows locked, she twirled around and faced the hallway head on. If there were at least some wind, she would feel better about why the door had swung open. She took a single step, keeping her knees bent, then another.

She would cut around through the opening to the walk-through kitchen, then around the living room to check on the front door. Except, she no more than made another single step when an arm swung around the opening from the kitchen knocking Nickie's gun from her hand.

The force from the blow was male. She ignored the rush of adrenaline and the prickling on the back of her neck. She was too damn pissed off. She grabbed the wrist before he had a chance to retract it. Yanking on the arm, she forced the man into the hallway. Simultaneously, she dropped her shoulder and dug in, toppling them both to the floor.

Hey, she knew that scent. Male soap. The slightest hint of the kind of cologne that made her feel something between dizzy and a secure sense of home.

"Duncan?" She squirmed out of the awkward position they had landed in and sat up, straddling him. He lay there rubbing the spot on his collarbone she had shoulder shoved him. "You're in LA!" she added honestly confused.

He lifted his brows to her as if the fact that he was lying in an apartment in upstate New York—not L.A.—made her dense.

"How did you know I was here? Who told you I was here? Why are you here?"

"Where is your car?"

"I got a ride with the locksmith."

"How were you going to get home?"

"I know people."

SAVAGE BETRAYAL
available in print and ebook

MEET THE AUTHOR

R.T. was born and raised in the beautiful Midwest, the youngest of six ornery children. She married at a young age and began her family shortly after. With three amazing small boys, life was a whirlwind of flipping houses and working two jobs in between swim lessons and games of Candyland.

Now that her boys are nearly grown, R.T. spends much of her time on the road, traveling from one sporting event to another, serving as mom and cheerleader.

When she isn't writing or traveling, she works with several non-profit organizations, promoting the work they do for those who cannot help themselves.

R.T. enjoys hearing from readers. You can contact R.T. through her website: www.rtwolfe.com